Adventures

Enid Blyton

The Boy Next Door
The Treasure Hunters

·PARRAGON·

This edition published in 1995 for
Parragon Book Service Limited
Units 13–17 Avonbridge Industrial Estate
Atlantic Road
Avonmouth, Bristol BS11 9QD
by Diamond Books
77–85 Fulham Palace Road
Hammersmith, London W6 8JB

First edition published 1992 for Parragon
Book Service Limited

All rights reserved

Printed in England

Conditions of Sale
This book is sold subject to the condition
that it shall not, by way of trade or otherwise,
be lent, re-sold, hired out or otherwise circulated
without the publisher's prior consent in any form of
binding or cover other than that in which it is
published and without a similar condition
including this condition being imposed
on the subsequent purchaser.

Contents

The Boy Next Door

First published in a single volume in hardback in 1951 by
William Collins Sons & Co Ltd.
First published in paperback in 1984 in Armada

Copyright © Enid Blyton 1951

The author asserts the moral right to be identified as
the author of the work

Chapter One

THE BOY NEXT DOOR

BETTY could hardly keep still one fine day at the end of July. "Robin's coming home from boarding school," she told everyone. "And my Cousin Lucy is coming to stay to-day. Two people on one day—I *shall* have fun after being all alone!"

Betty did have rather a lonely life. Her brother Robin went off to boarding school each term, and Betty had lessons at home with her governess, Miss Thomas, because there was no school near. Betty's parents lived in a lonely spot, in beautiful country, with hills and rivers all round. The only house near was a big empty one built as a pair to Betty's own house, which stood in its own grounds nearby.

But now Betty's cousin Lucy was coming to stay—and her brother was coming home. It would be marvellous to have two companions.

"Robin's eleven, Lucy is ten and I am nine," she thought. "We're like a step-ladder. Won't Robin be

9

pleased to find Lucy here, too!

Lucy arrived first, by car. She was not much bigger than Betty, but was quite different. Betty was fair, with blue eyes, like Robin—but Lucy was very dark, with short, curly hair and deep brown eyes. Betty rushed to meet her when the car drew up.

"Lucy! I'm so glad you've come! Robin isn't here yet, but he will be soon. Mummy, can I take Lucy to my room? Lucy, you're to share a bedroom with me!"

"Dear me, Betty, let me just get a look at Lucy!" said Mummy, with a laugh. "Did you travel all by yourself, Lucy? How grown-up you are!"

"Well—I didn't travel *quite* by myself," said Lucy, and she turned back towards the car. "Oh, Aunt Jane, I hope you won't mind—but I just *had* to bring Sandy!"

"Who in the world is Sandy?" said Mummy, astonished.

"This is Sandy," said Lucy—and out of the car jumped a brown and white fox-terrier, not much bigger than a puppy. "Aunt Jane, he got into the train with me and got under the seat when no one was looking—and the train went off with him—so I couldn't very well make him go back, could I? Will it matter having him, do you think? He's awfully good. He doesn't need a kennel. He can sleep on my bed at night."

"I don't think I want him to do that," said her aunt. "But as he's here we can't do anything but welcome him. Do you want a bone, Sandy?"

"Wuff!" said Sandy politely. He was on his very best behaviour.

"I hope you haven't any cats," said Lucy, going indoors with her cousin. "Sandy is awful with cats. Honestly, he thinks they're only made to chase."

"Well, we've got Tiger," said Betty. "But no dog has ever chased Tiger yet. She's too fierce. She's a ginger cat with stripes. I should think she'll quite probably chase Sandy. Come on. Let's go upstairs. I'm dying to hear all your news. I hope Robin will be here soon. He'll be awfully pleased to see you."

But Robin didn't seem too pleased to see Lucy. He arrived soon afterwards, and shook hands very politely. But Betty could tell that he wasn't as pleased as she had expected. She followed him into his bedroom when he went to unpack.

"Robin, don't you like Lucy? Aren't you glad to be home again with me? Robin, Lucy has brought a dog called Sandy."

"Oh, I'm pleased to be home," said Robin, unstrapping a trunk. "But it's going to be a bit dull with only two girls to play with. I hope you won't want me to play with your dolls."

"Robin! Don't be horrid!" said Betty. "You know I don't play with dolls when you're home. I like tree-climbing and things like that then. I thought you'd like having two people to play with in the holidays instead of one."

"Well, it's a pity one of them isn't a boy, that's all," said Robin, emptying all the things out of his trunk on to the floor. "After all, I live with boys all the term—and I feel pretty feeble when I get home and play with two little girls. Girls can't even catch!"

"I *can* catch!" said Betty indignantly. "You know I can. And I bet Lucy can, too. Oh, look—here's Sandy!"

Sandy came running in, wagging his tail. He went straight up to Robin, put his paws up on his legs, and licked him with a wet pink tongue.

"Oh, you're a nice little dog!" said Robin, pleased. "I bet you'll come out with me for walks, won't you? You won't want to stick with girls all the time!"

"Wuff," said Sandy, and wagged his tail so fast that it looked like smoke at the end of him.

"I don't expect Lucy will want him to go for walks with you without us," said Betty, looking so mournful that Robin suddenly laughed. He stretched out his hand and pulled Betty down beside him.

"I feel rather grown-up these hols," he said. "I've been put into another form, you know, and we all think a lot of ourselves, because we're not juniors any more! Cheer up! We'll have some fun together—but I DO wish there was another boy somewhere for me to play with."

Betty told Mummy what Robin had said. "He seems too grown-up for girls now," she said seriously. "It's all right for Lucy and me because we've got one another for

11

company. But it *would* be nice for Robin to have a boy. Haven't we a boy cousin we can ask to stay, Mummy?"

"No," said Mummy, laughing at Betty's solemn face. "Don't worry about Robin. He'll want you to go off walking and boating and climbing with him when he has settled down again! Anyway—there may perhaps be a boy coming to live next door!"

"Mummy! *Next door*—but it's an empty house!" said Betty. "No one's lived there for a long time."

"Well, I've heard that people have taken the house and are staying there for the summer," said Mummy. "It's to be let furnished, you know—the last people left it with all the furniture in. So, for all we know, there may be a boy for Robin to play with—in fact there might even be a whole family of children!"

This was exciting. The three children watched for the new family to come. They arrived in two or three days' time, but as they came just as night was falling, it was difficult to see how many there were.

Robin saw them quite by chance. He was in bed, and heard a car on the road. He hopped out and went to see if it stopped next door. It did. It looked a very big and expensive car. Out of it got three or four people, as far as Robin could see from his window, which had a view of the drive that ran round the front of the next-door house. One person seemed fairly small.

"Hope it's a boy!" said Robin to himself as he hopped back into bed. "We'll find out to-morrow. Maybe we'll hear him shouting about—or he'll go down to the village to shop or something."

But the boy, if it was a boy, didn't appear at all. The three children watched carefully the next day, but they neither saw nor heard anything of the boy. The tradesmen drove up to the house and delivered goods, and a chauffeur was seen cleaning the car outside the garage. But there was no sign of a boy.

"You must have been mistaken," said Lucy to Robin. "Look—there's the grocer coming. Let's ask him if he knows if there are any children next door now."

So they asked him. "I think there's a boy," said the grocer. "I had to take some things round the back way,

12

and I believe I saw a boy. You'll see him soon enough if there is."

But the boy didn't appear. "It's funny," said Robin. "I wonder what he does with himself. He never goes for walks. We never hear him in the garden. Let's climb a tree and see if we can see him anywhere. There's a big chestnut at the side of our garden, near next-door's garden. If we climbed that we could look down on their lawn, I should think."

They all three went to the big chestnut tree. Robin climbed up first, to show the girls where to put their feet. Betty was quite good at climbing, but Lucy wasn't so good. It took her ages to get up high. But how lovely it was sitting astride a branch at the top of the tree, looking down into their own garden, and into the next one, too!

"Isn't it untidy and overgrown!" said Robin. "I can't see anyone, can you?"

"Yes, look—over there!" said Lucy suddenly. The others looked where she pointed, and they saw a small summer-house. Outside it, in a deck-chair, sat rather a fierce-looking woman, knitting. As they watched she put down her knitting, settled herself comfortably, yawned, and seemed to go to sleep.

"No sign of any boy," said Lucy. And then all three children stared hard, down into the untidy space where the fierce-looking woman sat, asleep in her chair. Someone was creeping out of the hedge nearby! Someone was on hands and knees, crouching behind the chair!

"A Red Indian!" said Betty, amazed. "Look at those gorgeous feathers. What's he going to do?"

The Red Indian suddenly rose to his feet, gave an ear-splitting yell, ran round and round the chair in a very fierce manner, and then disappeared into the hedge again. The woman woke and sat up angrily.

"Kit! I won't have these tricks played on me. I've told you that before. Come and take off your Red Indian things at once. I've told you you can't wear them because you always behave so badly when you've got them on."

But Kit didn't appear. The woman went to the hedge and began to poke about with a stick.

13

"Come out! I shall tell Mr Barton of you. Your tutor told you not to make any noise at all, and you know perfectly well why. Yelling like that in my ear!"

The stick at last found the hiding Kit, and he wriggled out of the hedge, grinning. His face was painted in a very peculiar manner, with bright-coloured stripes across it.

"Sorry, Miss Taylor," he said, "but I'm just tired of hanging around here and never doing anything. I'm going to go mad just for a few minutes and then I'll take these things off and settle down."

And, to the watching children's great delight, Kit proceeded to go completely mad, dancing about round the angry Miss Taylor, brandishing what looked like a chopper, and yelling in a really fearsome manner. He then did a kind of war-dance, which was marvellous to watch, pulled off his wonderful feathered head-dress at the end, and bowed gravely to Miss Taylor.

"The show is now ended," he said, and took off his Red Indian costume. The children saw that he was a boy, well-grown, of about eleven or twelve, with dancing eyes, short-cropped hair and a wide grin. He lay down on the grass and began to read, with Miss Taylor grumbling away nearby.

"I think," said Robin, "I rather think—we're going to know that boy! Golly, what a war dance! I say—he's American, I should think, wouldn't you? He spoke with a kind of drawl."

"He's fun, anyway," said Betty. "How can we get to know him? Oh—*I* know! Let's all dress up in *our* Red Indian things, and squeeze through the hedge to-morrow! We'll pounce on him and give him an awful fright! That *will* be fun!"

"Right!" said Robin, sliding down the tree. "We will!"

Chapter Two

THE RED INDIANS HAVE A BAD TIME

THE THREE children felt excited about their plan for giving the boy next door a fright.

"It will be just the same kind of surprise he gave to that fierce-looking woman!" said Lucy. "Have you got a Red Indian suit, that will fit me?"

"You can have my old one," said Robin. "I had a fine new one last Christmas. Really, you should be a Red Indian squaw, and not wear a proper brave's head-dress with heaps of feathers—but it won't matter for once."

The children's mother was quite surprised to hear there was a boy next door after all. "Well, he's very quiet, I must say," she said. "I wish you three were as quiet! Really, I feel sometimes I might as well go and live in the monkey-house at the Zoo—or perhaps in the parrot-house. I am sure that either of those places would be very peaceful compared with our house!"

The children laughed. "Well, I'm jolly glad there's a boy next door," said Robin. "I shall like to play with him. He looks good fun. I should think he's about the same age as I am."

Nobody said what they were going to do the next day. Robin turned out his old Red Indian suit and Lucy tried it on. If she turned up the edges of the trouser-legs, it would fit her quite well. She tried on the feathered head-dress.

"I look grand!" she said. "I'd much rather be an Indian brave than a squaw! Oh, I'm longing for to-morrow!"

The next day came. Robin climbed the chestnut tree to see if the boy next door was anywhere about. At first he couldn't see him—and then he heard a cheerful whistling from the summer-house, and guessed Kit was there. The fierce-looking woman was nowhere to be seen.

"Good!" said Robin, getting down the tree quickly to tell the others. "The boy's there—but that woman isn't. It would be a good time to pounce on Kit now. Come on—let's get into our things quickly."

They all put on their Red Indian clothes. They looked really fierce, especially when they painted their faces red, yellow, blue and green.

"How are we going to get into the next-door garden?" said Betty.

"We'll squeeze through the hedge," said Robin. "It will be easy enough, though it's pretty thick. Come on!"

They went to the hedge that separated the two gardens. Both gardens were very big indeed, about five or six acres each, some of it orchards and fields. Robin tried to find a way through. At first it seemed impossible, because the hedge was mostly of prickly hawthorn.

"We shall tear our things to bits," said Lucy. "Oh, blow! I've scratched my arm. Robin, we can't get through this horrid hedge, we really can't."

But at last they managed to find a thinner place, and one by one they squeezed through. They were in the next-door garden! It was terribly overgrown and untidy. The paths were lost in weeds and moss. Untrimmed rambler roses hung everywhere, and posts stood crookedly, half dragged down by the weight of the overgrown climbers. There was a very thick copse of trees

Robin climbed the chestnut tree

just before the children reached the lawn where the summer-house stood, and they were well hidden in the shadow of these.

They lay on their tummies and wriggled along as Red Indians do. Robin and Betty had had plenty of practice at this sort of thing, for they had played at Red Indians for years, but Lucy was not so used to it, and the others frowned at her when she made a dry stick crack beneath her.

"Sh!" whispered Robin. "Don't you know that Red Indians never make a sound, silly? Now look out for that twig—it's so dry it'll pop loudly if you crack it in half."

They crawled as silently as they could through the little wood. It was dark and overgrown in there. A blackbird saw them and flew off in a fright, calling loudly to all the other birds to beware.

"Blow that bird!" said Robin in a whisper. "Lie still, everyone. Kit might be on the watch if he knows that blackbirds give the alarm when they see anything suspicious. Wait till I give you the word to go on again."

So they all lay quite still, whilst the blackbird shouted his alarm from the top of a nearby tree. After a while he grew tired of it and flew down into the children's own garden next door.

"Now we'll get on," whispered Robin, and one by one the three children crept nearer and nearer to the little enclosed lawn, where they hoped to find Kit.

They didn't see a pair of bright eyes looking in amazement at them from a tree under which they passed. They didn't notice Kit up there, sitting as still as a mouse, watching the three children below passing by in single file! They didn't hear him slither quietly down the tree when they had gone by. He was grinning widely. He guessed that a trick was to be played on him—and he was going to play a trick, too!

The three children came to the edge of the lawn. The grass had been cut and it was easy to look across to the little summer-house. No one seemed to be there now. What a pity! Perhaps Kit had gone out.

18

"We'll separate," whispered Robin. "Lucy, you go that way. Betty, keep here, and I'll go the other way. Then, when I give a whistle, we'll all dart out of our hiding-places and catch Kit when he comes."

So the three separated, and keeping well hidden in the undergrowth beyond the lawn, they wriggled along to surround the grassy patch.

Suddenly Betty had a terrible shock. A most fiercesome-looking face glared at her from out of a bush. It was red and blue all over, and was topped by a magnificent feathered head-dress. It was Kit, of course. He sprang on Betty, and before she could shout for help he had jerked her to her feet and set her with her back to a tree.

He whipped a rope from around his waist and even as Betty yelled in fright he tied her to the tree so that she could not escape.

"One prisoner!" said the boy with a grin. "Now for the others!"

Lucy was frightened when she heard Betty's yell, and she lay quite still in the undergrowth. But Robin went to his sister's rescue, standing up to see where she was and then rushing towards her.

"Look out, Robin, look out!" yelled Betty as Robin came running up. "That boy is up a tree—look, just there!"

But it was too late! As Robin looked up into the tree, Kit dropped down on him from a branch, and both boys rolled to the ground. Kit was very strong, and it was not long before he sat astride Robin and tied up his arms so that he could not struggle!

"Another prisoner to tie up to a tree!" said Kit with a grin. He shook back the enormous feathers on his head and grinned all over his brilliant red and blue face. "Come on!"

"Come and help me, Lucy, quick!" yelled Robin. But Lucy was too scared to move. Kit dragged the unwilling Robin to the tree next to Betty and deftly tied him there.

Robin was furious and strained at the rope, trying to free himself. But Kit knew all about knots and loops, and both Betty and Robin were proper prisoners!

And then it was poor Lucy's turn! Kit found her easily, because she really was frightened. He tied her up to a third tree, and then stood in front of them, grinning his wide grin. "Now for a war-dance!" he said, "and then maybe I'll try shooting a few arrows at you!"

He did this amazing war dance again, circling round the trees, making a wonderful noise of yelling and whooping as he went. The three children watched him, angry that they were prisoners, but admiring Kit very much because he really did seem exactly like a real Red Indian.

"I suppose you thought you'd creep into my garden and take *me* prisoner!" said Kit, stopping at last. "You can't trick Kit Anthony Armstrong like that! I'm going to get my bow and shoot a few arrows at you now! I'll be back!"

To the children's horror the boy sped off towards the house. Was he really going to do as he said? It wouldn't be at all pleasant to have arrows shot into them—or around them! Lucy began to cry.

Robin pulled hard at the rope that bound his hands. If only he could get free and untie the others! But it was no use at all. He couldn't undo the stiff knots.

Then he heard the sound of voices near the house. It seemed as if Kit had met someone. The children listened. Kit was coming back—without his bow and arrows!

"I say," he said, "the dragon's back from her walk! She'll be furious if she sees you here in our garden. I'd better set you free. No—I shan't have time! She's coming to the summer-house, look! Now listen—stay absolutely still and quiet and maybe she won't see you. I'll go and hide somewhere and hope to set you free when she goes back to the house."

Kit disappeared into the bushes. Almost at once the fierce-looking woman appeared, carrying a book. The children's heart sank as she took a chair from the summer-house and sat down in it, opening her book.

They could not be seen from where the woman sat, so they all stayed as still as they could. Betty thought the name Kit had for her was very good. She really was fierce enough for a dragon!

And then Lucy got a tickle in her throat! She hardly

20

dared to clear the tickle away, so she swallowed hard. But the tickle came back, even worse. She swallowed again—and then, alas! she coughed! It was rather a big cough, and it made the woman look up at once.

"Is that you, Kit?" she said. There was no answer. Poor Lucy tried to choke back her next cough, but it came loudly, though Robin frowned fiercely at her. The dragon got up at once.

She came round a big bush—and saw the three children tied up to the trees! She stared at them in such amazement that Betty wanted to laugh. It seemed as if the dragon really and truly could not believe her eyes!

Nobody said a word. Robin tried to look as if it was the most ordinary thing in the world to be tied to a tree in someone else's garden. And then the dragon found her voice!

"WHAT are you doing here?" she asked. "How dare you come into my garden without permission? Who are you? Why have you tied yourselves up to my trees?"

"We're the children from next door," said Robin. "We came to play with the boy here."

Then the woman said a most astonishing thing. "*Boy!*" she said. "A *boy* here! There's no boy here at all! You must be mad. I shall complain to your mother about you. You are never to come here again. As for there being a boy here, you are quite mistaken. Whoever told you that has not told you the truth. There is no child here at all."

The children listened to all this in the greatest amazement. Robin was about to say that the boy had tied them up, when he caught sight of Kit signalling to him from a bush behind the dragon's back. It was plain that Kit did not want Robin to say anything more.

The dragon undid Robin's ropes and the boy then set his sister and cousin free. "Now, if I catch you here again I shall quite probably spank the whole lot of you," said the fierce woman. "And remember what I've said—there is NO BOY HERE!"

The children fled home, puzzled and frightened. "It is a mystery," said Robin solemnly when they were safe in their own garden again. "A real mystery. Why should that woman tell such a story? Girls, we've GOT to find out what it's all about!"

Chapter Three

THE BEGINNING OF THE ADVENTURE

ROBIN, BETTY and Lucy discussed the happenings next door as they stripped off their Red Indian suits. "We had better not tell anyone," said Robin. "Perhaps we oughtn't to have slipped into the garden next door like that without permission. I say, wasn't Kit smart to capture us all? I can't say I liked being tied up like that—but he did come along to set us free when that fierce woman was near."

"I liked him," said Betty. "I wish he'd teach me that war-dance. We could go right down to the bottom of the garden to learn it. Mummy would have a fit if we all started yelling like that."

"Are we going in to see that boy again?" said Lucy. "I'd be rather afraid to, after seeing that fierce dragon-woman. And *why* did she say there wasn't a boy there? I suppose she didn't know we'd seen him. She must be silly if she thought we'd tied ourselves up to trees!"

"I vote we go in again to-morrow," said Robin. "Not to-day, because we've got to go out with Mummy—and, anyway, that woman might be on the watch. But to-morrow we might."

"I don't want to," said Lucy.

"Nor do I," said Betty.

"Pooh—cowards!" said Robin scornfully. "That is just like girls—always afraid when anything happens. All right, I'll go by myself!"

Before he went the next day, Robin climbed up the tree to see if the dragon-woman was anywhere about. He couldn't see anyone on the lawn at all. As he slid down the tree to the ground, Lucy came running up.

"That fierce woman has just gone out!" she panted. "I went out after Sandy, who ran out of the front gate, and I saw her going down the lane. Why don't you squeeze into the next-door garden now and find Kit?"

"I'm going to," said Robin, and he went to the hedge to find the thin part through which they had all squeezed the day before.

But a great surprise awaited him! It was quite impossible to get through into the next-door garden now—because somebody had erected strong, chain-link fencing all the way down the other side of the hedge!

"Look at that!" said Robin, in surprise. "That must have been done yesterday whilst we were out with Mummy. It's no good squeezing through the hedge now—we couldn't get past that fencing. It's a kind of extra-strong wire-netting—the kind they use to keep cattle in, I should think! Golly! Fancy doing all that to keep us out!"

"It makes me think there really *is* a mystery next door," said Lucy, feeling excited. "We can't get over the top of the fencing either—it's much too high. The boy next door is a sort of prisoner, it seems to me."

As the children stood looking through the hedge at the strange and unexpected fence, they heard the sound of distant voices. One was Kit's—and the other was a man's.

"Let's do a bit of shouting to one another," said Robin, "then Kit will know we are playing here, and perhaps come to the hedge to talk to us. We'd better not shout to *him*. For some reason or other the people next door plainly don't want us to know Kit lives there. Come—shout to me and I'll shout back."

23

So the three began to shout loudly to one another, hoping Kit would hear them and know they were there. But although they waited some time the boy did not come to the hedge.

"I'll climb the tree again and see if he's still there," said Robin at last. So he climbed high and looked down into the garden below. Kit *was* there—but a man was with him this time, not the fierce-looking woman. The man looked stern and rather old, from what Robin could see of him. He appeared to be teaching Kit.

As Robin looked, the man shut the book they were studying, and leaned back in his chair. Robin could not hear what he said, but he imagined that he was telling Kit he was free to play. Now perhaps the boy would come to talk to the others!

But he didn't, for the man still sat there. Kit went into the summer-house and brought out a ball. He threw it up into the air and caught it. The man bent his head and read his book.

Kit went on and on throwing the ball high, and higher—and then suddenly he threw the ball with all his force towards the next-door garden! It curved high over the tree and then disappeared into Robin's own garden, landing with a thud!

"How peculiar!" thought Robin, and watched to see what the boy did next. He produced another ball and began throwing that about, too. Then he sat down, took out his pocket-knife and began to whittle at a stick.

"I'll find his ball," thought Robin, and slid down the tree. "Perhaps he has thrown it over to give us an excuse to take it back to the house and ask for him."

The boy told Betty and Lucy what had happened, and they all hunted for the ball. Sandy came along and hunted, too, his tail quivering with excitement, for he had no idea what everyone was looking for, but he couldn't help hoping it was a rabbit.

The ball seemed to have disappeared completely. It was most tiresome. Everyone scraped about for it, in the most unlikely places. And then Sandy found it! He gave a whine and put his paw on it. He rolled it out from under a bush and then sat down to receive praise and pats, very sorry to find that it was only a ball that was lost, and not a rabbit.

24

Robin picked up the ball. "Good dog!" he said to Sandy. "You're worth a hundred cats! Tiger would just sit on a wall and turn her nose up at us if we lost anything."

"Do you think we *dare* to take the ball back next door?" said Betty. "*I* don't dare!"

"I'll take it," said Robin. "It's a pretty awful ball, anyway—it's got a tear in it. It wouldn't be any good for bouncing."

Lucy took it and put her fingers inquisitively into the hole. She was just about to take them out again when her eyes widened in excitement.

"What's up?" said Robin.

"There's something inside," said Lucy. "Wait—let me get it out!"

She wriggled her finger and thumb about inside the old ball, and heard the crackle of paper. She got hold of it at last and pulled it out.

"It's a note!" she said. "Golly, what a clever way of sending us a message!"

"Right under the nose of that man, too," said Robin. "I think Master Kit is very clever. I'd just love to have him for a friend! Give me the note, Lucy. What does it say?"

Lucy handed over the note and Robin unfolded it. It was quite short, written in a strong, bold handwriting.

"To My Three Prisoners—

"Don't believe the Dragon when she says I'm not here! She has a Reason. I'm very lonely and bored, and I should like to know you. But you mustn't be seen here. They've put a chain-link fence all round the garden now to keep you out. But holes can be dug underneath! What about it? Chuck this ball back with an answer when you get a chance!

"K.A.A."

This was really a very thrilling note indeed to get. The three children stared at one another in excitement. There certainly was a Mystery—and only Kit could explain it. They must—they really *must*—get into the garden next door again, somehow. But they would have to be very careful not to be caught.

They all read the note again. It seemed even stranger and more exciting the second time. "We'll write an answer," said Robin. "And of course, we'll dig a hole underneath a bit of the fencing and get through that way. It's an awfully good idea. But we'd better do it away at the bottom of the garden in case anyone sees us."

"We'll have to take turns at it," said Betty. "We'll have to keep guard. O-o-oh, it will be fun! I say—won't it be thrilling if we get into the next-door garden again and have to keep a lookout for the Dragon? It makes me shiver to think of it!"

"Shall we answer the note?" asked Lucy. "What shall we say?"

They went indoors to get paper and pencil, and Robin wrote an answer

To Our Captor—

"We're going to dig a hole. Can you get out at night? It would be best to meet then. Say, to-night at midnight, by the summer-house, if possible. Send the ball back with an answer.

"Robin, Lucy and Betty."

The ball was thrown back. Robin threw it, as he could throw really well. Betty sat at the top of the chestnut tree to watch if it fell on the lawn. She came down in such a state of giggles that the other two couldn't get a word out of her for some time.

"Oh, Robin—the ball fell right on that man's book!" giggled Betty. "It gave him such a jump! And then he turned round and began to scold Kit for throwing it at him. Kit took the ball and went into the summer-house with it."

"Golly, that must have been a funny sight to see," said Robin, with a chuckle. "I expect Kit's read the note by now. Come on— let's see where would be the best place to dig a hole. We could be starting that now, really. Where's Sandy? He can come, too, and scrape about with his paws. He would be quite a help."

So all four went off down the garden, carrying spades—at least, Sandy didn't carry one, though he would dearly have liked to. He felt very important following the children about.

26

They examined the hedge thoroughly, and found just the place to dig a hole.

"Between these two hawthorn trees would be best," said Robin. "We can cut away the lower branches so that they won't scratch us while we work. We can dig deep down here because the ground is nice and soft. I guess it will take us some time to burrow right under the fencing the other side.

"Well, we don't need a very big hole," said Betty. "We can wriggle down the passage like Red Indians do. I say, won't it be fun! Sandy, you go and begin the hole—just there, look!"

So Sandy obligingly went down between the hawthorn trees and began to scrape so violently that the earth flew up in the children's faces.

"Lucy, you keep guard," said Robin. "Betty, you and I will start digging. Come on. Get away now, Sandy. You've made a fine beginning!"

So the hole was begun, and the three children worked very hard indeed to make it big enough to wriggle down at night. What an adventure! Through the hole at midnight! They were all longing for twelve o'clock to come.

"I shall feel a bit frightened!" said Betty. "But that will be part of the fun!"

Chapter Four

THE HOLE UNDER THE FENCE

THE CHILDREN worked very hard indeed at digging the hole under the chain-link fencing. When Mummy called them in to their dinner they were tired and hungry, and also extremely dirty.

"Good gracious!" said Mummy. "What in the world have you been doing with yourselves? You look as if you've been trying to dig down to Australia or something!"

"Well—we have been digging," said Betty.

The others frowned at her. They thought Betty was silly even to hint at their secret.

"Shall I come and see what you've been digging?" said Mummy.

But to her surprise nobody seemed very keen on taking her down the garden to see their mornings' work.

"It's a sort of secret," said Robin at last. Mummy was very understanding about secrets. She nodded her head.

"I see," she said. "Well, you keep your secret! I'm sure it's something lovely."

Everyone heaved a sigh of relief. They ate their dinners hungrily, and then went out again to go on with their work. They talked about Kit in low voices as they dug.

"He must be jolly bored living in that house with the dragon-woman and that stern-looking man," said Robin. "Nobody to play with or have a laugh with."

"And people saying he isn't there at all!" said Betty. "What a story-teller that woman is!"

"Sh!" said Lucy suddenly. She was on guard, watching to see if anyone came down their garden or the next. "Someone is coming down next-door's garden!"

At once the children hid their spades under a bush and crouched down low in some tall grass nearby. They lay there quite quiet. They heard the sound of someone brushing against the overgrown bushes next door, and then came the sound of voices.

"This garden is very thick and overgrown. No one can see into it from the outside. That's good!"

"Have you been all round?" came the voice of the dragon-woman. Robin tried to see who her companion was. He felt sure it was the stern-looking man.

"Yes—I went all round when George put up the wire-fencing," said the other voice. "No one can get in now, and no one can *see* in."

The two people came near to where the children had been working. Sandy growled softly. Lucy put her hand on his collar to keep him quiet. All the children shivered with excitement, fearing that their digging might be discovered.

But luckily it wasn't. The two people went slowly by, and neither of them saw the deep hole under the fencing just there. When they had gone out of sight and hearing, the diggers began again. This time Robin was on guard.

By the time that tea was ready the hole was almost deep and big enough to wriggle through. "We can easily finish after tea," said Robin. "Gracious, my back aches! O-o-oh!—I don't like standing up straight at all!"

"We'd better clean ourselves up a bit before your mother sees us," said Lucy, looking at their dirty overalls and hands. So they all went and had a good wash, and brushed their clothes well. They ate such an enormous tea that their mother was really surprised.

"Anyone would think you had all been very hard at work, the way you are eating," she said, as plate after plate was emptied. "Robin, I can't believe you want another bun. That must be the fifth you've had!"

"Wrong, Mummy!" said Robin. "It's the seventh!"

The hole was finished by six o'clock. By that time it was quite big enough to wriggle through. It was like a curving trench that sloped downwards to the fencing, underneath it, and then up the other side. It had been very difficult to manage the other side, but somehow Robin had managed to scramble through underneath and dig the trench widely there, too.

"Now—we'll all wriggle through on our tummies," said Robin, and one by one they struggled to get under the fencing and into the next-door garden.

It was really very exciting. Sandy was most excited, too, and ran down the trench and back, his tail wagging nineteen to the dozen!

"Don't you think we'd better cover up the trench this side with branches, or something?" said Lucy, when they all stood among the overgrown grass and bushes in the next-door garden. "It can so easily be seen now."

"Yes—we'll do that," said Robin, and began to break some branches to spread over the hole. "We can drag these sprays across when we go back. The last one can manage to do it."

Sandy suddenly stood still, his ears up, his nose twitching and his tail quivering. He had heard something. He gave a little growl.

"Somebody's coming!" said Lucy in a whisper. "Come on back."

But there was no time to get back. The stern-looking man was taking an evening walk around the grounds, and the children caught sight of him between the trees.

"Climb a tree, quick!" whispered Robin. "Up you get, Lucy! I'll give you a leg up!"

He pushed poor Lucy up a tree, and then swung himself up, too. Betty had already climbed into one. The man came nearer. Luckily he was walking very slowly.

"What about Sandy?" whispered Lucy. "He can't climb a tree! Lie down, Sandy; lie down!"

But Sandy didn't! He stood under Lucy's tree, looking up at her and Robin in great surprise. "He'll make that man discover us!" said Lucy.

But as soon as the man came near, Sandy left the tree and ran up to him, his teeth bared, growling fiercely. The man stopped in astonishment.

"Well! How did *you* get in here!" he cried. "I shouldn't have thought there was any way through this fencing! You must have been here yesterday when we fenced in the grounds—and you couldn't get out. Well—out you go now—and stop that silly growling or I'll give you the WHIP!"

Sandy didn't like the sound of that word. His tail dropped. He let the man take hold of his collar and lead him sternly off up the garden towards the house.

"He's going to let him out of the gate," whispered Lucy to Robin. "Oh, good!"

"We'd better wait up here a little while in case the man comes back too quickly for us to get back," said Robin.

So they waited in silence, wishing that Kit would come along. But he didn't.

Suddenly they heard a pitter-patter of feet and a swishing of bushes as some little body came up to their trees.

"It's Sandy again!" said Lucy with a giggle. "The man let him out—and he just went down our garden, found our hole, and came through it to fetch us! Really, isn't he awfully clever? I hope the man doesn't come walking back again, because if he does he'll be frightfully surprised to see Sandy here once more!"

"You'd better shin down the tree and get back through the hole with Sandy," said Robin. "Then keep a watch out and give a whistle when you're sure it's safe for Betty and me to come down."

So Lucy slid down the tree and went to the trench, with Sandy licking her ankles in delight. The girl wriggled down on her tummy, and, like a real Red Indian, slid along down the hole and up the other side. It was very bad indeed for clothes. Lucy made up her mind to wear her very oldest things next time!

She stood up when she got to the other side and cautiously went up and down the hedge to see if anyone was about in the next garden. But it seemed quite all right. So she gave a whistle, and Robin and Betty slid down their trees and were soon wriggling through the hole. Robin went last and pulled the broken branches over the trench. It was quite well hidden then.

"I say—this is all rather exciting, isn't it?" he said as he tried to brush the dirt off himself. "Golly, aren't we dirty? I bet Mummy will want to know a bit more about our secret if we keep going in as black as this. We'd better look out some raggedy old things to wear for this tunnelling business!"

Their mother was certainly not at all pleased when they appeared for supper, although they had made themselves as clean as possible. She sent them to have a bath as soon as they appeared.

"This Digging Secret, whatever it is, has got to stop," she said. "You are ruining your clothes."

"All right, Mummy, we won't dig any more," promised Robin, and went off to have a bath. They ate a big supper, and then were so tired with their hard work that they began to yawn widely.

"Goodness me, you'd better all go to bed!" their mother said. "You are tired out. Lucy is quite pale."

For once in a way the children didn't argue about going early to bed. "We want to be awake at midnight, so we might as well get a bit of sleep first," said Robin to the others, when they were alone.

"How shall we wake up?" said Lucy.

"I've got an alarm clock," said Robin. "I'll set it for a quarter to twelve, and wake up you two then. Come on— let's go to bed. I really am tired out!"

So they all went to bed, and as soon as they had put their heads on their pillows, they were asleep. They dreamt of tunnels and passages and holes, and Boys Who Weren't There, and dragon-women who frowned! And at last Robin's alarm went off under his pillow! He had put the little clock there, afraid that it might wake up his mother if he stood it on a table. It awoke him with a jump and he groped under the pillow to turn off the alarm bell.

Then he went to wake the two girls. They sat up in bed, excited.

"Put on those old things we got ready after supper," whispered Robin. "Don't be long! It's a quarter to midnight!"

In five minutes' time three children and Sandy crept quietly out of the house, Robin's torch shining to light the way. Down the dark garden to the hole under the fence! Dear me, what a thrill it all was!

Chapter Five

THROUGH THE HOLE AT MIDNIGHT

THE THREE children made their way down beside the hedge that separated the two gardens. Sandy ran with them, astonished and excited. Could this be a rabbit-hunt in the middle of the night?

Two great gleaming eyes of green suddenly appeared in the light of the torch. Lucy gave a little scream of fright. Sandy stopped—then gave a glad yelp and rushed forward. The eyes disappeared, and there came the noise of something bounding up a tree.

"It was only Tiger," said Betty, relieved. "Gracious, how queer her eyes looked, gleaming out of the darkness like that. Lucy, get Sandy back before he starts to bark."

Sandy was hauled away from the tree up which Tiger sat, her eyes gleaming green again. The little company went on down the garden. Betty couldn't help feel a little shaky at the knees. It was a bit *too* exciting!

They came to the hole under the fencing. Robin shone his torch on it. "You go first," he said to Betty. "Then Lucy. Then I'll come with the torch. I'll stand here and shine it for you girls to see by."

One by one they wriggled through the hole, and at last they all stood safely on the other side with Sandy at their heels, his tail wagging with pleasure. Robin shone his torch on the thick undergrowth.

"I hope the light of my torch won't be seen," he whispered. "I'll keep my hand over it as much as I can. Let's all take hands and try and walk in a single file."

So they did that, and stumbled along in the long grass and round thick bushes until they came to the little wooded part that surrounded the lawn.

"Now, whereabouts is the summer-house?" said Robin in a whisper. "Oooh—what's that?"

They all stared at a red glow a little way off. It disappeared. Then it came again. Then it vanished once more.

"It's the light of a red lantern being turned on and off," whispered Robin. "I bet it's Kit in the summer-house. Look, we're on the lawn now. Keep hold of hands, and we'll go across the grass in the dark, towards the light."

So they went silently across the lawn, and came to a dark shape, which was the summer-house. Inside there came a red glow again, and vanished.

"Kit! Is it you?" whispered Robin.

A low voice answered him: "Yes! My, you're punctual! It's just striking twelve! Hark!"

A clock could be heard striking from the house. The children crowded inside the summer-house with Sandy at their heels, his tail banging against their legs as he wagged it.

"Are we safe here?" asked Robin, feeling for the seat that ran round the little summer-house. "What's that you've got? A lantern?"

"Yes," said Kit, and he switched on the dim red glow again. "I thought it would be a signal to show you where to come. We're quite safe here now. I heard my tutor snoring away in bed, and I know the dragon couldn't guess I'm out, because I left a bolster down the middle of my bed, in case she looked into my room."

They went silently across the lawn

"Good," said Lucy. "Kit, that was a smart idea of yours to send us a message inside your old ball. We dug a hole under the fencing, just as you said."

"Good for you!" said Kit. "I thought you would manage to do it. I'm glad you're next door. I may perhaps have a bit of fun sometimes now."

"Kit, why did the dragon say there was no boy here?" asked Robin curiously. "It was an awful fib."

"Well—there's a reason for it," said Kit. "If I tell you, will you promise faithfully not to tell a single soul?"

"Of course," said all three at once.

"You can trust us," said Robin.

Sandy licked Kit's leg, meaning to say that he, too, could be trusted.

"Well, I'll tell you," said Kit solemnly. He switched on the red glow again, and his face shone queerly in the crimson light. "There's somebody after my life!"

Nobody said anything for a minute. This was a very strange thing to hear!

"What do you mean, Kit?" asked Robin at last.

"It's like this," said Kit. "I'm an American boy, and I'm very, very rich. My grandfather left an enormous fortune to my father, and when he disappeared and was thought to be dead in an aeroplane crash, the money came to me."

"Oh—did your father die when the plane crashed, then?" said Robin, feeling sorry for Kit.

"The plane was burnt," said Kit. "Nobody could be rescued from it. My father was known to be travelling in it, so I expect he lost his life when it crashed and burnt out. Anyway—I came into his fortune."

"But I don't see why anyone should be after your life just because you're rich," said Betty, puzzled.

"Ah, but, you see—if I died, there's a horrible uncle of mine who would get my money," said Kit. "It's an uncle I've never seen. He's tried to kidnap me twice already. I guess I wouldn't have much chance if he got hold of me!"

This all sounded most extraordinary to the three children. They felt as if they must be in a dream, hearing about enormous riches, and a wicked uncle who was after a small boy! They looked at Kit's earnest face glowing in the red light.

"Oh—is that why you're in hiding, then?" said Lucy. "Because you *are* in hiding, aren't you? Is the dragon looking after you—and your tutor? What's a tutor?"

"Oh, a teacher," said Kit. "They found this lonely house in this desolate bit of country—sorry, I know it's lovely with its rivers and hills, but it's boring to a boy like me, who is used to living in towns—well, they found this house and rented it to hide me till they can track down my wicked uncle and stop him coming after me. We travelled over from America and gave him the slip."

"Will he come to this country and look for you?" asked Betty, a little shiver going down her back.

"You bet he will!" said Kit. "But don't you worry! I'm not afraid. The only thing *I'm* afraid of is being bored and lonely. I guess if the dragon had known there were three children in your house she'd never have come here! But she heard there was one little girl and that was all."

"Well, that's all there is usually," said Betty. "The little girl is me. But Robin comes home from boarding school in the hols, and this summer our cousin Lucy is staying with us, too."

"*And* we're going to have some fun," said Kit. "Like me to teach you that war dance? It was taught me by a real live Red Indian. And my Red Indian suit is a real one, not a toy one like yours."

Kit sounded very exciting. The three children thought he would be a marvellous friend to have—just right for Robin.

"Robin was feeling rather vexed these hols, because he only had two girls to play with," said Betty. "Now he will have you. But I hope you'll let me and Lucy play with you sometimes."

"You bet!" said Kit. "I haven't got any sisters, and I always wanted some. You can play with me any time. We'll have some fun!"

"Is that dragon-woman very fierce?" asked Betty. "Who is she?"

"Oh, she's not bad," said Kit. "My tutor, Mr Barton, got her to keep an eye on me, and to watch out that nobody came near me, or knew about me here—and I'm not supposed to leave this garden at all, or show myself. If

I obey her, she's all right—but honestly I believe she'd get a stick and spank me if I didn't do what she said!"

"I shouldn't be surprised if she did, either," said Betty. "She looks like that. I hope she never discovers us here!"

"Do you think you really *are* safe here?" asked Lucy anxiously. "It would be so awful if your wicked uncle discovered you and tried to get you."

"I don't see how he can possibly know," said Kit. "Anyway, as I told you—*I'm* not afraid! Now, don't you go and tell my secret to anyone at all, will you? I want to be friends with you."

"You did give us a fright when you tied us up to trees yesterday," said Lucy with a giggle. "We meant to give *you* a fright!"

"I know," said Kit with a laugh. "Now—let's make plans. I don't see why I shouldn't sometimes get through that tunnel of yours and go into your garden, if I can be somewhere that no one can spot me."

"Well—if you do that, why can't you come out boating with us on the river one day?" said Robin eagerly. "We know a secret way down to the river. You'll be quite safe. We've a boat of our own, and we can have fun. We could take our dinner out sometimes and picnic on a little island we know, and bathe there. Wouldn't you like that?"

"Would I not!" said Kit, and his eyes shone in the red light. "I'll have to think of some way to outwit the dragon, though. It would have to be some day she goes out, I expect, and leaves me safely penned up here in the grounds! We'd better wait till she's settled down here a bit. You can come in to see me, can't you? There's a big attic at the top of the house that Mr Barton has given me to play in. We could go there. I can lock the door so that no one can come in."

"Oooh, yes," said Robin. "And we could play all sorts of games in your grounds, too, because they are so thick and old and overgrown. Marvellous for Red Indians."

"Well, listen—you come along in again tomorrow," said Kit. "After dinner, see? The dragon often has a nap then, and we could have fine fun playing about at the bottom of our grounds. Bring that dog, too. I like him."

"All right," said Robin. "I say, this is going to be fun, isn't it? Sort of secret and exciting. I hope that wicked uncle of yours doesn't find out where you are. It would be tiresome if you had to leave and hide somewhere else just as we had got used to you!"

"We'll come to-morrow, then," said Lucy. "And we'll bring our Red Indian things. You can teach us that war-dance."

"We'd better go now," said Robin, getting up. "See you to-morrow. Come on, girls. We'll skirt round the edge of the lawn before I put on my torch. Take hands. Good night, Kit."

"Good night, and thanks awfully for coming," said the American boy in his nice drawly voice. "I'll be right at the very bottom of our grounds, waiting for you. So long!"

The three children went out of the little summer-house, with Sandy at their heels, his hot breath on their bare legs. It was exciting finding their way by the light of Robin's little torch to the hole under the fence. They wriggled through and then made their way up to their own house.

"Good night!" whispered Robin at his bedroom door. "Now, not a word about all this, mind!"

"Of course not!" whispered back Lucy and Betty. They slipped into their bedroom and snuggled into bed.

"It's going to be exciting!" said Betty. But she didn't guess quite *how* exciting everything was going to be!"

Chapter Six

AN EXCITING CLIMB

NEXT DAY the children got out their Red Indian things ready to go into the next-door garden and play with Kit.

"I shall love to learn that nice, yelly dance," said Lucy. "I say—shan't we spoil our Red Indian things when we wriggle down the hole?"

"Yes—we shall," said Robin. "It would be a pity to do that. Let's see—what can we do about it?"

"Easy!" said Betty. "Put them in a sack, tie up the neck of the sack with a long bit of string, and then drag it through after us!"

"Clever girl!" said Robin, and Betty felt pleased. She went off to find a sack, and soon came back with one from the garden shed.

They all stuffed their Red Indian things inside it. Then, with their very oldest things on, they set off down the garden.

Mummy called after them: "Now don't do any more of that dirty digging, please!"

"No, we've finished that," called back Robin.

"Take some plums from the Victoria plum tree to eat at eleven o'clock!" called Mummy. So the children went to the plum tree and stuffed their pockets full of ripe plums. They took enough for Kit, too.

Sandy went with them as thrilled as usual. He kept a sharp lookout for Tiger, longing to chase her, but she was nowhere to be seen. Never mind! Perhaps there would be rabbits that morning. Sandy hoped for rabbits to chase, no matter whether he went walking on the hills, down the garden, or in the busy streets of a town!

They came to the hole. It was still there, hidden by branches. "Good!" said Robin. "Come on. You go first, Bets. Then Lucy."

Soon the three of them were standing cautiously on the other side of the tunnel, brushing the dirt off their clothes, listening for the sound of anyone coming. But there was no sound to be heard except the wind in the trees and a yellowhammer bird calling somewhere.

Robin had pulled the sack of clothes after him, and it had come sliding along the tunnel, much to Sandy's amazement. He had pranced after it, trying to snap at it.

"It's a good thing Sandy is such a quiet sort of dog," said Betty to Lucy. "If he was a barky dog, we couldn't possibly take him with us."

"I wonder whereabouts Kit is," said Robin. "We'll find him before we change in to our Red Indian things. Oh, blow—I believe it's going to rain!"

The children looked up through the trees in dismay. The sky was over-clouded and looked very low and black. Big drops of rain fell on their upturned faces. It was too bad!

"Come on down to the bottom of the garden," said Robin at last. "We'd better find Kit and see if there is anywhere we can shelter till the rain is over."

They made their way down the overgrown garden to the bottom. Chain-link fencing ran all the way round. Kit was certainly a prisoner!

41

"Hallo!" said a voice from up a tree. Kit seemed to love being up a tree! "Glad you've come—I've been waiting ages for you."

"Hallo!" said Lucy and the others. "I say—I hope this rain will soon stop!"

It was now pouring down and the children were getting very wet. They stood under the trees, hoping the clouds would blow over.

"There's nowhere we can shelter except the summer-house, and I daren't take you there in case the dragon comes to find me," said Kit gloomily.

"What about that big attic you said you've got for a play-room?" said Robin. "Could we get there without being seen?"

"Well—there might be a way," said Kit, after thinking for a minute. "Are you good at climbing?"

"Yes," said Robin. "Quite good. Lucy's the only one who's not really used to it."

"I can climb all right!" said Lucy indignantly.

"Well, listen," said Kit, his eyes beginning to shine. "If we went right round the garden to the other side, we could creep almost up to the house without being seen, because the trees are so thick there. There's an enormous ash tree that reaches right up to the top of the house, and its branches touch the walls. We couldn't climb up the trunk; it's too tall. But we could get on to the flat garage roof, then into the tree and up. I believe we could easily get in through the attic window then."

"Oooh—let's try," said Betty. "It sounds fine! If only nobody sees us!"

"There are no windows that side of the house where the garage is, except for two attic windows at the top," said Kit, thinking. "It ought to be all right. I tell you what I'll do. I'll go to the house and make sure that no one is about that could see you—then when you hear me whistle a tune, you climb up on to the garage roof and into the tree."

"I'll try it first," said Robin. "I don't want the girls to do anything dangerous, you know."

"Sure!" said Kit. "What about the dog? He can't climb."

They all stood and thought what to do with the little fox-terrier. Sandy looked up at them inquiringly. He didn't want to be left out of anything.

"Couldn't you bundle him into the sack of clothes?" asked Kit. "Would he stay there without making a noise? I could carry him upstairs with me then, hidden in the clothes."

"I don't expect he'd mind a bit," said Lucy. "He's used to all kinds of queer games. Aren't you, Sandy?"

"Wuff," answered Sandy politely, his ears quivering.

"Let's try him now," said Robin. So they stuffed Sandy into the bag of clothes, and then Robin put the sack over his shoulder to carry. Sandy gave a muffled yelp and tried to wriggle—but when Lucy patted the sack and said, "It's all right, Sandy dear, it's all right!" he settled down and didn't mind at all.

"Well, we can take him up to the attic like that," said Kit. "That's good. Now come on. I'll take you up to the back of the garage, and show you what to do. Then I'll go in and scout round to make sure everything's all right."

Kit took them round the bottom of the grounds. The rain poured down and everyone was very wet and uncomfortable. They crept quietly up the other side of the big garden and at last, through a thicket of trees and bushes, they came to the back of the big garage, which was built on to the side of the house.

The children looked up at it. "How do we get up there, to begin with?" asked Robin. "We can't fly!"

"I'll get a ladder," said Kit. "There's one in the garage."

He disappeared, and came out a minute or two later carrying a light ladder. He set it against the wall of the garage and it just reached the top.

"Now, up we go!" he said. He set the sack on the ground and let Sandy out for a minute to get some air. "We can put him back again when I'm ready to go indoors," he said. He went up the ladder, climbed out on to the flat roof and hauled Robin up too.

"Now, you can easily get into the ash tree branches from here," said Kit, pointing to where an enormous tree spread out strong branches over the garage roof. "Once you are in the tree you can climb from branch to branch

43

till you reach the attic window. It's that one—the one on the left, see? I'll go indoors now and go up to the attic with the sack of clothes and Sandy. Wait till you hear me whistle before you do anything."

Sandy was popped into the sack again. He was rather astonished, but made no fuss. Kit put him over his shoulder, winked merrily at the three children, and disappeared round the garage to go into the house.

Before two minutes had passed they heard the sound of "Yankee Doodle" being whistled loudly from above. They looked up and saw Kit at the attic window, which he opened widely. He nodded and grinned at them.

"Come on," said Robin in excitement. "I'll get up on to the roof first and give you girls a hand."

He went up the ladder and got on to the flat garage roof. Lucy came next, and he pulled her off the top rung of the ladder on to the roof. Then came Betty. Robin looked at the ash tree and chose a sturdy branch that stuck out over the roof. "This looks a nice easy one to climb on," he said. "Lucy, do you think you can manage all right? It's a good way to go up."

"Yes, of course I can manage!" said Lucy. "I'm not such a quick climber as you two, but I'm all right, silly!"

It really wasn't very difficult to climb up the tree. It had good easy branches for climbing. The three children soon reached one that was level with the attic window and slid along it to the sill.

But how were they to get on to the sill? The branch dipped with their weight when they went towards the end of it. Kit watched, his eyes wrinkling up as he wondered how to help.

"Wait a minute!" he said. He disappeared and came back with a broad plank he had taken from the box-room. He pushed it out of the window and Robin caught the end when it came to him. "Tie it firmly to the branch with this rope, then it won't slip," said Kit, and he threw a coil of strong rope to Robin. The boy bound the plank tightly to the tree. One end rested firmly on a broad branch, the other on the sill of the attic window. "We can always come in this way without being seen if we want to. We'll leave the plank tied there. No one is likely to see it!"

They stood in the big attic and looked round. It had slanting ceilings, and a skylight set just about the middle. Boxes and trunks were piled in one corner. Here and there were toys and games belonging to Kit—a set of electric railways, a fretwork set, a big bow and arrows, and several other things.

"Now let's dress up in our things and you shall teach us that war-dance," said Robin. "Come on! I say—is that dragon-woman anywhere about—or your tutor?"

"No—they're both out! Isn't it lucky?" said Kit. "The cook is in the kitchen, and the chauffeur, George, is out with my tutor. So we can make what noise we like! Hurry up and we'll get going."

They all changed into their Red Indian things. "We'd better lock the door, hadn't we?" said Robin, feeling that he really didn't want anyone to burst suddenly in on them.

"Right," said Kit, and he locked it. Then he began to teach them the dance. How they yelled, how they whooped, how they stamped round in a circle, all dressed up in their Red Indian costumes and feathers! They enjoyed themselves thoroughly.

And then they got a dreadful shock! There suddenly came a banging at the door, and the noise of someone trying to turn the handle. A voice called out sternly: "Kit, what are you doing? What's all this noise? Unlock the door at once!"

"It's my tutor back!" said Kit. "Golly, what are we going to do?"

Chapter Seven

MR BARTON IS ANGRY

THE FOUR children and Sandy stared at one another in dismay. Sandy gave a little growl, but Lucy stopped him at once.

"You mustn't be discovered here," said Kit in a whisper. "Where can I hide you?"

"Open the door, Kit, open it at once!" cried the voice of Kit's stern tutor. The children knew there was no time to escape out of the window. They looked round in despair. Robin caught sight of two or three big trunks and ran to them, beckoning to Betty and Lucy. Maybe they could get into them!

"All right, Mr Barton, I'll open the door," said Kit. "I was only practising my Indian war-dance."

He whispered into Robin's ear. "You try and get into the trunks whilst I pretend to fumble with the key in the door. That will give you a little time!"

Robin nodded and opened the lid of a big old trunk. He pushed Betty inside and shut down the lid. Then he put

Lucy into another, and last of all opened an enormous box and crouched down in it himself. He pulled the lid over him.

Meanwhile Kit had gone to the door and was rattling the handle and jiggling the key as if he was trying his hardest to open the door. When he saw the children were safely hidden, he thought it would be all right to open the door. His tutor was calling out impatiently all the time.

"Kit! What are you doing? Can't you open this door?"

"I'm trying my hardest!" panted Kit. "Just be patient, Mr Barton. I think the key is turning."

He turned it—and the door opened. His tutor came in, looking stern and vexed. He gazed round the room as if he expected to find it full of children. But there was no one there except Kit, who looked remarkably innocent.

"Do you mean to tell me that it was only you making all that awful noise?" cried his tutor, disbelievingly. "I know that you can often make a noise that sounds like a whole menagerie going at once—but it's impossible to believe that all those yells and shoutings and stampings were made by one small boy!"

Then an awful thing happened! Everyone had forgotten about Sandy! The little fox-terrier had run into a corner in fright when the banging at the door had become extra loud, but now he came out to see what the matter was, and stood by Kit, wagging his tail a little. Kit was afraid he might go and sniff at one of the trunks in which the others had hidden, and he picked him up at once. His tutor stared at the dog in the greatest amazement.

"That dog again!" he said. "How did he get up here? Did you bring him? And where in the world did he come from? There is fencing all round the garden!"

"I brought him up here," said Kit truthfully. "I found him in the garden. I'm so lonely, you see, and I do like him."

"He must belong to the people next door," said Mr Barton. "But I wish I knew how he gets into the garden."

"Through a rabbit-hole," suggested Kit. "He's quite a little dog—not much more than a puppy."

"Wuff!" said Sandy, hearing the word "rabbit" with great pleasure.

47

"He must go back," said Kit's tutor firmly. "Well, well—to think you and a small dog could make such a fearful noise together. Kindly do not lock the door again, Kit."

"Shall I take the dog back?" said Kit.

"Of course not," said his tutor. "You know we don't want you to be seen at all. And especially I don't want those children next door to know you are here. You know what children are—and then the secret will be out!"

He picked up Sandy and went out of the door.

"I'm going to take this dog back now," he said. "I want to give you some lessons when I come back, so get your books and take them down to my study. Be ready for me."

"Yes, sir," said Kit dolefully. As soon as his tutor was out of the room he flew to the big box in which Robin was hidden. "You must come out at once!" he hissed.

Robin was just about to push up the lid when to Kit's horror his tutor came back again to tell him something he had forgotten. The boy sat down at once on the lid of the box to prevent Robin from opening it and popping his head up!

Robin did not know that Mr Barton was back, and he couldn't think why the box lid wouldn't open. He pushed hard at it and began to speak to Kit.

Kit sat hard on the box, drumming his heels against it and whistling to hide the sound of Robin's voice.

His tutor was vexed with him. "Kit! Don't drum your heels like that and whistle whilst I am talking to you! Get up at once!"

Kit had to get up—but luckily by that time Robin had guessed something was up, and sat quietly inside the box. The three children were all trembling with excitement.

"I came back to tell you to get out the big world globe," said Kit's tutor. "You know where it is. Put it in the study ready for us. And don't be long, Kit, because I shall be back in a minute. Take off your Red Indian things."

He disappeared again and Kit waited until he had heard him going down the stairs. Then he quickly shut and locked the attic door and ran to the trunks. He pulled out Betty and Lucy, and Robin jumped out of his box, too.

"That was a narrow escape!" said Robin. "We'd better go at once. Come on, girls—along the plank and down the tree we go! When shall we see you again, Kit?"

"Don't know," said Kit dismally. "It's still pouring with rain. No good doing anything out of doors to-day, and I daren't risk you coming back to the attic. What about to-morrow?"

"We planned to go down the river," said Robin eagerly. "There's a big bend of it we haven't properly explored—the bit that's just beyond the tiny island we know. Like to come with us? Can you escape for a few hours, do you think? You could wriggle through our hole."

"I'll come somehow!" promised Kit. "I'll get the Dragon to let me have a picnic lunch by myself at the bottom of the grounds—but I'll bring my lunch through the hole and join you. What time? Twelve o'clock?"

"Yes, that would be fine," said Robin, going to the window. "Come on, girls. Kit's tutor will be back if we don't hurry!"

They got on to the plank one by one and slid along it cautiously to the tree. Then down they went and jumped on to the flat roof of the garage. Down the ladder and on to the ground—then right round the grounds and through the hole. The rain had made it muddy and their lovely Red Indian suits were in a fine mess by the time they had reached the other side.

"Never mind—we'll wait till they're dry and then brush them well," said Robin. "I wonder where Sandy is?"

They soon knew, for he came rushing to meet them when they went back to the house. Mummy had been surprised when Mr Barton had brought him back. She had felt sure he was with the children.

"Mummy, can we go for a picnic down to the river to-morrow?" asked Robin. "We want to go to that tiny island we found last year, and then explore the bend in the river beyond. We don't know that very well. It would be fun. If it's fine we might bathe, too."

"Yes, you can go," said Mummy. "I'll put up a nice lunch for you."

So the next day the three children and Sandy set off down the garden to see if Kit would be able to keep his word and come with them. It was not quite twelve o'clock. The sun shone down warmly out of a blue sky. The rain had all gone and it was a blazing August day.

They waited for Kit. Twelve o'clock came, but no Kit. The children waited a little longer. Sandy suddenly ran down the hole and disappeared. He did not come back when Lucy whistled to him, which was very naughty.

"Smelt a rabbit, I suppose," said Lucy, in disgust. "Well, I only hope Kit's tutor doesn't catch him again."

"It's a quarter-past twelve," said Robin, looking at his watch. "We'll just wait for Sandy to come back then we'd better not wait for Kit any more. It's a pity. He would have enjoyed a picnic on the river."

"Here's Sandy!" said Lucy, after about five minutes had gone by. "Naughty dog! Where have you been?"

"Look, Lucy, he's got something tied to his collar!" said Betty suddenly. "It's a note, or something."

"So it is!" said Lucy, and she undid the screwed-up note. She unfolded it and read it out loud.

"Can you possibly wait for me? Mr Barton has made me do extra work as I asked for the afternoon off for a picnic in the grounds. I shall be free at half-past twelve and can come then, with my food. Do wait!"

"K.A.A."

"Good old Sandy!" said Robin, patting the dog. "You didn't go after rabbits then! You went and found Kit and he managed to give you a message for us! Well, girls, we'll wait, won't we? It's only about five minutes from half-past twelve, anyway."

So they waited patiently, and just after the half-hour they heard a loud whistling. "Kit!" said Robin, and he stood up to show the boy the hole.

Kit wriggled through it on his tummy, and grinned as he stood up in the children's garden. "A jolly good way in and out, if a trifle dirty," he said. "Thanks for waiting. Mr Barton said I could have the afternoon off if I did extra lessons this morning. I hope nobody goes hunting for me this afternoon! Come on. Which way is it? Golly, I feel just like an escaped prisoner. I *am* going to enjoy myself!"

Kit was a wonderful companion. He made such a lot of jokes, and was so merry and full of laughter that the other three were delighted to have him with them. They let themselves out of the gate at the bottom of their garden and went across the fields, carrying their bags of food on their backs, slung by straps.

"We've got a little boat of our own on the river," said Robin. "We thought we'd take it out to-day, and row to the little island we know, have our lunch there and then do a bit of exploring beyond."

"You never know when I might want a good hiding-place!" said Kit with a laugh. "We could pretend that we're looking for one—one where nobody would find me even if they hunted for weeks!"

"O-o-oh, yes, that would be fun!" said Betty. "I do think you're an exciting person, Kit! Look—there's our boat! Come on, let's hurry and push her off. I'm longing to be on the river!"

They got into the boat—and off they went. Robin rowed and they all sang as they went. What fun they were going to have!

Chapter Eight

THE HOUSE-BOAT ON THE RIVER

"YOU'LL LIKE our tiny island," said Betty. "You haven't seen it either, Lucy. One year a swan nested there. And there are heaps of kingfishers, too. There's a little sandy beach where we can bathe and lie in the sun afterwards."

"Good," said Kit. "It sounds fine to me! Let me take the oars now, Robin."

Kit rowed very strongly and the little boat shot along quickly over the blue river. After a while they came to a bend and then the river widened out a good bit. Tucked away in the bend was a tiny island.

"That's our island!" said Robin. "It's nothing but a mound on which grows a little wood, a few blackberry bushes and grass. But it's fun. There's no rabbits though, Sandy!"

"Wuff!" said Sandy dolefully. He was sitting at the prow of the boat, watching the water as if he meant to jump into it at any moment. Lucy had her hand on his collar in case he really did!

The children ran the boat on to the little sandy beach. They jumped out and hauled the boat up a little way. Then they went over the tiny island. It was so small that it took only about four minutes to walk all the way round it!

"It's grand," said Kit. "I wish it was mine. Now, what about lunch—or shall we bathe first?"

"Let's bathe," said Robin. "I'm boiling hot!"

So they stripped off their shorts and jerseys and went into the water. They all had swim-suits underneath, ready for bathing. Kit was a marvellous swimmer. Once he disappeared under the water for such a long time that the others were quite frightened—but he popped up almost half-way across the river!

It was very hot in the sun. The four children and Sandy lay on the little sun-baked beach of the island and let themselves dry. Their swim-suits felt dry almost at once. Then they had their lunch.

They were terribly hungry. Kit had not got such a nice lunch as the others, so they shared with him. Sandy had some biscuits and one potted meat sandwich which Lucy spared for him out of her share. After lunch they felt lazy and sleepy.

"But don't let's go to sleep!" said Kit, sitting up. "I haven't come out to sleep! I want to explore. I don't know what your countryside is really like, you know. It's quite different from America. Let's take the boat and go and explore the bit you said you didn't know. Round that bend where the water is so blue and where those cute little birds are swimming, bobbing their heads like clockwork!"

"Moor-hens!" said Robin with a laugh. "Come on then. Into the boat we get!"

They all got into the boat and Sandy took his place at the prow. The boys took an oar each and rowed off. It was lovely on the river that afternoon. A cool breeze blew every now and again. The water splashed against the boat and made a lovely gurgling noise. The children were very happy.

They rowed round the big bend of the river. The banks were thickly lined with trees and the water was very deep.

"It's lovely here," said Lucy, lying back and letting one hand drag in the water as they went along. "I could go on like this for miles."

"I dare say you could!" said Robin, "if somebody else rows you! I don't see why you girls can't take a turn, do you, Kit?"

So the girls were made to take their turn at the oars, and the boys lazed as they went along past the thickly-wooded banks.

"Look! There's a house beyond there!" said Robin suddenly. "See how the lawn slopes down to the river. That's the first house we've seen since we left home!"

"And look—what's that over by the bank there?" said Betty.

They all looked. They saw a house-boat there, badly in need of a coat of paint. It was very old and had been left to rot to pieces. It had once been a good one, and had had plenty of brass rails and white paint. But now it was a sorry sight. Plainly, no one had used it for ages.

"What's that you say—a house-boat?" said Kit. "I've never seen one before. What's it for?"

"Well—it's just what its name says," said Robin. "A boat that is used as a house by its owners. They live there—cook their meals, sleep there in bunks. A house-boat is fun. But this one hasn't been lived in for years, I should think. It's almost falling to pieces."

"I'd like to see what it's like inside," said Betty. They all thought the same. They sat in the boat and stared at it.

Sandy gave a little "wuff." Perhaps rabbits lived there?

"Do you think it would matter if we pulled up alongside and had a look at it?" said Lucy.

"Well—I don't know," said Robin. "Perhaps it belongs to the people who live at the big house beyond. What about going and asking permission? I'm sure they wouldn't mind."

"All right," said Betty. "You go, Robin, and take Kit."

"No, thanks," said Kit at once. "I'm not appearing in public just now!"

"Oh, I forgot!" said Betty. "Well, you go alone, Robin."

They rowed to the bank, near the big house-boat. Robin jumped out and walked up the green lawn that led to the big house. It was shuttered, and he wondered if there were anyone there. He came to a door and knocked loudly on it.

An old woman opened it, looking most surprised. Robin felt sure she didn't have many visitors in that lonely spot!

"Excuse me," he said politely. "I just wondered if you knew about that house-boat down there? Do you think I and my friends could have a look at it?"

"I don't know anything about it," said the old woman, peering at Robin. "I'm caretaker here till the house is let. No one ever said anything to me about a house-boat. But don't you do any mischief now."

"Oh no, I won't," said Robin, and scuttled off down the lawn. He hadn't been forbidden to look over the boat, and that was all he cared about! He told the others and they looked thrilled.

"We'll explore it straight away," said Kit, and they rowed right up to the big house-boat. They tied their boat to a rail and then climbed up to the deck.

There were windows and doors leading right into the boat, but they were all shut and locked. Betty peered into a window and exclaimed at what she saw.

"It's a little bedroom, with bunk-beds at the side and a dear little wash-basin and a hanging wardrobe and chest. Do look! It must be so exciting to live in a house-boat!"

"I've found a door whose lock has rotted!" called Kit. "We can get right inside now!"

They all trooped along the wide deck to Kit. He swung open a door and Sandy trotted inside at once, his tail straight up. Any rabbits here? it seemed to say.

The children went in. Everything was dirty, damp and spoilt, but to the four boys and girls it was all lovely. How they would love to live here! What fun to wake up in the morning and hear the water go splash-plash, gurgle-gurgle, against the sides of the boat. What fun to get water from the river to fill their wash-basins! How lovely to cook a meal on the little stove in the kitchen and eat it in the open air on the deck! And how gorgeous to watch the night stealing over the water, and then to go to bed on a house-boat that rocked slightly every time the river swelled a little!

"It looks as if the owner has forgotten all about this boat," said Betty. "I wish it was ours."

"Let's make it ours," said Lucy suddenly.

"What do you mean?" asked Robin in surprise.

"Well—why shouldn't we come here and clean it up and wash the decks and polish the brass and pretend it's our very own boat?" said Lucy. "I'm sure the owner wouldn't mind, because we should only be making the boat more valuable, not spoiling it. We could have meals here. We could even sleep here one night, if your mother would say 'Yes'!"

The children stared at Lucy, thinking it was a perfectly grand idea! A house-boat of their own! It would be marvellous.

"Let's," said Kit at last. "There's nobody to stop us except the old caretaker Robin saw, and she didn't even seem to know there was a boat here! It can't be seen from the house, anyway. Let's come tomorrow and clean it up. And I say—wouldn't it make a fine hiding-place for me if ever I needed one? No one would ever dream of looking for me here!"

"That's true," said Robin. "I don't think you *will* need a hiding-place, Kit, because kidnapping and things don't happen here as they do in America—but if you did, this is the Very Place!"

"We'll bring cleaning things to-morrow and have a good time," said Lucy. "This is going to be fun. If only we could sleep here at night. How I'd love to wake up in the morning and hear the water gurgling and feel the boat rocking whilst I lay in my bunk."

The children thoroughly explored the house-boat. There were two bedrooms, very small, with two bunks apiece. There was a tiny kitchen, hardly big enough to hold the stove and a dresser! There was a small room that could be used as a sitting-room in bad weather.

The decks were big and wide, and had clearly been used for eating and sitting, for there were little tables and rotted deck-chairs piled under a kind of porch at the back end of the boat.

"Oh, I say! It's half-past four!" said Kit in dismay. "I must get back or I shall get into a dreadful row. I bet the whole household is looking for me all over the grounds by now!"

"Come on, then," said Robin, scrambling back into the boat. "It won't take us long to get back if we both take an oar. Off we go! Hi, Sandy, you're left behind. Jump, silly dog, jump!"

Sandy took a leap from the house-boat into the little boat and landed on Lucy's lap. The boat soon left widening ripples behind it as the boys rowed strongly away.

Kit wriggled through the hole under the fencing when they got back. They could hear the strong voice of the Dragon calling for him in angry tones.

"Kit! Kit! Where are you? It's tea-time. Are you asleep? Come at once!"

Kit winked at the others and then gave a yell. "Hi! I'm coming! Just a minute!"

He sped up the garden, and the others went into their own house. "To-morrow!" said Lucy to Betty, rubbing her hands. "I *am* looking forward to making that boat our own!"

Chapter Nine

THE "BLACK SWAN" IS CLEANED UP

THE CHILDREN talked a good deal about the old house-boat they had discovered. They were all longing to go back and clean it up. "We didn't decide with Kit what time he could get free to-morrow," said Robin. "How silly of us! But we were in such a hurry to get him back in time for his tea."

"Let's go to-morrow morning," said Lucy. "It's Saturday, isn't it? Perhaps Kit could get the morning off. Let's ask him. Robin, you climb the tree and see if Kit is anywhere about. If he is we'll throw a ball over with a message inside."

Robin climbed the tree. Kit was on the lawn next door with a book. The Dragon was nearby, reading, too. Robin slithered down and told the others. He wrote a short note, stuffed it into an old split ball, and sent it over into the garden next door. In a few minutes the ball came back with an answer! It really was a very good way indeed of sending messages.

Robin read out the note from Kit. "I'm free on Saturdays, hurrah! I'll go off into the garden directly after breakfast, and hope no one will miss me till lunch-time. I'll be in your garden as near as I can to nine o'clock."

"We'll pack up cleaning things now, shall we?" said Lucy, who liked to get everything ready well beforehand. "What's the time? Half-past five. Will the shops be shut? Could we go and buy what we want? I've got some money."

"We can get the things from Mummy," said Betty.

"No, we can't, silly," said Robin. "This is a secret, remember. You can't expect Mummy or anyone else to hand out soap and cloths and polish and dusters without knowing what they are for! Don't be stupid."

"I didn't think of that," said Betty. "Well—it will be much more fun to buy them, anyway. I've got some money in my money-box, too, Robin. Let's see if the shops are still open. We can get our bikes and ride down to the village."

The village was a good way away—about three miles. The children's house and Kit's were lonely places, far from anywhere—but the children had bicycles, and didn't mind cycling down to the village whenever they wanted anything. They got them out now and were soon cycling quickly along the little narrow lanes. The village stores was still open, so they were able to get exactly what they wanted. They had already made out a list.

"One bar of soap," said Betty. "Two large floor-cloths. Two smaller cloths. One tin of Vim. Three dusters. That's all."

They stuffed everything into their bicycle baskets and cycled back home, all longing to put the soap and cloths to good use. They would make that old boat really beautiful!

"I wish we could paint her nice and white, too," said Robin. "I know where there is a big tin of white paint and some brushes."

"Oooh! Why couldn't we take those too, then?" said Betty eagerly. "Then you two boys could paint the boat whilst Lucy and I did the cleaning."

"Well—we might take them," said Robin, seeing in his mind's eye a beautiful, spick and span house-boat, painted a dazzling white, rocking gently on the blue river. So as soon as they got back home they went to look for the paint. They found it, and two big brushes, with some turpentine to clean the brushes if they wanted to.

"Quite a lot of things to carry!" said Lucy as she looked at the collection of things laid ready. "Is there anything else?"

"We'll take some chocolate and some plums and a few biscuits," said Robin. "If we start at nine and don't get back till one, we shall want something to eat."

So four bars of chocolate, a packet of biscuits and a dozen or so ripe plums were put ready, too. Everything went into satchels, to be slung across the children's shoulders.

They went to bed that night full of excitement. It was lovely to have a secret. It was fun to have a friend like Kit. It was gorgeous to think of that old house-boat waiting for them on the river!

Just before nine o'clock the next day the three children and Sandy were waiting outside the tunnel, on their side of the garden. This time Kit was punctual. He arrived just exactly at the hour, and scrambled through the tunnel at once. Sandy ran half-way down it to greet him, and licked him rapturously on the nose.

"Stop it!" said Kit, trying to turn his head away from the wet tongue, as he wriggled through the hole. "Lucy, call your dog off. He's awfully licky this morning, and he's been eating kippers or something."

Everyone laughed. Soon Kit was standing beside them, his eyes taking in their big, bulging satchels. "You seem to be taking a whole lot of things!" he said. "Here, let me carry yours, Betty, and I'll carry Lucy's for her on the way back."

"We've got some white paint to paint up the old boat and make her nice," said Robin proudly. "Don't you think that will be fun to do, Kit?"

"*Rather!*" said Kit. "I'm a marvel at painting! Slip-slap, spatter-dash, my word, we'll slap the paint on that old boat in a trice! Come on. Let's run to your boat. I can't go slowly this morning."

They all ran across the fields to the river. They untied their boat and got in, thankfully putting down their loads. The boys took the oars. Off they went in the sunshine and did not stop rowing until they reached the old house-boat.

"There she is," said Robin as they saw her, half hidden by drooping willows. "I say—did anyone notice her name? I didn't."

"There it is," said Kit as they drew near. "The *Black Swan*. That's a nice name, except that she must once have been a very white boat! Tie our boat up, Robin. Then up we go on deck!"

The children took a look at the house in the distance. A spire of smoke came from one chimney, but otherwise it looked as deserted as it had done the day before.

"I don't think anyone is likely to disturb us," said Robin, climbing up on the deck. "Give me your hand, Bets. Heave ho—there you are! Come on, Lucy. Shove her up, Kit."

All four stood on the dirty decks of the *Black Swan*. They hardly knew where to begin their cleaning.

"We'll do the outside before we start on the inside," said Lucy at last. "Can you boys begin to paint her white? You could do the house part first—all round the windows and wooden walls. Then you could do the doors."

"We'll wash the decks," said Betty, and got out the soap, and a cloth. "Oh, dear—they really want scrubbing. We didn't think of a scrubbing-brush—or a pail either for the water."

"There's probably both brush *and* pail somewhere in the tiny kitchen," said Lucy, and the two girls went to see. There *was* a pail there, and two scrubbing-brushes, a big one and a small one. The girls were very pleased. They dipped the pail in the river and filled it with water. Then they set to work to scrub the dirty decks.

It was fun. The decks came beautifully clean, though they were hard to scrub. When the water was dirty the girls emptied it into the river and drew up some fresh water. It was even easier than turning on a tap!

Meanwhile the two boys were splashing about with the white paint. Kit was right—he really did know how to set about it, and he showed Robin how to lay the white paint on evenly. The piece they had done looked very fine.

The girls cleaned the windows and then tried to polish the brass rails round the deck, but these were really too tarnished. By this time it was eleven o'clock and the children were tired and hungry.

Drooping willows hid the house-boat

"Let's sit down and have biscuits and chocolate," said Robin. So down they sat on the clean deck, and began to munch happily.

"The walls you have done do look nice," said Betty to the boys. "And the decks look better now they're clean, don't they? Lucy and I had better go and clean up a bit inside the boat cabins after we've had a rest. Everything's in a mess there. We'll bring out some of the cushions and things to air. They smell damp."

The children really worked very hard indeed at cleaning and tidying the old house-boat. Lucy and Betty carried out piles of cushions, bedding and pillows into the hot sun to air. They opened all the doors and windows of the boat and let the breeze blow inside to take the musty dampness away. By the time that half-past twelve came and they had to go, the boat really did begin to look very different.

"Good-bye, *Black Swan*!" said Betty as they rowed away. "We'll come again soon—to-morrow, perhaps. We've left all our cleaning things inside you, and we can soon smarten you up."

They were all a little late for lunch, but that couldn't very well be helped, because they hadn't really left themselves time enough to get back. They knew Mummy wouldn't mind a great deal if they were a little late, but it was different for Kit. It mustn't be found out that he escaped from his garden! If his secret was discovered, the tunnel would be filled in, and he would never be able to play with Robin and the others again.

"So long!" said the boy, disappearing into the tunnel. "See you to-morrow!"

Chapter Ten

LUCY'S BIRTHDAY CAKE AND A SURPRISE

KIT COULD not go with the children when they next
went to visit their house-boat. Mr Barton, his tutor, was
keeping rather a strict eye on him, because Miss Taylor,
the Dragon, had complained that he hid himself in the
garden and didn't come when he was called. Actually, of
course, Kit had been out on the river, and hadn't heard
anyone calling him at all! But he couldn't very well explain
that.

Robin, Betty and Lucy went on with the cleaning and
painting of the old house-boat. Before another week had
gone by it looked really lovely. It was dazzling white, and
the brass had actually begun to shine a little! The windows
were bright, the little stove shone, all the crockery was
washed, and the chairs and couch well pummelled to rid
them of dust.

"We ought to give a party!" said Lucy, looking at the
house-boat proudly. "We could get out those little red

tables and chairs from the back of the boat and use those. They are all clean because we've scrubbed them."

"A party! Who for?" asked Robin. "There's nobody to give a party to, silly."

"We could give one for ourselves," said Lucy. "It's my birthday next week. I don't see why we couldn't have my birthday here, cake and all! It would be marvellous!"

"It *would* be rather a good idea," said Robin. "Let's ask Mummy if we can take our tea out on your birthday. We can ask Kit to the party, anyway."

So when Lucy's birthday came, four children and a dog went to the cleaned-up house-boat and climbed on to its spotless decks. Robin had the birthday cake in a tin. "It's got eleven candles in the tin, too," he said. "They are loose, so we can stick them on the cake when we're ready. There are chocolate biscuits, too, and three different kinds of sandwiches."

Kit had managed to get the afternoon off by a bit of luck. Both his tutor and Miss Taylor had gone out. The cook was supposed to give him his tea, but Kit had told her he was not hungry and wouldn't want any. He had simply wriggled through the hole and joined the others, who were impatiently waiting for him. Sandy gave a welcoming yelp.

When they got to the house-boat the children set out the gay tables and chairs. They put the food on them and fetched cups, saucers and plates from the tiny kitchen. They were pretty cups, red and blue and yellow.

Lucy had a look at the little stove. What a pity they couldn't make some tea!

"Not that we really want tea to drink," she thought, "because we've got lemonade. It would be fun to boil a kettle on the stove. One day we'll bring some water with us and make tea or cocoa."

The others called her. "Lucy, what are you doing? Do come on. We want to begin."

Lucy took out some more plates and set them on the gay tables. Then the children sat down and had their party. Sandy was given a chair to sit on, too, because he really behaved very well indeed at table. He ate his food off the plate and drank water out of his cup—rather noisily, it is true, but still, as Lucy pointed out, he had to drink with his tongue, and that was not very easy.

The birthday cake had been taken out of its tin and set on a big plate in the middle of one of the tables. It looked fine. Mummy had set eleven pink and white roses round it, to hold the eleven candles. Robin carefully put them into the rose-holders.

"There!" he said, "That looks lovely! When shall we light the candles, Lucy?"

"Now," said Lucy. "They won't show much in the open air, but we simply must light them."

But unfortunately nobody had any matches, so the candles couldn't be lighted. It was a great pity. "I do hate to cut the cake without lighting the candles first," said Lucy dolefully. "I'll see if there are any matches in the little kitchen." She disappeared into the kitchen and rummaged about. She came out in delight. "I've got a box," she said. "They were in that tiny cupboard by the larder. You light the candles, Robin, please."

But alas! the matches were so damp and old that they wouldn't strike. It really was most disappointing. The children sat at the gay little tables, striking matches that wouldn't light, getting quite cross about it. Sandy watched everything with the greatest interest. He couldn't think why the children didn't stop fussing about candles and cut the cake. He knew of old that dogs at birthday parties usually got a share of the cake!

"Well—we must cut the cake without the candles lighted, that's all," said Robin at last. "Now remember everyone—you must wish when you eat your first bit of cake. Birthday-cake wishes are magic, and always come true!"

"Woof!" said Sandy, pleased. He knew what *he* was going to wish! He'd wish for rabbits to chase!

Then suddenly Sandy sat up straight on his chair and growled. The children looked at him in astonishment.

"Sandy, what are you growling for?" asked Lucy.

"Are you cross because you haven't got a bit of my cake yet? You *are* an impatient little dog!"

Sandy growled again, and the children saw that all the hairs on the back of his neck were rising up. They did that when Sandy was angry. But what could he be angry about?

Sandy was staring through the drooping willow trees on the bank that hid the house-boat. Was somebody coming? The children couldn't hear anyone. But then footsteps over grass wouldn't be heard. Nobody wanted to be caught on the house-boat because, although they *felt* it really was theirs, now that they had cleaned and painted it so beautifully, they knew that it really wasn't.

"Listen," said Kit in a low voice. "If it's anybody snooping round, don't give me away. I shall have to pretend to be dumb, because anybody knows I'm an American boy as soon as I open my mouth. I can't talk the way you do. And so if anyone . . ."

He stopped short and stared between the trees. He had seen something moving there. Someone was walking on the bank!

"Let's hope they won't see us," whispered Robin. "Lucy, make Sandy be quiet. He's going to growl again."

Lucy put her hand on Sandy's collar. He stopped rumbling inside at once. He knew when he had to be quiet! Everyone sat as still as mice. They heard a little cough behind the trees. They could see no one yet, and felt certain that no one could see them.

Then there came the sound of a match being struck, and after that they smelt the smoke of a cigarette just being lighted.

Then the somebody began walking again, and appeared on the bank, where the willows ended, staring at the house-boat! It was a tall man, with twinkling blue eyes, and a cigarette in the corner of his mouth. He stared at the boat and at the children in the greatest astonishment.

They stared back. They didn't know what to say or do, so they just stared. Sandy gave a growl.

"Well, well, well!" said the man at last, and he stepped on board the house-boat. "Quite a nice little party? A birthday party, too, by the look of the grand cake!"

Still nobody said a word. The man took a look round the decks and popped his head in at the sitting-room and bedroom windows of the boat. He seemed more surprised than ever.

67

"I suppose none of you has a tongue?" he said, sitting down in an empty chair. "If you had, I should love to ask you a few questions."

"We *have* got tongues," said Robin. "What do you want to ask us?"

"Well, I'd love to know what you are doing on my old house-boat," said the man, and the children heard his words with dismay. *His* house-boat! What an unlucky thing for them that they had chosen that day to come!

"And I'd love to know who gave the old *Black Swan* such a dazzling coat of paint," said the man. "And who cleaned up the rooms inside. Most mysterious. I suppose you don't know the answer to these questions?"

Robin couldn't help rather liking the man, though he also wondered if by any chance he could be that wicked uncle of Kit's! Just suppose he was!

"Is it your boat?" he said. "I'm very sorry, sir, if we're trespassing. I did go to ask permission from the caretaker at the house to go over the boat, but she didn't seem to know anything about it. We haven't done any damage. We just gave her a coat of paint and cleaned her up a bit. We thought she was rather nice, you see, and it was a shame to see her falling to bits."

"I quite agree with you," said the man. "Well, I must say you are different from most children I know. They would do just as much damage as they could—but you seem to have gone out of your way to put my boat in good order. What's your name?"

"I'm Robin, sir," said Robin, "and that's my sister Betty and that's my cousin Lucy."

"And who are *you?*" said the man, turning to Kit, who, of course, had not said a word the whole time, but had tried to look as dumb and stupid as possible.

Kit stared at the man and didn't answer. "That's Sammy, sir," said Robin, saying the first name that came into his head. "You won't be able to make him speak. He's dumb."

"Poor lad!" said the man, and he really did look sorry. "I wonder if anything could be done for you. I'm a doctor, and I might be able to do something."

"There's nothing that can be done, sir," said Robin hastily. He didn't want the man trying any cure on poor Kit. "Well, sir, we'd better clear up and go, since it's your boat. We're sorry if we've trespassed, as I said before."

"Well, of course, you *have* trespassed," said the man. "But it's what I would call very satisfactory trespassing from *my* point of view—very!"

He smiled and the children were relieved to see him looking so good-tempered. "I suppose, sir," said Robin, smiling also, "I suppose you wouldn't let us trespass again, would you?"

"Well, I might, on one condition," said the man. "And that is—that you ask me to your party and give me a piece of that delicious-looking cake. Why don't you light the candles?"

"We've no matches," said Lucy. The man took out a box and handed it solemnly to her. She struck a match and lighted the eleven candles! Then she cut the cake. She gave a piece first to the man. "Here you are, Mr—Mr . . ." she said.

"My name is Cunningham," said the man. "Thank you, Lucy. Many happy returns of the day—and please treat my house-boat as yours whenever you like! I will rent it to you for one piece of birthday cake!"

What a bit of luck! The children stared at one another in delight. So the house-boat could be theirs to play on whenever they liked!

Chapter Eleven

WHO IS DUMB SAMMY?

MR CUNNINGHAM ate his piece of cake and said it was the best he had ever tasted.

"Did you wish?" asked Lucy. "You have to wish, you know."

"I did," said Mr Cunningham. "Where do you live, by the way? I didn't know there were any houses nearby."

"There aren't—only that one over there," said Robin. "We live in one of the two houses away up the river. We come here in our boat. Where do *you* live?"

"I used to live in that house beyond the lawns there," said the man, nodding towards the house away in the distance. "But now I want to let it, and I think I *have* let it, so that's lucky for me."

"Will the people want the house-boat?" asked Betty in dismay.

"No—I thought it was all fallen to bits, so I said nothing about it," said the man. "You needn't worry. The boat

70

will be nothing to do with them. You can say you have rented it from me if anyone asks you. And I must say it was very good rent you paid me—a most *delicious* piece of cake!"

"Have another bit?" said Lucy, taking up the knife.

"Well—if I do, that must be rent for *two* years," said Mr Cunningham. "Thanks very much."

All this time Kit had been munching his cake and saying nothing.

Mr Cunningham glanced at him. "Has he always been dumb?" he asked.

Robin went red. He hardly knew what to say. He was a truthful boy, but he couldn't possibly give Kit away. "Well—not always," he said at last.

Lucy saw that Robin was feeling awkward, and she hurried to change the subject. "Have another bit of cake, Sammy?" she asked.

Betty wanted to giggle when she heard Lucy calling Kit Sammy. Kit made a curious noise in his throat and took another piece of cake.

"Is that all the noise he can make?" said Mr Cunningham. The others thought of the fearsome yells and whoops that Kit could make when he wanted to.

"No—he can make other noises," said Robin. "Have a biscuit, sir?"

"No, thanks! I must be off," said Mr Cunningham, and got up. "Well, thank you very much for two years' rent, and remember what I say—you are welcome to use my boat whenever you want to! Good-bye!"

"Good-bye," said everyone except Kit, who made another curious noise in his throat. Sandy gave a polite yelp. He had quite taken to their visitor.

They all watched the man walk away and disappear behind the trees. Then Betty giggled.

"Poor Sammy!" she said. "I do feel sorry for you. Are you awfully dumb?"

Kit made a few more noises and the others shouted with laughter. Then Kit grinned and found his tongue.

"Thanks for playing up so well," he said. "I think that chap is perfectly all right—but you never know when any of my wicked uncle's spies might come around. Anyway,

71

if Mr Cunningham is one, he won't think that a dumb boy called Sammy is Kit Anthony Armstrong, who is anything but dumb!"

"I don't think he is anybody horrid," said Lucy. "I thought he was nice—and fancy letting us have the boat in return for two pieces of cake. Grown-ups do do funny things, don't they?"

"Well, we got the candles lighted, anyway," said Betty. "Look—they've all burnt down now. Blow them out, Lucy—one big blow for the whole lot."

Lucy blew and the candles went out. "You're a good blower," said Kit, feeling his head. "Is my hair still on?"

They all laughed. They felt very pleased to think that they hadn't got into trouble over the boat—and the thought that is was theirs to do as they liked in was simply marvellous! What fun they would have!

"I say—do you think Mummy would let us spend a night here?" Betty said suddenly. "Wouldn't it be simply wonderful!"

"Well—we'd have to tell her all about the boat then," said Robin. "But it won't matter now, because we have got permission to use the boat, anyway. She *might* let us come here for a night—or even a weekend."

"What about Kit?" said Lucy. The boy's eyes had begun to sparkle at the thought of a night on the boat.

"Oh, I'd slip off late at night and get back early in the morning," said Kit at once. "You don't suppose I'd be left out of an adventure like that, do you? No fear! I shall come too. But listen, I simply *must* get back now, or the Dragon will complain about me to Mr Barton. I don't want to be locked up in my bedroom or anything awful like that."

The children cleared away everything and then got into their little boat. They rowed off, well pleased with their afternoon. They looked back at the gleaming house-boat. It did look nice in the afternoon sunshine.

"See you soon, *Black Swan*!" called Betty. "You are ours now! We've rented you. We'll come and sleep in you one night soon!"

Kit luckily got back in time and no one knew he had escaped for the afternoon. Lucy gave him another piece of her birthday cake to smuggle up to his bedroom.

"You ask your mother about sleeping a night on the boat," he said. "We'll do that as soon as we can, whilst the fine weather lasts. And, I say—ask your mother if she's ever heard of our Mr Cunningham. If he really did live at that house, he must be all right."

So the children told their mother all about Mr Cunningham and his house-boat. She listened in amazement when she heard how they had discovered the boat and painted it and cleaned it.

"But you mustn't do things like that," she said. "You really mustn't! You might have got into serious trouble, you know. It was very nice of Mr Cunningham to say you might go there again."

"Do you know him, Mummy?" asked Betty.

"I have heard of him," said Mummy. "He used to live at the house there, but now I think he is trying to let it."

"He told us he *has* let it," said Robin. "But the people aren't going to have the house-boat. Mummy, can we spend a night there? Do let us!"

"Well—I'll have to find out if Mr Cunningham really means what he said," said Mummy. "I'll go and telephone him now. I can find his number."

Mummy went off to telephone. The children looked at one another gleefully.

"I bet we'll be allowed to sleep on board!" said Robin. "Golly, what sport! Think of having breakfast there, and cooking bacon and eggs on that little stove!"

The children could almost smell the bacon and eggs already. They waited impatiently for their mother to come back. She soon came into the room again, but she looked rather puzzled.

"Yes—it seems quite all right," she said. "Mr Cunningham was amused at finding you having a birthday party on the boat, and pleased that you had painted and cleaned it so nicely—but he said something about a boy called Sammy, who couldn't speak."

The children looked at one another in dismay. What a bit of bad luck that Mr Cunningham had mentioned Kit! *Now* what were they to say? They said nothing, and hoped their mother would say no more.

"Who's this Sammy?" she asked. "And why have you never told me about him? Is he really dumb? What's he like, and where did you meet him?"

"He's just a boy," said Robin at last. "He's about as old as I am. We met him, that's all."

"Mr Cunningham says he's dumb," went on their mother. "He's a doctor, and wondered if he could have anything done for him. He thought he was your brother or cousin, it seems."

"Oh!" said Robin.

His mother looked at him impatiently. "I shall begin to think *you're* dumb next!" she said. "Where does this boy live?"

This was a most awkward question—but very fortunately Sandy changed the subject so completely that nobody had to answer. Tiger the cat happened to come into the room at that moment, and Sandy saw her. With an excited yelp he jumped at her, and in a moment there was a regular circus in the sitting-room! Tiger jumped here and there, and Sandy leapt like a mad thing after her, knocking down everything that got in his way. Mother shouted, and Lucy yelled.

Then Tiger decided that she had had enough of it. She turned on Sandy and put out her claws. She dug ten sharp needles into him, and he yelped with pain. He turned himself about and ran to hide behind Lucy—but Tiger came after him.

Poor Sandy! He ran out of the door with Tiger chasing him for all she was worth. She jumped at his back and dug her claws into him again. He ran upstairs and she ran after him. He tore downstairs and she tore after him. Into the sitting-room again and all round it, between everyone's legs went the two excited animals, and Mummy was quite furious.

Somehow or other Lucy caught Sandy and Mummy shut the door on Tiger.

"Well, really!" she said, sinking into a chair. "It's bad enough when a dog chases a cat—but it's far worse when a cat chases a dog. Lucy, go and put Sandy into his basket up in your room and shut the door on him. I don't want to see him for at least two hours."

74

The children all went out of the room with Sandy, and shut the door quietly. They put the panting dog into his basket, examined him for scratches and then heaved a sigh of relief.

"Tiger came in at *just* the right moment!" said Robin. "I simply can't *think* what I could have answered about Kit. I do hope Mummy forgets about him."

Mummy did. It was very lucky. She asked no more questions at all, but simply said that if they were really good for the next few days she would let them spend a night on the house-boat!

"We *must* tell Kit!" said Robin. "Won't he be thrilled?"

Chapter Twelve

IS IT THE WICKED UNCLE?

THE CHILDREN talked of nothing else but going to spend a night in the house-boat.

"There are two little bedrooms, with two bunks in each," said Robin. "Just right for the four of us. Sandy can sleep with one of us in our bunk."

"With me, of course," said Lucy. "You don't suppose he'd sleep with anyone else, do you? Won't it be fun undressing at night in the boat—we'll have to light candles to see by."

"We'll get the stove going," said Robin. "And we must remember to get water for the kettle. We can't drink river water."

"I should think the old caretaker would let us have some water," said Lucy. "We could tell her that Mr Cunningham said we could use the boat."

"Yes—that would save us having to take water with us,"

said Robin. "We'll get Mummy to give us bacon and eggs and bread and everything we want."

Mummy said they could go the next Friday, as they planned for that. They slipped in to next door and told Kit what they were going to do. He was very thrilled.

"I'll join you," he said. "I can't go out of any of the downstairs doors because they are always locked and bolted at night, and if I went out and left one unbolted, as I would have to do, Mr Barton would be sure to discover it next morning. He often gets up early to work. I'll slip out of the attic window, across the plank and down the ash tree."

"What! In the dark?" said Lucy.

"It won't be dark," said Kit. "There'll be some kind of a moon. Anyway, I could do it in the dark, silly."

"Can you come for a picnic with us to-morrow?" asked Robin. "We are going to take our tea to Bracken Hill. We can lend you a bike if you can come."

"I'd love to," said Kit. "But I can't. Both the Dragon and Mr Barton will be in to tea to-morrow, and I'll have to be there. I can't keep on and on disappearing for various meals."

"What a pity!" said Robin. "Never mind—look forward to a night on the boat."

"I certainly will!" said Kit. "Look out—here's the Dragon!"

The fierce woman came along over the lawn. All the children were at the back of the summer-house, behind a bush. The Dragon called Kit.

"Kit! I want you to do something for me. Where are you?"

Kit appeared, whistling. The Dragon was about to sit down on a deck-chair nearby when something caught her eye. It was a small blue handkerchief belonging to Lucy!

The Dragon picked it up. "Whose is this?" she said. "A hanky with L on it! Kit, have those children been here again?"

"What children?" asked Kit in the most innocent voice imaginable.

"You know quite well I mean the children next door," said the Dragon impatiently. "I don't see how they can get in, I must say, now that that fencing goes all the way round.

77

But children always seem to manage to squeeze through somewhere. Are you sure they haven't been in the garden, Kit?"

"In the *garden*?" repeated Kit. "Did you say in the *garden*, Miss Taylor? How could they get in?"

"Oh, I don't know," said Miss Taylor crossly, opening her book. "I suppose the wind blew the hanky over. Don't stand there looking like a perfect stupid, Kit. Go indoors and see if you can find my knitting for me. Hurry, now!"

Kit went indoors. The other children stood still behind the summer-house, hardly daring to breathe. Sandy stood perfectly still, too. He really was a very good dog for that sort of thing.

Kit appeared again. He caught sight of Robin peering anxiously from behind the summer-house and winked at him.

"Here you are, Miss Taylor," he said, and he held out some knitting. Miss Taylor gave a grunt of annoyance.

"That's not it," he said. "That belongs to Cook. Dear me, what a stupid boy you can be at times. I suppose I had better go and look for it, or you'll bring me out the housemaid's embroidery next!"

And, to the children's great relief, the Dragon got up and walked towards the house.

"Good for you, Kit!" whispered Robin, and the three children and Sandy moved off quickly into the little wood beyond the lawn. It wasn't long before they were scrambling down the hole to safety.

"It's a pity Kit can't come to-morrow," said Robin. "Never mind—we three will go."

"And Sandy, too," said Lucy at once.

"Sandy can't cycle," said Betty.

"Well, we can't leave him out of a picnic," said Lucy. "I'll take him in my bicycle basket."

So the next afternoon the three of them set out, with Sandy in Lucy's basket, sitting up and feeling very high and mighty indeed when he passed other dogs. He didn't like it when Lucy suddenly rang her bell, but otherwise he enjoyed his ride very much.

The children had a lovely picnic and ate every single thing they had brought with them. Then they wandered about looking for early blackberries, but there were very few.

"I'm jolly thirsty," said Robin, mopping his hot forehead. "Have we drunk all the lemonade?"

"Every drop," said Lucy. "Can't we go and buy some at the nearest village?"

"I've got sixpence," said Robin, feeling in his pocket. The others had a little money, too, so they mounted their bicycles and set off to the village nearby. It was set at the forking of three roads, and had quite a number of shops that sold lemonade and ices.

They went into the biggest shop and sat down at a little table, meaning to have lemonade and ices, too. As they sat there, a big car drove up outside, and a man got out. He came into the shop.

"Excuse me," he said to the woman there. "Could you tell me if I'm anywhere near Faldham?"

"Not far," said the woman. "Take the middle road, sir."

"How far is it in miles?" asked the man.

"About eight miles, I'd say," said the woman, taking the three children their lemonade and ices.

Betty spoke up at once. "It's not as much as eight," she said. "I've measured it on the speedometer of my bike—it's exactly six and a half."

"Do you live at Faldham, by any chance?" asked the man, coming over to the children.

"We live outside Faldham," said Robin.

The man sat down and ordered an ice for himself. "Bit of a lonely spot, isn't it?" he asked.

"Yes, very," said Betty. "There are only two houses outside the village—ours—and another close by."

"Who lives there?" asked the man, eating his ice.

"I don't really know," said Betty. Then she got such a kick on the ankle from Robin that she nearly swallowed the spoon with which she was ladling ice cream into her mouth!

"Have new people come there lately?" asked the man—but by this time Betty was choking over her swallowed ice cream, and Robin answered:

79

"I've just come back from boarding school, so I don't know much about things," he said. "They may be a family of Eskimos, for all I know!"

"Ha, ha!" said the man, laughing as if he didn't really think it was a funny joke at all. "You don't happen to have seen a small boy about there at all, do you?"

"How small?" asked Robin solemnly, scraping his ice cream round.

"Small as you," said the man.

"I'm big," said Robin.

"Well, *big* as you!" said the man impatiently.

"What colour eyes?" asked Robin.

"Blue," said the man.

"What colour hair?" said Robin.

"Fair," said the man.

"How many fingers?" asked Robin, again very solemnly. The man stared at him with annoyance.

"Do you think you're being funny?" he asked at last.

"Yes, I do rather," said Robin, and Betty and Lucy gave explosive little giggles. The man got up impatiently.

"I'll send you a telegram if I see a small, big boy with blue eyes, fair hair—and how many fingers did you say?" said Robin.

"Don't be rude," said the man shortly. He paid his bill and went. He got into the car, spoke to another man there and drove off.

"Golly!" said Robin, letting out a big sigh of relief. "I bet you anything you like that's the wicked uncle! And somehow or other he's found out that Kit is in our district. We'll have to warn Kit. Oh, blow—I suppose this means he will have to go off somewhere else and hide! I say, Bets, I really thought you were going to give the game away! Sorry I kicked you so hard."

"It's all right," said Betty. "You only made me choke. I didn't for one moment think that man was after Kit. I do hope he won't find him."

"Come on—we must rush back and warn him," said Robin, getting up. "Put Sandy into your basket, Lucy."

Off they all went again, tearing back to warn Kit of danger. What a strange thing that they had happened to be in the shop when the wicked uncle came by!

Chapter Thirteen

AN UNWELCOME VISITOR

THE CHILDREN rode home quickly, and only stopped
once. That was when Lucy went over such a large stone in
the road that poor Sandy was jerked right out of her
bicycle basket! She had to stop to put him back again. He
didn't seem to mind at all.

"Did you have a nice picnic?" called Mummy as they
put their bicycles into the shed.

"Lovely!" cried all three of them.

"Come and tell me all about it," said Mummy. But that
was just what the children didn't want to do! They wanted
to warn Kit as quickly as ever they could.

"You two girls go in and tell Mummy everything, and
I'll slip under the fence and tell Kit," said Robin in a low
voice.

He called to his mother.

"We ate everything!" he said. "Lucy, tell Mummy how
Sandy fell out of the basket."

"You didn't take Sandy in your basket, surely!" cried Mummy.

The girls went to tell her all about the picnic, and Robin slipped out of the garden door and down to the tunnel under the fencing. He crawled underneath and stood up in the next-door garden. He wondered where Kit was.

It was raining a little, so he thought probably Kit was up in his attic-room, playing there by himself. He decided to go up and see. He carefully made his way all round the grounds, keeping in the thick bushes and trees, and at last came to where the garage backed on to the house. The ladder to get up to the roof was not there, but it took Robin only a minute or two to get it from the empty garage. He set it against the wall, climbed up, stood on the flat garage roof, and then swung himself into the branches of the big ash tree nearby. Up he went like a cat, and came level with the attic window.

He whistled a low whistle, rather like a blackbird. No answer. He whistled again, and this time Kit's head appeared at the window. He grinned in delight when he saw Robin.

"Come in and see my electric train," he said. "I've got it going."

Robin slid along the plank that stretched from the sill to the tree, and jumped down into the big attic. Kit locked the door.

Robin spoke in a low voice. "Kit, I believe that wicked uncle of yours is in the district!"

"Don't be silly," said Kit. "He couldn't possibly know I'm here yet."

"Well, listen," said Robin and he told Kit about the man in the car, and the questions he had asked.

"'Golly! It does sound a bit queer," said Kit. "Thanks for being clever enough not to give me away. What's the man like?"

"Fairly tall. Fair hair, a bit like yours. Blue eyes—very blue," said Robin. "But you've never seen your uncle, have you?"

"No," said Kit. "Although he has kidnapped me twice, he has always employed other people to do the dirty work. But it looks as though there was a family resemblance between us, doesn't it? Blow! I did think I was going to settle down here for some time. It's nice knowing you. You're great kids." Now—shall I tell Mr Barton and the Dragon—or not?"

"I think you ought to," said Robin. "Listen—is that your uncle's car coming back?"

They went to the window to see—and Robin gave a cry of alarm. "I say! That's the same car the man was in! But he's gone past your house—he's turning in to our house!"

"Funny," said Kit. "You'd better go back and find out what he says, Robin."

So Robin hurriedly went back down the tree, under the hole, and up his own garden. He rushed into the house and bumped into the man in the hall!

"Hallo!" said the man. "Here's the rude little boy again!"

Robin's mother was coming out of the sitting-room at that moment to see who her visitor was. She heard what he said.

"Rude!" she said in astonishment. "Robin, have you been rude?"

Robin felt most uncomfortable. He stood and said nothing. The man looked at the boy's mother.

"I am looking for a small boy who is supposed to be in this district," he said. "I am very, very anxious to find him. I thought perhaps he might be in this house or the next one, as these seem to be the only two there are here."

"Well, there's only Robin here," said his mother.

"I don't know of any other boy. I am sure there isn't one next door. But wait—there *is* another boy!"

"Really?" said the man. "Where is he? What is he like?"

"Well, I've never seen him myself," said Robin's mother. "I know two things about him that might perhaps help you. His name is Sammy—and the poor boy can't speak. He is dumb."

"I'm afraid he's not the boy I'm after," said the man. "The boy I want is called Kit Anthony Armstrong. You are sure you haven't heard of another boy anywhere here?"

"Well, there are only these two houses here," said Mummy. "I would be sure to know if any boy was near. If this Sammy isn't the boy you want, I'm afraid you won't find him in Faldham!"

"Well, thank you very much," said the man, and picked up his hat to go. "I must have been mistaken. But, madam, I'd take it as a very kind act on your part if you'd telephone to this address should you hear of any boy of twelve years of age called Kit."

"Very well," said Mummy, feeling quite puzzled, and taking the man's card as he spoke. "I'm sorry my boy was rude to you. It's most unlike him."

"Oh, that's all right," said the man, and went out of the hall door and got into his big car. He drove off without calling in at Kit's house at all.

"Robin! What does this mean? Were you really rude to that man?" asked Mummy, shocked. "What happened?"

"Well—he just asked me a lot of questions, and I didn't see why I should answer them," said the boy, rather sulkily. "I didn't like him."

"You mustn't be rude to strangers just because you don't like them!" said his mother. "I really do feel ashamed of you. I'm sorry I couldn't help the man—he really seemed quite concerned about this boy called Kit. I didn't like to ask him why he was so anxious to find him."

Robin could have told her, but he didn't want to. He hurried to find the two girls and to tell them that the man had actually come to call on their mother! They listened in horror.

"Fortunately, Mummy doesn't think there's a boy next door, and she told the man the only one she had heard of was called Sammy and was dumb," said Robin. "It was a good thing Mr Cunningham said that to her—it must have put the man off properly. Oh, dear—I suppose Kit will have to go soon."

"I don't see why," said Lucy. "After all, the man doesn't think any longer that Kit is anywhere about here—so he's likely now to go and look somewhere else! Kit would be best to stay where he is. The man won't come looking in the same place twice!"

"No—you're right, Lucy," said Robin, cheering up. "Quite right! If he doesn't come back within a day or two, I vote we tell Kit not to say anything to the Dragon or to Mr Barton, but just to sit tight and hope the man won't appear any more, but will go hunting in other places called Faldham!"

"That man talked like an American," said Betty thoughtfully. "He didn't look very wicked, did he?"

"Wicked people often look awfully good," said Robin. "You can't tell. Anyway, he simply MUST be Kit's uncle, because he's awfully like him."

"Robin, Kit will be able to spend the night on the house-boat with us, after all, if that man doesn't turn up again—won't he?" said Lucy eagerly. "It would have been horrid if he hadn't been able to do that. Things are much nicer if Kit's with us. He's such fun."

Robin and the girls couldn't manage to go down the garden and under the fence to tell Kit what had happened that evening. Mummy insisted that they should all have a game of Snap, as it was raining, so they sat there, snapping and gathering up the cards. Meanwhile, Kit was feeling rather anxious, wondering whatever had happened. Why had the man gone next door?

At the children's bedtime, when they were undressing in their rooms, a shower of little stones came against the windows. Robin jumped, and then went to look out. In the garden below was Kit! He signed to Robin to know if anyone was about.

"It's all right," said Robin, whereupon Kit leapt up the pear tree by the wall, and was soon astride the window-sill. The girls came into the room, and soon Kit was being told all about the man's visit.

"He really is after you; there's no doubt about that," said Robin. "But Mummy put him off properly, though she didn't know it! We think he'll go off to another Faldham now—there are about seven places called Faldham, you know—and he won't come back here. So don't you think it would be best not to say a word to Mr Barton or the Dragon till we see if there's any more sign of the man?"

"Anyway, if there is, you can always hide on the house-boat!" said Lucy, her eyes shining.

Kit nodded. "I shan't say a word," he decided. "Not a word. And, as you say, I can always rush off to the house-boat. Nobody would ever think of me being there! Thanks awfully, all of you. Now I must go, or the Dragon will come after me with smoke and flames pouring out of her nostrils!"

The children giggled as Kit slid to the ground. Just as he landed there, Mummy happened to draw the curtains downstairs, and gazed in the greatest astonishment at the dark shadow dropping to the ground.

"Robin!" she called. "Is that you? You naughty boy, what are you doing?"

Robin heard her and groaned. "Oh, my! Now Mummy will know there was someone here to-night. The cat will be out of the bag."

"*You* drop down the tree quickly," said Lucy, "and then climb up again. You'll get into the bedroom just when your mother comes into the bedroom, and she will never guess it was Kit then. Quick!"

The two girls shot out of the room. Robin dropped down the tree and then climbed up again, appearing at the window as his mother came into the room.

"Robin! So it *was* you! What do you mean by behaving like this when you are supposed to be in bed?"

"Very sorry, Mummy," said Robin humbly, and got into bed.

"I should think so!" said his mother, and turned the light out with a click. Really, what would these children be up to next?

Chapter Fourteen

OFF FOR A NIGHT ON THE BOAT

THE CHILDREN all made great preparations for Friday.
Mummy said they were to take rugs with them, because
she felt sure the bedding would be damp.

"You must spread each bunk with a rug," she said.
"And be sure to drag the bedding out into the hot sun to
give it another airing before you sleep on it. Now—what
do you want to take with you to eat?"

"Oh—heaps of things," said Robin. "You've simply no
idea how hungry we get on the river, Mummy."

"Well, I can guess," said Mummy with a laugh. "All
right—I'll pack you up a hamper of things. I'll get
somebody to carry it down to the boat for you. You will
have plenty of other things to carry. Don't forget your
pyjamas and nightdresses, and your toothbrushes."

There *were* a lot things to take just for one night on the
boat! But Mummy said they could leave some of the
things there for another time, so that was good.

"It looks as if we'll often be allowed to spend the night there," said Robin. "I hope Kit will, too. I always miss him when he doesn't come. Lucy, are you taking dog biscuits for Sandy?"

"Of course!" said Lucy.

"Don't forget his tooth brush and pyjamas," said Betty solemnly.

"Idiot!" said Lucy. "Sandy, will you enjoy spending a night in a boat, I wonder?"

"Woof," said Sandy, and wagged his tail joyously. He was happy to be anywhere with Lucy.

The day came at last, sunny and hot. The children were sorry to set off without Kit. But the American boy did not care to escape from the Dragon until night-time.

"I'll go to bed early, though," he promised, "and then I'll be able to come about nine, I hope. Will you come and fetch me in the boat, Robin? It's a fag for you to have to come all the way back for me, I know—but I can't think what else to do. I *could* follow the river-bank, I suppose, till I come to the house-boat—but I expect I'd have to go a good bit out of my way at times."

"Yes, you would," said Robin. "Of course I'll come and fetch you in the boat. I'll be waiting at our usual place at nine o'clock. It will be getting dark then. No one will see you."

The three children and Sandy set off in the early afternoon. Harry, the gardener, came with them, carrying the hamper of food, and a couple of rugs. The children carried the other things between them. They were all in a great state of excitement. To go to bed in the boat seemed to them a really tremendous thrill.

"We'll go to bed quite late," said Robin. "For one thing, I won't be back until at least half-past nine with Kit—then we'll want to talk."

"And won't it be LOVELY to sit in that little sitting-room, lighted by candles, with the darkness outside, and the water lap-lapping against the boat!" said Lucy. "Oh, I *am* glad I came to stay with you these hols!"

Harry, the gardener, put down the things he was carrying when he arrived at the boat. "Well, there you are," he said. "Good luck to you! Sleep well!"

"Thanks, Harry," said Robin. The children began to pile the goods into the small boat. Then Robin took the oars and they set off. It was very hot indeed, and the sun baked their shoulders.

"I vote we bathe off the house-boat," said Lucy. "I simply must get cool somehow!"

They came to the white-painted house-boat and clambered up the side. Robin handed the things up to the girls, and they piled them on the decks, ready to be sorted out.

Then the boy tied up his little boat to the big one and clambered up, too.

"We'd better put the bedding out into the sun," he said. "Mummy said we must."

"Oh let's bathe first," said Lucy. "I'm so hot."

"No—we might forget about the bedding," said Robin. "Come on—we promised."

So, before anything else was done, all the bedding from the four bunks was dragged out and strewn over the decks in the hot sun.

"It'll be absolutely baked!" said Robin. I'm sure it won't have a scrap of dampness left in it. Now—shall we bathe?"

"Yes," said Betty. "I'll just put the milk into the little larder in a pail of water to keep cool. And put the hamper of food out of the sun, Robin, will you? We'll arrange everything after we've bathed."

They had a gorgeous bathe in the cool river water. All three children were excellent swimmers, and Sandy, of course, swam in the way dogs always do swim—"scrabble, scrabble, scrabble with all four paws at once!" as Lucy described it. He looked about for rabbits as he swam, for he thought there might possibly be a few bathing in the river that hot afternoon. But, as usual, Sandy was disappointed.

The children were tired at last. They climbed to the deck of the house-boat and lay drying themselves in the hot sun. "I'm getting burnt as brown as a ripe acorn," said Lucy, looking at her tanned legs. "I say—what about a drink? I'm awfully thirsty."

"Get it yourself, then," said Robin lazily. "I can't move."

They came to the white-painted house-boat

"Nor can I!" said Lucy dreamily. "Can you feel the boat moving up and down a little as the river flows beneath it, Robin? Isn't it lovely? I do love this old boat."

The children lay there lazily for half an hour and then got up to arrange their things and get some tea. It was fun choosing their bunks. The girls had one little bedroom, and Robin put his things on one of the bunks in the other. "Kit will bring his own things, I expect," he said. He stuck new candles into the candlesticks that abounded on the boat, and put matches there, too. All the children were secretly looking forward to night-time.

The girls unpacked the food and put it neatly into the tiny larder. Then they set tea on one of the little red tables outside in the sunshine.

"There's ginger-beer to drink," said Betty. "But when we have supper to-night, we'll boil water to make some cocoa. That will be fun."

"We'll have to go and ask the old caretaker for some water, then," said Robin. "Hope she won't mind!"

"You go, Robin," said Betty. "She's seen you once before. Take the kettle with you."

So, about six o'clock, Robin took the big kettle from the little stove and set off up the lawns to where the big house stood in the distance. Smoke curled up from a chimney so the boy knew there was someone there. He wondered idly if the new people had arrived yet, the ones to whom Mr Cunningham had let the house. There seemed no sign of them.

He went round to the back door and knocked. No one answered. He knocked again, more loudly, and then pushed open the door. The old caretaker was working in the kitchen there. She looked up with a jump as she saw Robin.

"Bless us all!" she said, annoyed. "What do you mean by making me jump like that! What do you want?"

"Please would you be good enough to let me have some water for my kettle?" asked Robin politely.

"Why? Are you picnicking anywhere here?" asked the old woman. "You'd better not! Mr Cunningham has let the house now, and the people are here already. You'll get into trouble if you trespass on these grounds."

"It's all right," said Robin. "We are in the old house-boat on the river."

"Oh—is that the house-boat you spoke about the other day when you came?" said the caretaker. "I haven't had time to go down and have a look at it yet. I've been so busy getting ready for the new people. But you'd better be careful about using that house-boat. You might be turned off it!"

"No, we shan't," said Robin. "Could I get the water, please?"

"There is a tap you can use just outside the kitchen door," said the old woman. "Use it when you like, and don't come bothering me any more."

"All right," said Robin. "I'm sorry to have bothered you. I won't again. I'll just get the water when I want it."

He shut the kitchen door and went to find the tap outside. There was one just under the kitchen window. As Robin went to fill his kettle, he heard a man's voice speaking to the old woman in sharp tones.

"Who was that here just now?"

"A little boy," said the caretaker.

"Where does he come from?" said the voice. "I don't want children messing about here. We came here to be perfectly quiet and private."

"He said something about being on the house-boat at the bottom of the garden," muttered the caretaker crossly. "You'd better ask him yourself where he comes from. I don't know anything about him."

"A house-boat—at the bottom of the garden!" said the man's voice in surprise.

"I haven't heard anything about that. That must belong to the property, then. I'll have a look at it. Mr Cunningham must have forgotten to tell me about that. It might be useful when I want to work by myself."

Robin heard all this in dismay. He hoped the man wouldn't make any difficulties about the house-boat. It would be tiresome if they had to take it away and tie it up somewhere else. He wondered if he should have a word with the man—but as there was silence after that, it was clear that he had left the kitchen. Perhaps he wouldn't bother any more about the boat.

"Anyway, Mr Cunningham rented it to us!" thought the boy as he sped off with the kettle. "That man can't turn us out! I hope he won't turn up at the house-boat to-night!"

But that was just what he *did* do! It was most upsetting.

Chapter Fifteen

A HORRID SHOCK

ROBIN WENT back to the house-boat and told the girls what he had overheard. They were rather worried. When grown-ups got cross they did unpleasant things. It would be horrid to be turned out of the boat just as they had planned to spend the night there.

"I hope the man doesn't come to-night when you are off to fetch Kit," said Betty. "I should be afraid."

"Oh, he'll come before dark, if he's coming," said Robin. "I'll be here. You needn't worry. After all, so long as we've got permission from the owner, that's all that matters!"

But somehow the evening was a bit spoilt. The children bathed again, and then stood watching the scores of little fishes that swam by the boat. A blue and green kingfisher, brilliant in the evening sunshine, sat on a low branch nearby, his head on one side, watching the fish, too.

Then suddenly down he swooped into the water and came up again with a fish in his beak. A toss of his head and it was gone!

"I wish we could catch fish like that," said Betty. "Just a dart into the water—and back again with a fish in our mouths!"

"Wuff!" said Sandy, quite agreeing. He was watching the water, too—but not for fish. He couldn't understand the dog that was looking up at him out of the water. He didn't guess that it was his own reflection!

About half-past seven, when the water was purple with the long shadows of trees in the evening sunshine, the children heard voices in the distance. Sandy pricked up his ears and growled a little.

"Oh," said Betty, looking scared, "do you think it's someone coming to the boat?"

It was! The voices came nearer, and then two men appeared at the side of the drooping willows that hid the boat. They did not look at all pleasant. In fact, they looked as stern as the Dragon. The children looked at them and said nothing.

"What are you kids doing here?" said one man in a sharp voice. He had cold blue eyes and short, fair hair. The other man was smaller and dark.

"We're spending the night on this house-boat," said Robin politely.

"Oh, no, you're not!" said the man. "You're going to clear out of here in double-quick time! We've rented this property, and we're not having any kids messing about. This house-boat belongs to us now."

"It doesn't," said Robin boldly. "It's been rented to *us*!"

This was quite true, but the man didn't believe a word. He gave a short laugh. "And what do you pay?" he asked in a scornful voice.

Nobody answered.

"Well, speak up!" said the man. "I suppose you're telling fibs, so you can't answer. Well, clear up your things and be gone in half an hour."

This was too much for Betty. "We've *paid* our rent—for two whole years!" she said indignantly. "You just ask Mr Cunningham!"

"And what rent did you pay?" said the man mockingly. "Twopence a week?"

"No—we paid Mr Cunningham two slices of Lucy's birthday cake," said Betty. "He said that was quite enough rent."

The two men burst into loud laughter. "Do you really expect us to believe that?" said the smaller man. "Well, whatever rent you paid you'll have to clear out. We want to be private here. We shall probably use the house-boat ourselves."

Betty began to cry. Sandy growled deeply in his throat—"Urrrrrrrrrr". Robin went red with anger.

"Please ring up Mr Cunningham on your telephone," he said. "He will tell you that he gave us permission to have this boat. We shan't interfere with you at all. We won't even come for water if you'd rather we didn't."

"You certainly won't set foot on our grounds again," said the first man roughly. "As for Mr Cunningham, he's gone abroad, as you probably very well know."

"Well—ring up our mother, then," said poor Robin, still scarlet in the face. "Mr Cunningham told her about us and the house-boat. She knows all about it. Her number is Faldham 5."

"We'd better do that," said the first man, turning to the other. "The sooner we get these kids off the place and they understand they're not to come back, the better. Come on—we'll ring up Faldham 5."

They went up the green lawn. The three children looked at one another, dismayed and angry. It was too bad! Mr Cunningham *had* said they could have the boat. But how awfully horrid these men were! They had spoilt everything.

"I bet Mummy will say we're not to come here again if those men don't like us about," said Robin with a groan. "I just bet she will! Oh, why did Mr Cunningham go away? We could have telephoned to him and everything would have been all right. It's a great pity he didn't tell those men about us and the boat."

Meantime the men were telephoning Faldham 5. They got on to the children's mother at once. In most polite tones the first man explained things to her. "We think there must be some mistake," he said smoothly. "We have taken over the whole property from Mr Cunningham who is, as you probably know, now away. We cannot have children over-running our grounds, as we only took this place on Mr Cunningham's assuring us we would be completely private."

"Of course. I quite understand," said the children's mother. "It is true that Mr Cunningham *did* say they might have the boat, but I don't want any trouble to be caused over that. I will tell the children they must not use it."

"Thank you, madam," said the smooth tones of the man. "This is kind of you. If we can make it up to the children in any way—say by making them a handsome present—we shall be glad to do so."

"No, no, of course not," said the children's mother hastily. "But if you would just let them spend this night there, it would please them. They have taken everything there, and it would be such a disappointment if they had to come back now. I am sure they won't do any damage."

"We will tell them they can spend to-night there, of course," said the man. "Good night, madam!" He put the receiver down, and once more went down the lawns to the house-boat. Sandy growled, so the children knew he was coming. They were all afraid they might be turned out that very night.

. The man hailed them. "I got on to your mother, and she agrees with me that it would be impossible to have you messing about here, now that we have taken the house. But you can stay for the night. After that don't come near here at all. Understand?"

"Yes," said the children sulkily.

The man turned and went back up the lawn. The three children scowled after him. How they disliked him!

"I believe he's another wicked uncle!" said Betty. "He talks like the other one did—sort of drawly."

"Well, it's no good thinking that every American we come across is Kit's wicked uncle!" said Robin. "These men can't have anything to do with him. The other man even knew Kit's name! Oh, I say—isn't it sickening to think we're not to come here again?"

"I don't see why we shouldn't," said Lucy. "Why should we give up something we've every right to have just because that horrid man says we must? I vote we don't! I

97

vote we come whenever we want to—providing that man isn't here!"

"I vote that, too," said Betty. "Just to show we don't care tuppence what he says! We know quite well that when Mr Cunningham comes back he'll say he meant us to have the boat and use it."

"I might ask the man if we could use the boat if we took it somewhere else farther down the river," said Robin thoughtfully. "If we were out of his way he wouldn't mind about the boat. We might moor it outside our little island."

"Ask him to-morrow," said Lucy. "What's the time, Robin? Oughtn't you to be fetching Kit? It's getting quite dark now!"

So it was. The sun had gone, and evening was coming. The water looked very dark. It splashed against the house-boat with a pleasant sound.

"You girls get ready some supper, and see that the kettle is boiling," said Robin, looking at his watch. "I'll fetch Kit. Pity we haven't got better news for him!"

Robin slipped down into the boat below. The girls went into the tiny cabin sitting-room and lighted two candles. At once the cabin looked very cosy. They set up the little flap-table there and laid the supper. It looked good.

"Cold ham, tomatoes, fresh lettuce, bread and butter, cheese, biscuits, ripe plums, apples," said Lucy. "A very fine feast! I hope Robin and Kit won't be too long. I'm glad we've got Sandy with us. I'm sure he'd fly at those men if they tried to be horrid to us again."

"I'll put the kettle on the stove," said Betty. She lighted the stove in the tiny kitchen. It made a pleasant glow. The little girl put the cocoa tin ready, fetched the milk, and set beside the tin a big jug for the hot cocoa when it was made. It really was fun doing all these things on her own!

After some time there came a shout from the dark waters. "Hi, there! Here we are! Show a light, *Black Swan*!"

Betty lighted a lantern and hung it over the side to show Robin where to tie up his boat. Then the two boys clambered up to the deck. They peered through the window of the little cabin, and looked with delight at the feast there brightly lighted by the two candles.

"What-ho for a night on board!" said Kit. "*Now* we're going to enjoy ourselves?"

Chapter Sixteen

KIT GETS INTO TROUBLE

IT WAS COSY in the little cabin, sitting squashed together round the table. All the children were very hungry, and the ham and salad soon disappeared. So did the cheese! Betty had made the cocoa, and they drank it thirstily. It was very good.

"The kettle boiled ages before you came," said Betty. "I was afraid all the water would boil away, so I had to take it off the stove, and put it on again just before you arrived. We hadn't any more water."

"I could have got some," said Robin boldly. "I shall get water from that tap outside the kitchen if I want to, no matter what that man says!"

"Hear, hear!" said Kit, cutting himself a large lump of cheese. "The man has no right to act as he did."

"Kit, did you manage to escape from your house without the Dragon or Mr Barton seeing you?" asked Betty eagerly. "Tell us about it."

"There's nothing to tell," said Kit. "I just said I was

going to bed early, so I went. I stuck the bolster down the middle of my bed to look like me, and then I got out of the attic window in the usual way. And here I am! I had only waited about two minutes on the river-bank before Robin came."

They finished supper and then went out on deck to see the moon coming up.

It swam up through the trees, looking very bright and lovely. The river shone silver, and every now and again the children could hear the plop-plop of a fish jumping. An owl called in the distance, a lovely long quavering sound: "Oooo! Ooo-oo-oo-oooooo!"

"Isn't it lovely here?" said Lucy, enjoying every minute. "We're far away from our beds—all by ourselves—and we needn't go to bed till midnight if we don't want to."

"Well, I'm getting awfully sleepy," said Robin, yawning. "I've had a long row here and back twice, don't forget! You girls go and wash up quickly. Then we'll all go to bed."

So Betty and Lucy cleared the supper away, washed the things, and set the table for breakfast. Then they lighted candles in the tiny bedrooms, and drew the little curtains there across the windows. How small and cosy the rooms looked!

The children went into the little sleeping cabins. It was fun to undress there. Sandy jumped up into Lucy's bunk and curled himself round sleepily. Lucy laughed.

"You'll have to move up a bit, Sandy!" she said. "You're right in the very middle. Move up!"

The children snuggled into their narrow bunks. Not one of them had ever slept in a bunk before, and it seemed very exciting. They pulled the bedding up round them and blew out their candles.

"Good night!" called the girls, and the boys answered sleepily: "Good night! Sleep well!"

"Woof!" said Sandy, which was his way of saying good night, too. He was now on Lucy's feet, warm and comfortable. Everyone except Lucy fell asleep at once.

The little girl lay for a time and listened to the noises around. The house-boat creaked a little as the river ran underneath and lifted it now and again.

The waves went plash-lash-lash against the sides, and the owl called again, much nearer.

"It's all lovely," said Lucy to herself, trying her hardest to keep awake and enjoy every single minute. "I love to hear the gurgling noise the water makes. I love to feel the boat moving. It's fun to sleep on the water."

Then she, too, was fast asleep, and not one of the four children stirred until the morning sun put hot fingers through the cabin windows. It was nearly eight o'clock!

"KIT!" said Robin, looking in dismay at his watch. "We meant to wake at six and take you back—and it's almost eight. You'll get into trouble!"

"Crumbs! I certainly shall!" said Kit in horror. "We have breakfast at eight. I say, let's go at once! My word, isn't this sickening?"

Robin and Kit dressed hurriedly and tumbled into the little boat. "Have breakfast ready when I get back!" called Robin as the boys rowed off hurriedly. "And tell those men we shall be leaving soon if they come again."

Robin left Kit on the shore where he had picked him up the night before, then rowed back again to the house-boat. He was very hungry by the time he arrived. He smelt bacon and eggs frying, and thought it was the best smell he had ever known in his life.

"Poor Kit!" he said as he and the two girls ate their breakfast. "I bet he really will get into awful trouble this time. I wonder what will happen."

A shout from the bank made the children look up. The two men stood there. "You're to clear off now," shouted the first man. "And remember this—you don't come here again!"

No one replied. All the children had made up their minds that they *would* come if they wanted to—so it wasn't a bit of good the man saying they weren't to! They washed up everything and made the deck tidy and neat.

Then they slipped down into their boat and rowed back home. It had been fun. Not such fun as they had hoped, because those men had spoilt things a bit—but still it had been lovely. They worried a little about Kit, and hoped he would be able to let them know how he had got on.

Robin climbed up the chestnut tree as soon as they got home, but there was no sign of anyone next door at all. He slid down, wondering if he dared to go in and find out anything.

"Can't you get in at the attic window without anyone seeing you?" said Lucy. "Poor Kit might be locked up in his bedroom or something!"

"I'll try after dinner," said Robin. He and the others went indoors to tell their mother all about the night on the boat. They said nothing at all of Kit, of course.

"Well, I'm afraid you mustn't go there again," said their mother. "The new people at the house object to children using the boat at the bottom of their garden—and I must say I think it was queer of Mr Cunningham to allow it when he had let the house! So don't go there again."

Nobody said they would, and nobody said they wouldn't. They just changed the subject and told their mother about the brilliant kingfisher they had watched catching fish.

After dinner Robin climbed the chestnut again, but still there was no sign of Kit. So the boy got under the fencing and slipped into the next-door garden. What *had* happened to Kit?

He ran silently round the grounds and up the other side to where the garage stood. The ladder was still against the wall. Kit had left it there. Up it went Robin, on to the flat roof, and then into the big ash tree. Down the plank to the window-sill he slid, and in at the window. No one was there. The room was quite empty.

The boy tiptoed to the door. His heart was beating fast. He was afraid of being caught by the Dragon or by Mr Barton. He tried to remember which was Kit's bedroom.

He went out on to the landing and looked over the banisters there.

There were three bedroom doors below, that he could see. Which one was Kit's?

No one seemed to be about. The boy slipped quietly down the stairs and stood in front of the bedroom doors. He opened one and peeped in. Nobody was there at all. He shut the door quietly. He tried the next.

It was locked! Was Kit locked in there? The key was on Robin's side of the door.

The boy knocked gently. There was no answer. He knocked again.

Kit's voice came: "Who is it?"

In a trice Robin had unlocked the door and was in the room! He closed the door behind him and looked round the room. It *was* Kit's bedroom! The boy was sitting huddled up before a desk, an open book in front of him. He looked woebegone and miserable.

"Robin!" said Kit, starting up and speaking in a loud whisper. "However did you dare to get in here? The Dragon may come at any moment!"

"Can't help it," said Robin. "I just *had* to come and find out what had happened to you!"

"The very worst," said Kit gloomily. "For some reason or other the Dragon came into my room early this morning, about five o'clock—and she spotted the bolster down my bed. She woke Mr Barton, and the two hunted all over the house for me.

Then they hunted in the garden, though they didn't see how I could be out of doors because all the doors and windows were securely bolted. They haven't spotted my way of escape from the attic-room yet."

"What happened when you got back?" asked Robin.

"Well, I climbed up into the attic and walked down to my bedroom," said Kit, "and on the way I met the Dragon! She looked so astonished that I had to laugh. She clutched hold of me as if she wanted to make sure I was really there. Honestly, I think she's quite fond of me!"

"Did you tell her where you had been?" asked Robin.

"Of course not, idiot!" said Kit. "She thinks I was hiding somewhere in the house to give her and Mr Barton a fright. I won't say a word—and that's what has made them both so angry. I'm to be locked up in my room for two days, and do an awful lot of hard studying. I couldn't think how to get word to you—but now you've come it's all right. Don't worry about me. They'll let me out the day after to-morrow—only I won't be able to vanish at night any more, I'm afraid. I guess they'll keep a sharp eye on me in future! I shouldn't be surprised if they lock my bedroom door every night!"

103

Suddenly the boys heard footsteps coming, and Robin felt his heart sink. He didn't at all want to be caught just then. He looked round for a hiding-place.

"Under the bed!" hissed Kit, sitting down at his desk again. "Quick!"

There was the sound of a key being jiggled in the lock, and then an exclamation as the Dragon discovered that the door was unlocked. She opened it and looked inside.

"Kit, who unlocked the door? It isn't locked—and I *know* it was locked before. Who's been here?"

"Was the door unlocked?" said Kit, putting on a most innocent face.

"Yes—it was—and it's no use trying to pretend to *me*!" said the Dragon, losing her temper. "Someone's been here—and is here still, for all I know!"

She looked round the room and then gave a scream. She pointed to the bottom of the bed. Kit looked, and, to his horror, saw that one of Robin's feet was clearly showing under the valance.

"Who's that?" cried the Dragon. "Come out, whoever you are!"

Chapter Seventeen

PLENTY OF EXCITEMENT!

ROBIN DID not move. He did not know that his foot was showing from underneath the bed. The Dragon shouted to him again.

"Come out! If you don't, I shall drag you out!" And drag him out she did! She caught hold of Robin's foot and pulled him roughly and strongly out from under the bed. He sat up and looked at her. "Oh! it's the boy from next door again!" she said angrily. "Didn't I tell you never to come here?"

"Yes, and you told me there wasn't a boy here," said Robin. "You told a fib!"

"How dare you come here like this?" cried the Dragon. "Oh—here is Mr Barton. *He* will deal with you!"

Mr Barton was a very stern-looking man, who, so Kit said, never smiled at all. He looked in astonishment and anger at Robin as the Dragon told him what had happened.

"Mr Barton, I've told this boy all about myself," said Kit. "He knows I'm in hiding, and he knows why. He wouldn't tell anyone. He's my friend."

"Your friend!" said Mr Barton scornfully, in a horrid dry voice. "You are a most foolish and tiresome boy. You know quite well that we have been given instructions to keep your hiding-place a secret, and to let you make no friends until that unpleasant uncle of yours is caught and dealt with. And you make things as difficult as possible for the people who are doing their best to guard you. You deserve to be whipped—and so does this boy, too, coming into other people's houses without permission!"

Robin felt quite frightened of Mr Barton. His eyes were so cold and piercing, and his mouth was thin-lipped and cruel.

"I'm sorry sir," he said.

"*Sorry!*" said Mr Barton. "It isn't enough to be sorry. You will keep out of this house and out of the garden, too, unless you want me to complain to your parents and have you sternly punished. Do you wish me to do that?"

"No," said Robin, who didn't want any more complaints about him to go to his mother.

"And you will tell me exactly how you got into this house," said Mr Barton.

Robin caught a warning glance from Kit. He shut his lips tightly and did not answer.

Mr Barton lost his temper. He banged on Kit's desk, making the book jump in the air and fall to the floor.

"DO YOU HEAR ME, BOY?" he roared. "You will tell me what I ask you."

Robin was badly afraid he would have to tell. He didn't see how he could stand there for ages and not say a word, because he was already a bit shaky at the knees. An idea came to him. No one was between him and the door. He could rush out, bang the door and slip upstairs before anyone caught him. Then he wouldn't have to say a word!

Without waiting to think about it, the boy carried out his sudden plan. He rushed to the door, banged it shut behind him, and tore up the stairs to the attic-room as quickly as he could.

Mr Barton was at first too astonished to do anything. Then he ran to the door and flung it open. He did not know whether Robin had gone up or down the stairs. He called to the Dragon:

"Go up to the attics and see if he is hiding there. I'll go downstairs. And if I catch him I'll give him a good whipping!"

Mr Barton ran down the stairs, and the Dragon ran up to the attics. Kit remained where he was, hoping and hoping that Robin would have time to slide out on the plank to the ash tree and get down in safety.

He did! The Dragon looked into the other attic-room first and then into the one that was Kit's play-room. By that time Robin was half-way down the tree. It did not occur to the Dragon that the boy could have got out of the window, for she did not for a moment think there was any way down to the ground. She felt sure that Robin had gone down the stairs, and she hurried down, too, to help in the search.

After about four minutes the telephone rang in the house, and Mr Barton went to answer it. It was Robin telephoning from his home next door!

"Is that Mr Barton? Please sir, don't bother to go on looking for me. I'm home. I'm sorry I can't tell you how I get in and out, and please don't be angry with Kit because I went to see him. I'll keep his secret, I promise you. I haven't told anyone at all about Kit."

Mr Barton was still in a furious temper. He flung down the receiver with a snort, and went to tell the Dragon.

"It beats me how those children next door get in and out! But if ever I catch one of them again, they'll be sorry!" he stormed. "As for Kit, don't let him out of your sight in future!"

The girls listened to Robin's story, holding their breath with horror when he told them how the Dragon had seen his foot coming out from under the bed. "It was terribly exciting," said Robin, feeling quite a hero, and decidedly clever as he related the whole story.

"I think things are getting a bit *too* exciting!" said Betty. "And oh, Robin—what do you think? I've left my dear little silver watch on the house-boat! I put it under my pillow last night and forgot to put it on my wrist again this morning! I am so sad about it, because I'm sure that horrid man will take it if he finds it."

"He jolly well won't," said Robin. "I'll go and get it for you myself to-morrow. *I'm* not afraid of that man. I can't go to-day because we've got to go out in the car with Mummy. It's a good thing she's out now, or I couldn't have telephoned to Mr Barton. It was funny to think of him and the Dragon looking upstairs and downstairs for me, and me here all the time!"

The children were sad to think of poor Kit being locked up. They did not dare to try and see him again. They went out in the car with their mother, to have tea with friends about ten miles away, and when they came back Robin wondered if he could slip away and go to the house-boat to fetch Betty's watch for her. But he decided not to.

"That man might be on the watch to-day to see if we come back," he said. "I'll go to-morrow, after tea."

So the next day, about five o'clock, he and the girls set off to walk to the river. He got into the boat and waved good-bye to them. They were going to take Sandy for a nice rabbity walk. He was so thrilled. Robin rowed along, thinking of all that had been happening. He thought with dislike of Mr Barton and of the horrid man at the lonely house. "The Dragon's not so bad," he thought. "I'm scared of her, but I don't dislike her. Now, where's that house-boat? I should be getting near it!"

He saw the lonely house in the distance and glanced over his shoulder to see the house-boat. He couldn't seem to see it. So he stopped rowing, and twisted himself right round.

And, to his enormous astonishment, the boat wasn't there. It simply—wasn't—there!

Robin sat in his little boat, staring at the empty space by the willow trees where the boat had always been. He wondered if he were dreaming. The house-boat had been there the day before. They had spent the night on it. And now it was gone. It was simply extraordinary. Robin couldn't make it out at all!

"*Where* has it gone?" he thought. "Can it have sunk? No—impossible!"

All the same the boy rowed over to the spot where the boat had been, and looked down into the deep water there. But no house-boat was sunk below the river. Only little fishes darted about by the hundred. It was most mysterious.

"Well, this beats everything!" said Robin to himself. "It really does! Whatever has happened to our boat?"

The boy made up his mind to find it. The men must have taken it somewhere. But why? And where? It was really very queer. Robin began to row farther up the river.

Not very far up, a little backwater ran into the river, so overgrown with drooping willow trees that it was quite difficult to see. But some of the branches of the willows were broken, and Robin's sharp eyes saw them.

"They've taken the boat up that hidden backwater!" he thought to himself, in excitement. "It'll be up there. I'll go and find out."

The boy rowed under the weeping willow trees and came into the little backwater. It was very pretty and very quiet. Plainly it ran alongside the grounds of the lonely house. The men must have taken the house-boat there for some reason.

"To hide it from *us*, I suppose!" said Robin crossly. "Well, they'll just be wrong. I'll find it."

And find it he did! It was moored to the side, some way up the backwater, under a very big drooping willow, that practically hid it. The branches drooped all over the decks, and if Robin had not been looking for the boat, he might easily have passed it by unseen, it was so well hidden!

The boy sat silently for a moment, listening for voices or sounds that might warn him of people about. But he could hear nothing. So in a trice he was up on the deck and into the little cabin where Betty had slept the night before. He slid his hand under her pillow—and felt the little silver watch. "Good!" he thought, putting it into his pocket. "Betty will be pleased. Now I'll go back and tell the girls the news."

He slipped down into his boat and rowed back again, feeling puzzled and excited. Surely the men wouldn't have taken all that trouble to hide the boat just to prevent the children from using it? And yet, what other reason could there be? It was very extraordinary. Robin wished Mr Cunningham was home so that he might ask him a few questions.

109

He got back and met the girls. When he told them his news they were most astonished.

"How clever of you to find the boat, Robin!" cried Betty. "And, oh, I *am* so glad to have my watch! I wish we could tell Kit our news. I hate to think of him locked up like that!"

"I'll slip in to-night, about twelve o'clock," said Robin. "Everyone next door will be asleep then. I'll give Kit a fine surprise!"

But it was Robin who got the surprise, not Kit!

Chapter Eighteen

ROBIN MAKES A DISCOVERY

THAT NIGHT Robin set his alarm-clock for midnight, and put it under his pillow. It woke him up with a jump. He was warm and sleepy and comfortable and thought after all he would not get out of bed and go adventuring in the middle of the night. But the sound of a car made him suddenly sit up.

The car stopped somewhere near. Robin jumped out of bed. The car was in the drive next door. Robin could see its lights. Funny that a visitor should come at that time of the night!

"Perhaps it's Kit's tutor come back late from somewhere," thought the boy. "Well—now I'm wide awake I'll go next door after all, I think. I'll be jolly careful not to walk into the Dragon or Mr Barton, though!"

He got out of bed and slipped into shorts and jersey. He put on his rubber shoes and slid down the pear tree outside his window. He landed with a light thud, and, in the clear moonlight, ran down the garden to where the tunnel was under the fencing.

He was up by the garage in no time. The ladder was still there! Good! Up he went, and then into the ash tree, along the plank to the sill, and into the dark, quiet attic. He paused at the door. He could hear no sound at all.

The landing was in darkness. All the doors were shut. The whole house seemed still. Robin wondered where the late visitor was—or could it have been Mr Barton himself? Well, he must have gone to bed pretty quickly then! Robin made up his mind to make no noise at all, in case Mr Barton began to wander about.

He crept down to the landing where Kit's bedroom was. He tried Kit's door. To his enormous delight, it was not locked! The boy opened it cautiously and stepped inside.

The room looked a little different, somehow. Robin was a bit puzzled. The moonlight shone in at the window and showed everything quite clearly. And then the boy saw how it was different! There were two beds there, instead of one!

And in each bed someone slept. Robin was cold with fear! Kit was in one bed—and golly! the Dragon was in the other! The moonlight showed up her face quite clearly. She was fast asleep.

"I suppose they've decided to have someone sleep with Kit in case he does another disappearing trick!" thought Robin. "Goodness me—I hope the Dragon doesn't wake. I daren't wake Kit in case the Dragon hears me!"

The boy tiptoed out of the room and shut the door very quietly. He heaved a sigh of relief as he stood there in the darkness.

And then he heard something that made him jump. It was a voice, coming up the stairs! It had an American drawl in it, and it was not Mr Barton's voice! Robin stood there, wondering whether he dared slip up the stairs to the attic. He could not see who was coming, for a bend of the stairs hid the two men. Then, with a sigh of relief, he heard them go into a little room on the half-landing below.

"What a funny time for someone to come and talk to Mr Barton!" thought Robin. "Oh, dear—I do hope Mr Barton isn't going to send Kit away, now he knows that I know his secret. That would be too bad."

The boy tiptoed down the stairs a little way, wondering if he could hear whether Kit was to be sent away or not— and what he did hear sent a shock of horror down his back!

"You can have five thousand pounds as soon as the boy is in our hands," said the American voice. "No more, and that's flat!"

Robin could not move. What did this mean? Why should Mr Barton have five thousand pounds? And was Kit the boy they spoke of? If so—that meant that Mr Barton was a traitor! He was bargaining with Kit's enemies! Perhaps Kit's wicked uncle was the man in that little room down there!

"Come here to-morrow night and I'll hand him over," said Mr Barton's voice. "Bring the money with you in cash. You can't have him to-night. That woman insisted on sleeping with him. Have you got a safe place to put him in? There's sure to be a great uproar if he disappears. I'll have to tell the police and pretend all kinds of things."

"We've got a fine place," said the other man. "No one would ever look there. Have him ready as soon as it's dark to-morrow. Bring him in the car to that spot we arranged, and I'll take him over from you. If you play your part well no one will ever know you had anything to do with it. It's up to you."

"Where will you take him?" asked Mr Barton.

"Never you mind!" was the answer. "Now, I'm going. See you to-morrow. So long!"

The door was opened and the two men came out. Robin darted up the stairs a little way. He wished he could have seen the other man. He felt so certain that it must be the man who had questioned him in the ice-cream shop. The wicked uncle! Somehow he must have found out where Kit was, after all!

He heard the men go downstairs. He heard the front door open and a car door slam. He heard the roar of the engine being started up—and then the car was gone! Mr

Barton came indoors and locked and bolted the door. Robin fled upstairs to the attic. He slid down the tree and was back in his own garden in record time. He was trembling. Things were really very serious. He wondered what he had better do.

Somehow or other he had to warn Kit. That was certain. Should he tell his mother? No—she would not believe such a tale, and might go straight to Mr Barton, and then he would be warned. Should they tell the Dragon! No! She might perhaps be a traitor, too. Robin couldn't tell if she was or not. Poor Kit! It was awful to be in someone's power like that, and be handed over to a wicked man.

The boy went into the girls' room and woke them. He poured out his tale in whispers. They were horrified. Betty began to cry. "Let's tell Mummy," she sobbed. "I don't want Kit to be kidnapped. Let's tell Mummy."

"No," said Robin. "I've got a much better idea. *We'll* kidnap Kit and hide him! We'll keep him safe till we can think what's best to do. We can't plan things all in a hurry."

"But where can we hide him? Here, in the house?" said Lucy, astonished. "Your mother would soon find out."

"Of course not here," said Robin scornfully. "I've got a much better place than that. We'll hide him in the house-boat!"

"In the house-boat!" echoed the girls. "Of course—what a fine idea!"

"Nobody would ever think of looking for him there," said Robin. "We'd be the only people who would know. We could take him food each day. His enemies would never, never think of looking in a place they've never even heard of!"

"That's exactly what we will do!" said Lucy. "Kit will be quite safe there. When shall we take him?"

"We must watch our chance and take him as soon as we can to-morrow," said Robin. "We must be as quick as we can. Mr Barton is supposed to hand him over in the evening. What a horrid creature he is!"

"I never did like the look of him," said Lucy.

"Nor did I," said Betty. "O-o-o-oh!—this is getting most terribly thrilling. I feel as if I must be in a dream."

"Well, you'd better go to sleep again now," said Robin, getting off to bed. "We'll have some work to do to-morrow!"

They all fell asleep after a time, and when they awoke in the morning they could hardly believe that it was all true! Robin climbed up the chestnut tree to see if Kit was by any chance on the lawn below. He was—but the Dragon *and* Mr Barton were there as well.

Kit glanced up at the top of the chestnut tree. He was longing to get a glimpse of the children. Robin waggled a branch wildly, and Kit felt certain the boy was there. He picked up a ball and began to throw it idly. Robin slid down the tree again.

"He's seen me, I'm sure," he said. "He picked up his ball—and I'm sure it was a signal to me to throw him over a message. I'll write one now. You girls find the old split ball."

Soon the message was crammed inside the ball, and Robin threw it over into the next-door garden. Kit was on the watch for it. Neither the Dragon nor Mr Barton noticed the second ball dropping on the lawn. They merely thought it was one that Kit was playing with. The boy picked it up and went behind the summer-house. He read the short message:

"Kit! You are in great danger. Go to the tunnel as soon as you can. We shall be there."

Kit put the note into his pocket. He threw his ball high into the air, and it fell with a crash into the bushes beyond. Kit made as if he would go to get it.

"You're not to go out of sight, Kit," said Mr Barton sharply.

"I'm only just going to get my ball, sir," said Kit meekly, and went into the bushes. He ran rapidly down the garden as soon as he was out of sight and came to the tunnel. The others were there, on the other side. In a few words Robin told the surprised boy all about the happenings of the night before, and how he had found out that Mr Barton was a traitor, ready to hand Kit over to the kidnappers that night.

"We're going to hide you on the house-boat," whispered Robin. "Can you come now, this very minute? Oh, blow—there's Mr Barton yelling for you. He'll be along in half a tick. Escape into our garden the very first chance you have, and go down to our boat by the river. We'll come there with food as soon as ever we can."

Kit's eyes nearly fell out of his head as he heard all that Robin had to tell him. He went back to meet the angry Mr Barton, planning how to escape down to the boat the very first minute he could.

"What a blessing we've got such a good hiding-place for me," he thought. "No one in the world would ever think of hunting for me there!"

Chapter Nineteen

KIT TRIES TO ESCAPE

KIT HAD to go back to Mr Barton, who was very angry indeed with him for going out of sight.

"Didn't I forbid you to go out of my sight?" he shouted, and actually gave the boy a cuff, a thing he had never done before. The Dragon spoke up at once, much to Kit's surprise.

"Don't hit Kit! You know you've no right to do that!"

"Hold your tongue," growled Mr Barton. "This boy has to learn to do what he is told. How can we keep him in hiding and look after him if he disappears whenever he wants to?"

"I don't think you ought to hit him," said the Dragon, in an obstinate tone. "The boy doesn't have a very good time. Let him alone."

Kit felt grateful to the Dragon for sticking up for him. He went to her and picked up her knitting wool, which had fallen to the ground.

"Thank you, Dragon!" he said in a low voice. Miss Taylor looked a little less fierce, and her eyes gave the boy a kindly glance. Mr Barton sat down again in his chair, muttering something.

"Don't anger him," said the Dragon. "He's in a funny mood to-day."

Kit sat quietly beside the Dragon, pretending to read a book. He worried about what Robin had told him. He simply MUST escape as soon as he could. He had plenty of courage, but the thought of being kidnapped and held prisoner in some unpleasant place once again filled him with horror. He wished he had a father and mother as most children had. His mother had died when he was a baby, and his father had been missing ever since his aeroplane had crashed and burnt out. He had nobody but his wicked uncle and a great-aunt who had put him in charge of the Dragon and Mr Barton.

"All I've got to do is to run down the garden and escape under the fencing," he kept telling himself. "I wish it didn't take so long scrabbling through that tunnel. Mr Barton would discover me long before I could get through. How and when shall I escape?"

Kit tried two or three times to give Mr Barton the slip that day. When he went to wash his hands for dinner, he turned into the kitchen instead of into the wash-place, hoping to be able to slip out through the scullery door before anyone noticed him.

But Mr Barton had followed him into the kitchen! He ordered him out at once.

"What are you doing here? I sent you to wash your hands, not bother the cook! Go at once and do what you are told!"

Kit meekly washed his hands and took his place at the meal. He wondered if he could get permission to go up to his attic play-room after dinner—then he might escape down the tree. So he asked Mr Barton.

"May I set out my railway this afternoon in the attic?" he asked.

"No—you are going to study with me out in the summer-house," said his tutor, who was quite determined not to let Kit out of his sight once that day.

So poor Kit had to sit in the summer-house and learn some Latin until tea-time. Then Mr Barton took him firmly by the arm and led him indoors.

It was the same after tea. Mr Barton kept Kit close beside him, and the boy began to despair. "Could I take a run round the garden, sir?" he asked at last.

"Yes," said Mr Barton, and Kit got up joyfully. Now was his chance. But his heart sank as Mr Barton rose, too.

"I will come with you," he said. And he went with Kit all the way round the grounds. Kit did not go near the passage under the fencing! He was not going to give Mr Barton the chance of discovering *that*!

"I don't think you need sleep in Kit's room tonight, Miss Taylor," Mr Barton said to the Dragon at supper-time. "That room is really too small for two people."

"I think I would rather sleep with him," said the Dragon.

"I have had your bed taken out of Kit's room," said Mr Barton. "I will see him into bed myself and then lock the door. He will be quite safe."

The Dragon said no more, but she was angry. She had never liked the surly Mr Barton, and now she liked him even less. Kit looked and felt miserable. How in the world could he escape if Mr Barton did things like that? If he was locked into his room he could not possibly get out. There was a sheer drop to the ground from his bedroom window. He would break his neck if he tried to escape that way.

"Mr Barton wants to make sure I'm under lock and key when darkness comes, so that he can hand me over," thought the boy desperately. "Whatever am I to do?"

There really did seem nothing he could do at all, as long as his tutor kept him under his eye. It was no good running off. Mr Barton was on the watch for any tricks. The boy sat down with a book, trying to plan something.

"You had better go to bed early to-night, Kit," said Mr Barton, in smooth tones. "You look tired. Come along upstairs now."

"I'm *not* tired," said Kit indignantly. "It's only a quarter to eight!"

But he had to go. Mr Barton took hold of his arm and held it firmly. Kit found himself in his bedroom and had to undress.

"Get into bed," ordered Mr Barton, and into bed poor Kit got. Then Mr Barton said good night and went out of the room. He locked the door behind him—and took the key out of the lock. Now, even the Dragon could not go in.

Kit got up and dressed. He put his pyjamas on over his clothes, in case Mr Barton suddenly came back. He knew now that his only chance of escape was to slip quickly out of the door when Mr Barton opened it later on to get him out.

"And I bet he'll say that somebody is after me, and I've got to go away with him and hide!" thought the boy. "That would be his way of getting me to my wicked uncle! Well—I'll make a bolt out of the door as soon as ever it's opened! I'll take the bulb out of the electric light so that when Mr Barton turns on the switch—it won't light! That will give me a chance to escape."

He took the bulb out of the lamp. Then he settled down on a chair behind the door, waiting for Mr Barton.

About nine o'clock he heard him coming and stood up, his heart beating fast. Now—he must take his chance, for he wouldn't have another!

Mr Barton put the key in the door and unlocked it. He opened the door and put his hand in to turn on the switch for the light. Click! went the switch, but there was no light! The room remained in darkness.

Mr Barton gave a vexed hiss and went into the room to turn on the lamp beside Kit's bed. Kit took his chance! In a trice he was round the door and up the stairs to the attic.

Mr Barton heard him and saw him go round the door, for he had left on the light in the passage outside. He gave a shout and was after the boy at once!

Kit knew it would be no good to try and escape out of the attic window with Mr Barton so close behind him. He wouldn't have time even to slide across the plank to the tree. He must try and hide somewhere for a few minutes and then, when he saw his chance, he could try the attic window. So, quick as lightning, the boy stood on a chair beside a cupboard, and then, with a deft leap, he was on the top of the cupboard. He lay down flat, very cautiously. It was a big cupboard and tall.

Mr Barton rushed on to the landing and up the attic stairs. He passed by the cupboard and went straight into Kit's playroom. No one was there!

The man was in a real fury. "Kit, I shall give you a good hiding for behaving like this! What do you think you are doing? These silly ways you have of hiding have got to stop! Come out at once!"

Kit lay on top of the cupboard and made no sound at all. Mr Barton went on and on talking, trying to get Kit to come, and his voice became more and more angry.

Then Kit heard a car driving up outside, and he guessed it was his wicked uncle, come to find out why Mr Barton hadn't handed him over at the time and place arranged. His heart began to beat so fast that he was afraid Mr Barton would hear it!

Mr Barton heard the car, too. He did not dare to go down and answer the door, because he was afraid that Kit would give him the slip if he did. So he called down to the Dragon.

"Miss Taylor, open the door and bring my visitor up here, please!"

In a minute or two the visitor came upstairs. "What's up?" he asked in a low tone. "Where's the kid?"

"I was just going to bring him along when he dashed out of his bedroom and upstairs here somewhere," said Mr Barton in an angry voice. "Wait till I catch him! I'll box his ears and give him the best hiding he's ever had in his life!"

Kit lay still on the top of the cupboard. He felt certain he would be discovered sooner or later. Then an idea came to him. He had his ball in his pocket. Suppose he took it and threw it hard into the box-room opposite him! It would make a noise there, and the men would be sure to think it was he, Kit, there! They might rush into the box-room—and then maybe Kit could slip down from the cupboard, run to his playroom and escape!

The boy did not wait another moment. He took out his ball quietly, and then, with a violent jerk of his arm, threw it with all his might into the little box-room opposite the cupboard. It made a great noise there, bouncing and rolling about, and the two men at once thought that the boy was in the box-room. They rushed into the room,

121

Kit slid across the plank

switched on the light and shut the door so that the boy
could not run out of it if he was there!

This was just what Kit wanted! He slipped down from
the cupboard and ran to the play-room. He shut the door
and turned the key in the lock! Now, those two men would
have a job getting in, and give him a chance to escape!

The men saw at a glance that the box-room hid no boy,
and when they heard the sound of Kit going to the
attic-room they rushed over to it—just in time to see the
door close and to hear the key turned!

They hammered on the door. "You bad boy!" yelled Mr
Barton. "Open this door at once!"

Kit ran to the window. Mr Barton put his shoulder to
the door and heaved hard. The lock began to splinter, for
it was not strong! In a moment the door would be broken
in! Kit slid across the plank, trembling.

"I *may* do it!" he said to himself. "I *may* do it! Come on,
Kit— don't you be caught!"

Chapter Twenty

AN EXCITING NIGHT

THE DOOR of the play-room fell in with a crash, for both men had thrown their weight and strength against it. Kit heard the crash as he slithered down the ash tree. He was so excited that he almost lost his hold and fell, but just managed to save himself in time.

Mr Barton had run to the window, and at once saw the plank reaching across to the ash tree, for the play-room light shone on it and showed it up clearly.

"Look at that!" he cried. "This is how the boy has escaped from the house whenever he wanted to—and how that boy next door came in! Let's go downstairs quickly and catch him in the garden."

Both men tore down the stairs, but by this time Kit was on the ground and speeding as fast as he could down the garden to the passage under the fencing. The men saw his dark shadow and went after him. Mr Barton had a torch and sent a beam of light to find Kit.

The boy plunged into some thick undergrowth and then

made his way quietly to the place where the tunnel had been made. The men plunged about in the undergrowth, trying their best to find the boy.

Kit lay on his tummy and began to slide beneath the fencing, down the curving passage the children had made. He was almost through when the two men came up, panting, and Mr Barton saw the curious passage by the light of his torch. He was almost speechless with rage.

"Look at that!" he cried. "Those children next door must have done this. This is how they've been getting in and out of the garden—and that tiresome dog, too! Kit, how dare you behave like this? Come back at once!"

But Kit didn't. He tore off into the darkness, leaving the two men standing there, helpless, for they were both too big to wriggle down that tunnel! It was only big enough to take children on their tummies!

Kit wondered what to do. Would it be any good going down to the boat now it was dark? The children would hardly be there. He decided to go quietly to the house and see if there was a light in Robin's bedroom.

There was! A shower of small stones brought Robin to the window at once. In a trice he was down the pear tree and standing eagerly beside Kit.

"I say, old thing, we'd almost given you up, and were wondering whether to tell Mummy or the police about you," said the boy. "We've got all the food into the boat. Come along to it now and I'll row you to the house-boat. You can tell me what's happened when we're in the boat. We must go whilst it's dark."

The two boys hurried down to the river. The boat was there, waiting. In it was a hamper of food and drink for Kit. The boys got in and Robin took the oars.

Kit told him all that had happened, and Robin listened in growing excitement. Kit had only just escaped in time!

"I think you've been jolly clever," said Robin admiringly. "I really do. Throwing that ball to make a noise in the boxroom was a simply marvellous idea. Golly, how angry those two men must have been when they saw you wriggling through our tunnel and couldn't get through it themselves!"

Robin came to the little backwater and slid up it in the boat. He shone a torch towards the trees when he had gone some way up, and Kit caught sight of a bit of the house-boat.

"I say—it's jolly well hidden, isn't it?" he said. "I bet no one will ever find me here!"

They rowed to the *Black Swan* and climbed up on its deck. Then down into one of the little sleeping cabins they went.

Someone had been there! Someone had prepared one of the bunks as a comfortable bed! Someone had put food and water on the little chest of drawers! How queer!

"I suppose one of the men from the house must have slept here yesterday," said Robin puzzled. "Well, it's a good thing he's not here to-night! Shall I open a window, Kit? It feels awfully hot in here with the window closed."

"I'll open it," said Kit, and tried to push open the little window. But it wouldn't open. Kit shone a torch on it outside and saw that it had been nailed in such a way that it could not be opened from the inside.

"I don't know what those men have been doing here," he said. "They must like a fug if they nail up the windows, that's all I can say!"

"I'll have to go now, Kit," said Robin. "But I hope you won't feel too lonely here. No one will come along to-night, that's certain. Anyway, if you hear anyone, just slip off the boat and hide up in a willow tree. The branches come down low over the deck."

"Right!" said Kit. "Thanks for all you've done, Robin. Come again to-morrow and we'll decide what to do. I'm out of Mr Barton's clutches for the time being, anyway!"

Robin slid down the side of the house-boat and got into his own little boat. He called a low good-bye to Kit and rowed away down the quiet backwater to the river. Kit couldn't help feeling a bit lonely as he heard the sound of oars getting fainter and fainter in the distance.

He threw himself on the bunk fully dressed, and then saw that he still had his pyjamas on over his clothes! "I'll be too hot!" thought the boy, and took them off. Then he lay down again, feeling tired out with excitement. His eyes shut—and very soon Kit was fast asleep. The house-boat rocked gently every now and again. The water gurgled round it, and a little water-vole swam across, making tiny ripples behind him. A moor-hen said "krek-krek" once or twice, but Kit did not hear him.

Robin rowed back quickly, longing to tell Betty and Lucy what had happened. He tied up the boat and made his way across the fields, letting himself in at the gate at the bottom of the garden.

Suddenly he heard sounds nearby! He flattened himself against a tree and listened breathlessly. He saw the light of torches being flashed around, and he guessed that Mr Barton and the wicked uncle had found their way into the garden and were searching for Kit, thinking he might be hiding there.

The boy grinned to himself. Kit was far away in a safe place now! He, Robin, had managed to defeat the two men. They couldn't get Kit now, that was certain.

He stayed behind the tree, listening to the low voices of the men and watching the flashing of the torches. He wondered what the men would do when they didn't find Kit. Well—they wouldn't get a word out of the two girls or Robin! Robin began to wonder what Kit himself ought to do. It rather looked as if Mummy had better be told a few things soon. He decided to tell her in the morning.

Suddenly, as Robin stood behind the tree, he felt something cold pressed against his bare leg, and he jumped violently. Then he gave a sigh of relief! It was only Sandy putting his nose against Robin's calf. He had come to find the boy, and had actually not barked or growled at the two men. Sandy was a most remarkable dog the way he knew when to keep quiet!

Robin decided it was time to get back to the house. He felt tired, and it really seemed as if the two men meant to spend the whole night hunting in the garden! So he cautiously made his way towards a little path a good way off from where the men were searching. But Sandy did not move so cautiously, and made a noise in the undergrowth!

At once the men called to one another. "What's that? Is that the boy? Over there, quick!"

Robin slipped behind another tree. Sandy discovered a rabbit-hole and put his nose down it. As Robin did not seem to mind the men, he did not mind them either. Sandy smelt rabbit so strongly that he began to get very

127

excited. He scrabbled at the hole with his front paws and sent a whole lot of earth flying into the air. It fell to the ground and made a noise.

The men darted over to the sound at once, and got a shower of small stones and earth all over them. Robin chuckled quietly. Good old Sandy! The boy slipped away as the men came near, and ran quietly down the path to the house. He could escape nicely whilst the men were bothering themselves with Sandy!

"Why, it's only a dog!" said Mr Barton in disgust, as his torch showed up Sandy's back legs. His front ones were in the hole, with his head. "That tiresome dog again! He's always appearing. Come on—we can't find that boy now. He's gone into hiding somewhere—but he won't feel quite so cheerful in the morning, after a night in the open, and no breakfast to look forward to! He'll probably come creeping back to the house, and we'll get him then. I'll pay him out for leading us a dance like this!"

"And so will I," said the other man grimly. They went quietly out of the garden by the back way and into the gates of their own house. Robin heard the front door slam as he leaned out of his window to see whether the men were still anywhere about.

The girls came creeping into his room. They hadn't been able to sleep because they had been so worried about Kit. Robin grinned at them.

"It's all right," he said. "Kit had a frightfully narrow escape—but he's safe on the house-boat now. When I came up the garden I nearly ran into Mr Barton and the wicked uncle hunting all over the place for Kit! Sandy scrabbled earth over them from a rabbit-hole."

"Oh, Robin—what's happened?" said Lucy.

Robin told them Kit's exciting tale. They listened with wide eyes. It sounded like a story from a book.

"We'll wait till to-morrow before we do anything more," said Robin, yawning. "I'm going to sleep. Good night!"

"And *what* a to-do there was in the morning.

Chapter Twenty-One

A VERY STRANGE THING

THE NEXT morning the Dragon was astonished not to see Kit at breakfast. She ate her porridge and said nothing for a few minutes, expecting Kit to come. Then she spoke to Mr Barton, who was reading the newspaper, looking surly and stern.

"Why isn't Kit down?" she asked.

"He's having breakfast in bed," said Mr Barton. This was an untruth, of course. Kit was far away on the house-boat!

"Why? Is he ill?" asked the Dragon.

"No," said Mr Barton.

"I shall go up and see him," said the Dragon, and she rose.

"Sit down," said Mr Barton, beginning to lose his temper again. "I'm in charge of this boy."

"I am, too," said the Dragon, and she began to look very fierce.

"You're only supposed to see to his clothes, food, and health," said Mr Barton. "If you interfere with me, I shall have you discharged."

The Dragon rose from the table, and, before Mr Barton could stop her, she was out of the door and up the stairs. She came to Kit's door. It was shut—and locked! The key had been taken away. The Dragon fowned. She did not like all this locking up.

She knocked at the door. "Kit! Have you got your breakfast? Are you all right?"

There was no answer, which was not surprising considering that the room was empty. The Dragon knocked again. As there was still no answer, she looked worried.

"Kit! Are you there? Answer me!"

But there was no reply at all. The Dragon went downstairs and faced Mr Barton.

"I don't believe Kit is there! There isn't any reply when I knock at the door. I demand that you open that door, Mr Barton! If you don't, I shall go to the police."

Mr Barton was feeling worried himself, but about his five thousand pounds, not Kit! If the boy did not turn up he would lose his money—and it really seemed as if the boy had escaped. Though why he should run away Mr Barton could not think. He did not know that Kit had been warned against him.

The Dragon rapped angrily on the table. "Mr Barton! Do you hear me? Unless you open Kit's door at once, I shall ring up the police!"

There was nothing for it but to open the door. The Dragon would certainly do what she said, and then Mr Barton might get into trouble. He would open the door—and then pretend to be most astonished that Kit was not there. He would try to persuade the Dragon that Kit was off on another of his pranks and would soon be back.

So he got up from the table, took the bedroom key from his pocket and went upstairs with the Dragon. "He is probably feeling in a sulky mood and won't answer you," he said as he fitted the key in the door. He opened the door—and the Dragon gave a cry.

"He's not here! His bed is empty! What has happened to Kit! Mr Barton, do you know anything about this?"

Mr Barton was doing his very best to seem as astonished as the Dragon. He opened his eyes wide and looked all round the room in surprise, as if he expected Kit to be hiding behind the door or a chest of drawers.

"Now where can he be?" he said.

"Mr Barton, has Kit been kidnapped again?" cried the Dragon, looking rather white. "How could he have disappeared out of this room, when the door was locked? He couldn't possibly have jumped out of that window. He would have broken his neck!"

"Ah—but someone might have come *in* at the window and taken Kit!" said Mr Barton. "Now don't let's worry for a little while, Miss Taylor. The boy may possibly have slipped out of the room before I locked the door, and may be hiding from us—you know how full of silly pranks he is."

The Dragon stared at Mr Barton, hardly believing a word he said. "What was all that running about and shouting I heard last night?" she asked suddenly. "Just after I sent that visitor upstairs to you?"

"Running and shouting?" said Mr Barton in an innocent voice. "I don't know. You must have been mistaken. Now let's go downstairs and finish our breakfast in peace. Probably Kit will turn up before we have finished."

"Well—if he hasn't, I'll ring up the police at once!" said the Dragon, and she sounded as if she was almost in tears! She was fond of Kit in spite of her fierceness.

They sat down and finished breakfast. Mr Barton felt furious with the Dragon for interfering, and he quickly made plans. If she wanted to ring up the police, he couldn't stop her, that was certain. Well, he must pretend to be as upset and puzzled as the Dragon herself. No one could suspect *him* of kidnapping the boy.

"The police will soon find Kit, wherever he is hiding," he thought, "and then they will bring him back to me, of course. That will be my chance to hand him over to his uncle straight away! So I shall get my five thousand

131

pounds after all. Yes—I think on the whole I shan't do too badly if I *do* let Miss Taylor ring up the police. She will certainly begin to think there is something queer about my behaviour if I try to stop her."

So when the Dragon went to the telephone and asked for the police, Mr Barton said nothing to prevent her. He spoke to the police himself, too, and told them how Kit had twice been kidnapped before in America.

"But this time I am sure the boy has not been kidnapped," said Mr Barton in his smoothest tones. "I feel certain he has run away, as a boyish prank. Naturally it annoyed him to have to be kept in hiding almost like a prisoner. If you could find him for us it would be a great relief."

A police Inspector was round at the house in about half an hour, questioning the Dragon and Mr Barton. He seemed to agree with Mr Barton that Kit had only run away for a prank.

"Boys will be boys!" said the Inspector. "Leave it to me. We'll let you know as soon as we hear of any stray boy in the district. Anyway, he'll probably come back of his own accord as soon as he feel hungry."

"Quite likely," agreed Mr Barton. The tutor wished he could get hold of Robin and question him about Kit. He felt sure that the children next door had had much more to do with Kit than he had known. That tunnel under the fencing must have been used very often by one or other of them.

When the police Inspector had gone, the telephone rang. Mr Barton went to answer it. He heard the cautious voice of Kit's uncle speaking.

"Any news?"

"None," said Mr Barton, "except that Miss Taylor got the police here. But if they find the boy they're going to hand him over to me—and you can come and get him at once."

"No," said the voice. "I'm not risking being caught through coming over to your house. I'll show you the hiding-place I've prepared for him, and you can take him there yourself. Meet me the other side of Faldham in half an hour."

"Where's this wonderful hiding-place?" asked Mr Barton impatiently. "You're always talking about it."

There was a pause. "It's a house-boat!" was the reply. "You know we took that lonely house on the river? Well, we found there was a house-boat that went with the property. Some children were playing in it, but we turned them off. We towed it up into a little backwater near the house, and hid it under some willows. We've got it all ready for the boy. Nobody in the world would guess he was there. We've nailed up the windows and have got a padlock for the door, so that he can't possibly get away."

Mr Barton gave a long whistle. "A very—good—place," he said. "All right—I'll meet you outside Faldham in half an hour and you can show me the place. Then, when I get the boy again, I'll take him straight to the boat so that he won't be seen going to your house. I can take him there by going up the river, can't I?"

"That's the idea," said Kit's uncle. "If you take him at night, no one will see you. We'll look after him then!"

"And what about my money?" said Mr Barton.

"You don't get a penny unless the boy is delivered to us," was the answer. "As soon as that boy is on board the boat, you will have your reward."

Mr Barton put down the telephone receiver and went to get the car out. He would see exactly where this wonderful hiding-place was—and then take Kit there just as soon as ever he could lay hands on him again!

And Kit was there all the time! He was actually hiding himself in the very hiding-place that the kidnappers had themselves got ready for him—but he didn't know it. And *they* in turn didn't know that Kit was there! This was surely one of the strangest things that could possibly happen!

Now Mr Barton was on the way to see this hiding-place—and Kit was there. Look out, Kit—you're in danger again!

Chapter Twenty-Two

A NARROW ESCAPE

NOW THAT morning Robin decided to go and talk things over with Kit before he told his mother anything about all the exciting happenings of the day before. So the boy took his boat and rowed off down the river. He passed the little island, went by the lonely house, and then slid up the hidden backwater. He came to the house-boat and cautiously tied his boat on the farther side of it, under a bush so that it could not be seen.

Then he clambered on to the bank and went to the weeping willows that hid the big house-boat. He stood there for a moment listening. He could hear nothing. He stepped on to the deck of the house-boat and made his way to the cabin where Kit was to sleep the night before.

Kit was there, reading a book. He did not hear Robin, for the boy was so quiet, and he jumped violently when he heard his voice.

"Kit! Is everything all right?"

"Golly! You made me jump almost out of my skin!" cried Kit. "I say—it's good to see you! I had a very good night— slept like a top and I couldn't think where in the world I was when I woke up this morning!"

Robin grinned. "You didn't worry much about enemies, then," he said. "I and the two girls hardly slept a wink for worrying about you. Listen Kit—I want to discuss with you what you think is the best thing to do now. Shall we tell our mother? I have a feeling she just *might* not believe us, and if Mr Barton is very clever and tells her a whole lot of fibs, it will be awfully difficult for us to stop you being handed over to him again."

"Yes," said Kit thoughtfully. "Perhaps it would be best to wait a bit. But, Robin, I really do believe you'd be safe to tell the Dragon. I think she's fond of me, and I know she hates Mr Barton. Couldn't you just go to see her and find out if she's upset about me disappearing? If she is, then tell her what you know, and then, if ever I'm captured by Mr Barton again, she won't let him have charge of me."

"She's such a fierce person," said Robin, not at all liking the idea of talking to the Dragon by himself.

"She looks as fierce as twenty dragons, I know," agreed Kit. "But she's not really. How I wish I knew for certain whether she is my friend or my enemy. I don't see how we are to know!"

But they did know—and in a very short time, too!

There suddenly came the sound of voices from the bank, and the two boys in the sleeping cabin sat up straight in alarm. Who was coming? It was Mr Barton and the wicked uncle, of course! The uncle was showing Mr Barton the hiding-place he had prepared for Kit when he had been kidnapped. Little did they know that the boy was already there!

"It's somebody coming!" whispered Robin.

"Get into the little hanging cupboard, quick!" said Kit. "Look—behind that curtain there, where people hang their coats. I'll hide behind the one in the next cabin."

There was a door between the two sleeping cabins, and Kit was soon in the next one, hiding behind the curtain. He heard the footsteps of the men as they came on board the house-boat.

They stood on the deck, talking. Kit peeped out from behind the curtain and caught a glimpse of them through the nailed-up windows. His heart went cold and his knees began to shake.

One of the men was Mr Barton, but the other was his wicked uncle! Kit was as sure of it as he could be. He had never seen his uncle, but there was a distinct family resemblance in that cruel face, with its cold blue eyes and thin-lipped mouth. The voice had an American drawl in it.

"Well, Mr Barton, what do you think of the hiding-place we've got for my nephew?" said the American voice. "Right away from anywhere, isn't it?"

"Yes—it's a good place," said Mr Barton. "How do I get to it from the river? Let's see—I could get a boat where the river bends round, not far from the bottom of our garden—row straight up—and then look out for this backwater."

"You'll know where the backwater is because it's not far past the house," said Kit's uncle. "It's the only house on the banks for miles, so you can't mistake it. Look—come down into the cabins—you'll see the boy will be *quite* comfortable—if a little lonely! We've had the windows nailed up and I've got a padlock for the door, as I told you. He can't possibly escape once we get him here."

To the horror of the two hidden boys the men walked into the little sleeping cabins. Kit tried to think whether he had left any of his belongings about. The hamper of food was in the kitchen under the table. They might not see that. But he had left out his book—and he thought his pyjamas must be over the chair, where he had thrown them the night before.

The men looked round the cabins. They had no idea at all that the boy they were hunting for was within two feet of them, behind a curtain either of them could have touched at that very moment!

Kit and Robin were trembling from head to foot. For the first time they knew that the very hiding-place they had chosen for Kit was the same one that the enemy had also prepared for the boy. Now they knew why the windows had been nailed up! Now they knew why the sleeping cabin had been prepared, and why food and

136

drink had been set ready on the chest. It was all for Kit—Kit who should have been handed over to the enemy the night before, and brought to the boat as a prisoner!

And by a very strange chance, Kit had chosen the same hiding-place for himself, under the very nose of the enemy. Could anything be queerer—or more frightening?

Both boys felt quite certain that at any moment the curtains would be pulled aside and they would be discovered. Kit hoped desperately that he wouldn't cough or sneeze. He felt sure a sneeze was coming.

"I wish we knew where that wretched boy is," said Mr Barton eagerly. "I had him all locked up, and was just going to get him, as you know, when he sprang out of the door past me. He must be hiding in the country-side somewhere now. But the police are looking for him, so he should soon be found."

This was news to the two boys.

"It's a pity you couldn't stop that interfering Miss Taylor from getting in the police," said Kit's uncle irritably. "I suppose we couldn't buy her help, could we? Would she stop bothering about the boy, and go away and leave us a free hand, if we gave her a few hundred pounds?"

"No, I'm certain she wouldn't," said Mr Barton at once. "She's fond of the boy; goodness knows why. She has a funny way of showing it, for she's a sulky kind of woman—but I really don't think you could possibly get her on your side. She knew the boy's father very well, and went to the boy at once when she heard of the aeroplane crash."

"Well—we can't count on *her* help, then," said Kit's uncle. "I'll tell you what we'll do—we'll send *her* the ransom notes when we've got the boy! We'll say that we will set Kit free on payment of a large sum of money, and she shall be the go-between. If she hands over the money, which she can get from the boy's great-aunt, who's in charge of his fortune, we'll hand over the boy! I shan't appear in this at all of course. I've plenty of go-betweens who can't possibly be traced back to me. All *you've* got to do is to keep your mouth shut, say nothing at all, take your money and quietly disappear, when we get hold of the boy."

"I know that," said Mr Barton. "If only I could find that boy! I'd give him a good hiding before I handed him over to you, I can tell you that!"

"He'll get one from me, too," said Kit's uncle in a grim voice. "Causing us all this trouble! If only I could get hold of him this very minute!"

He could have if he had wanted to—merely by stretching out his left hand! The boys listened to every word, and Kit felt furious when he heard what a traitor Mr Barton had turned out to be. But he was glad to know that the Dragon was on *his* side, and not on his uncle's. That was something to be thankful for.

"Well, come on!" said Mr Barton at last. "I've had enough of this stuffy cabin. I can find my way here all right, *if* I get hold of the boy. I'll bring him here, lock him up, and then go back and telephone to you. I'll simply say that 'the parcel has arrived.' You'll know what I mean."

Kit's uncle laughed. "Yes—I shall know," he said. "Look, the padlock is there on the window ledge. Come along to the house now, and have a drink before you go."

To the great relief of the two boys the men left the house-boat and made their way back to the house. They had not noticed either book or pyjamas after all! Kit darted out from the cabin and peered between the willows to make sure they had all gone. Then he went back to Robin. Both boys were pale; the whole affair had been far too exciting for them.

"Well—to think that I came to the very hiding-place prepared for me!" said Kit at last.

"You'd better stay here," said Robin. "After all, it's the last place your uncle would expect to find you! You have plenty of food. I'll get right back now and tell the Dragon everything at once. Then she can go and tell my mother, and between them they'll know what to do. You keep safe here till I come and tell you what's been decided."

"Righto!" said Kit. "My word, when those men know we were just under their noses in these cabins, won't they be FURIOUS!"

Chapter Twenty-Three

A MARVELLOUS SURPRISE

ROBIN SLIPPED into his little boat and began to row down the backwater as quickly as he could. He wanted to tell the grown-ups all the story now. It seemed suddenly to have grown very serious. Before, it had been rather fun and very exciting—but since Robin had stood trembling behind the curtain, within reach of two bad men, he hadn't felt it was fun at all!

"It's getting horrid!" he thought as he rowed strongly back down the river. "We've got to do something now. I'll go in and see the Dragon as soon as I get back!"

First of all he went to tell Betty and Lucy the latest news. They could hardly believe it!

"Oh, let's tell Mummy, quick!" said Betty. "I feel afraid."

"You've forgotten your mother's out for the day," said

Lucy. "We'd better go in and tell the Dragon. Come on, let's do it now!"

"Well—Mr Barton may be back," said Robin, who didn't at all like the idea of running into that horrid man. "I'll go and see if his car's in the drive first."

It was—so he was back already! This was a blow. Then Robin climbed up the chestnut tree to see if the Dragon was on the lawn by herself. If so, they might perhaps squeeze through the tunnel and go and call to her. So up the tree he went, and came down beaming.

"Yes—she's there knitting, and Mr Barton isn't anywhere to be seen. Come on—we'll get through the tunnel."

So down the garden they went to the passage under the fencing. But to their anger and dismay somebody had filled the whole thing in! They could no longer use that way in and out. They stood there, red with rage.

"Blow Mr Barton!" said Robin angrily. "*He's* done this, I'm sure! Well—*now* what are we to do? I really don't feel like going and knocking at the front door!"

"We'd better watch until Mr Barton goes out again—if he *does* go out," said Betty gloomily. "I'm not going into that house whilst he's there. *I* don't want to be captured!"

"Well, we'll take turns at watching the house next door to see if Mr Barton does go out," said Lucy. "I'll take first watch. If I hide just over there, in the hedge, I can easily spy anyone going in or out."

"Right," said Robin. "We'll take turns of half an hour each. Then as soon as he goes out we'll pop in and tell the Dragon everything."

So Lucy took the first watch. She saw the cook go out on her bicycle and return with some shopping. She saw the chauffeur clean the car. She saw Sandy wander in at the front drive, look around for possible rabbits and then go back again. She saw Tiger sitting in the sun and washing herself. Sandy didn't go near Tiger now. He had had a lesson from her, and had learnt it very well!

After half an hour Robin came to take his turn, and then Betty. After dinner they watched again, and got very tired of it. Tea-time came and still Mr Barton didn't go out. The children began to despair.

And then, about half-past six, Robin, who was on watch, saw, to his great delight, the figure of Mr Barton going down the drive. He was going to the post, for he had a letter in his hand. Good! Now was the children's chance!

Robin gave a low whistle, and the others came running up, their eyes eagerly looking for Robin. Sandy was with them.

"He's gone out!" said Robin. "Come on. It's the only chance we'll have. We'll take Sandy with us, because I shall feel a bit safer if we have a dog to guard us."

"Come on, Sandy," said Lucy, and the little terrier ran beside her, his tail wagging.

The children walked up the drive to the house next door. They knocked and rang the bell. The maid opened the door.

"Can we speak to—to—Miss Dragon?" asked Robin, who had forgotten for the moment what the Dragon's real name was.

"No one of that name lives here," said the maid, and began to shut the door.

"I know—it's Miss Taylor!" said Robin. "She lives here, I know she does."

"Well," said the maid, opening the door a bit wider again. "I don't think I ought to let you in, because I've been given orders not to—but I'll fetch Miss Taylor if you'll wait here a minute."

"Please be as quick as you can," said Robin, who was afraid that Mr Barton might come back at any moment.

The maid disappeared. She was away for a long time, it seemed to the children. Then at last she appeared again, this time with Miss Taylor, who was frowning.

"What do you want?" she asked.

"Miss Taylor, please can we speak to you for a minute in private?" asked Robin. "We've got important news for you."

The Dragon looked hard at Robin. "About Kit, do you mean?" she said.

Robin nodded. Miss Taylor beckoned them to come inside. "Mr Barton will be back soon," she said. "You can tell him, too."

"No," said Robin, "we can't. He's in the pay of Kit's wicked uncle!"

"WHAT!" said the Dragon in the greatest astonishment. "Now what in the world do you know about wicked uncles and Mr Barton?"

"We know an awful lot," said Robin. "Please take us somewhere private. It's very, very important."

"Do you know where Kit is?" said the Dragon in a low tone.

Robin nodded again. Miss Taylor led them all into a little room and shut the door. Sandy went in too and ran round, sniffing.

"Now what is all this mystery?" asked the Dragon, sitting down. "Begin at the beginning and tell me."

So Robin began at the very beginning and told his story. The Dragon was good at listening and did not interrupt once. Only when she learnt what a traitor Mr Barton was did she move. Then she got up and walked once round the room, her face grim.

Robin went on with his tale to the very end. When at last he stopped, he saw, to his great surprise, that there were tears in the Dragon's eyes!

"Poor Kit!" she said. "Poor little boy!"

The children stared at her, astonished. Not one of them had ever dreamed for a moment that the fierce Dragon could shed tears! She got out her handkerchief and mopped her eyes.

"I think you're very clever, brave children!" she said. "I really do. I *am* glad you've come to tell me!"

Robin opened his mouth to say something—but at that very moment there came such a terrific hammering on the front-door knocker that everyone jumped.

"Now who's that?" said the Dragon, astonished. "What a noise to make!"

The children hoped it wouldn't be Mr Barton coming back! They heard the maid almost running to the door. They heard the door opening. They heard a loud American voice say something—and then a frightened-looking maid came into the room and spoke to the Dragon.

"Miss Taylor, there's a gentleman here who says he's got to see Master Kit. I said he wasn't here, but he won't believe me."

142

Footsteps sounded down the polished hall, and a man came in at the door. He was the same man who had spoken to Robin in the ice-cream shop—the one Robin had been rude to. He was looking worried and angry.

The Dragon leapt up from her seat. "Peter!" she said in a half-choked voice. "PETER! It can't be you!"

The man looked at her, and his face creased into affectionate, smiling lines. "Why, Jane Taylor!" he said. "So it's *you* who had charge of Kit!"

"Peter! We thought you were dead!" said the Dragon, and she began to cry again. "I feel I'm in a dream. I don't understand what's happening!"

"Cheer up, Jane!" said the tall man with a laugh that sounded very much like Kit's. "I'm not dead. I never was! I wasn't in that aeroplane that got burnt out. I'd had a crash somewhere else, flying with Roy, my friend. We were both taken to hospital, badly burnt from blazing petrol, and no one knew who we were. I was off my head for months."

"Oh, Peter! Is this all really true?" said the Dragon, smiling through her tears.

"Quite true," said the man. "When I came to my senses again and remembered who I was, I remembered I had a boy called Kit! And then I heard that that wicked fellow Paul had kidnapped him twice for his money. So I lay low, meaning to get him if I could. I knew Kit had been shipped off to England in charge of two people my aunt said she trusted. Then I heard Paul had gone to England, too—and I guessed why. He was after Kit again! So along I came to look for Paul—and to make myself known to Kit once more."

"Oh, dear—and we put you off properly," said Robin with a groan. "We thought *you* were Kit's wicked uncle—but—but—you're his father, aren't you?"

"I am!" said the tall man. "And I want to see Kit. Where is he?"

"Well, at the moment he's not here," said Robin. "He's on a house-boat we know, in a backwater up the river. We hid him there when we knew his wicked uncle was after him."

It was a pity that Robin spoke in such a loud voice, for at that moment Mr Barton was walking in at the front door! He had let himself in with his latch-key, and he overheard what Robin said.

He stopped still in amazement. Then, without a sound, he walked out of the front door again and made his way to the garage. So Kit was actually on that house-boat! Those children had hidden him in the very place that his enemies had planned. What a bit of luck!

"I'll go right away to Paul and tell him his parcel has arrived!" said Mr Barton with a hard smile as he started up the car. "And we'll both go and look at the parcel together! Ha, Master Kit, you're in for a little trouble now!"

And so Mr Barton drove off in the darkening night, not knowing that Kit's father had arrived, alive and well, ready to find his son and take him into safe keeping as soon as ever he could!

Chapter Twenty-Four

KIT HAS A WONDERFUL IDEA

THE CHILDREN and Miss Taylor had no idea that Mr Barton had overheard Robin's words. They went on talking eagerly, telling Kit's father the whole story. He listened as if he could not believe his ears.

"Well, I always thought American children were pretty tough," he said, "but you beat everything, you three! Tunnelling under the fence like that—and climbing up the tree to the attic—and taking my boy off to the house-boat! You've been pretty good friends to him. I'll say you have!"

"Don't you think we ought to go and tell Kit you've arrived?" said Robin, going red with pleasure at so much praise. "For one thing, he oughtn't to be on the house-boat longer than we can help, now we know it's the hiding-place his enemies arranged for him. They might come and find him when he was asleep or something! And, for another thing, he'll be wild with delight when he sees you again, Mr Armstrong!"

"I'll just go and have a word with the police first," said Mr Armstrong in a very grim tone. "I've a feeling that Mr Barton, Paul and whatever other friends they've got will be better locked up in an English prison before they do any more damage. I'll get the police to surround the house they've got, and you shall take me by water to the house-boat. Then, if the men should try to escape, they'll find all their paths are blocked! The police will be on land—and I'll be on the water!"

Mr Armstrong went off to the telephone. The Dragon hugged all the children hard, one by one, much to their surprise. She seemed suddenly much younger and didn't look at all fierce.

"Things are coming right!" she said. "Dear old Kit—what a wonderful surprise he'll get!"

"I wonder what he's doing now," said Robin. "I say, wasn't it a good thing Mr Barton didn't come back whilst all this was happening? He's a long time going to the pillar-box to post his letter!"

Mr Barton had reached Kit's uncle by then. He poured out to the surprised man what he had overheard Robin saying. "The boy's actually on your house-boat!" he said. "Those children you turned off must be the ones that live next door to us—and they made friends with Kit, got to know his secret, and for some reason have hidden him on the house-boat!"

"We'll go and see," said Paul. "What a bit of luck for us, if so! I suppose he couldn't have been there when we went to visit the boat this morning? No—we didn't see a sign of him."

"Come along quietly," said Mr Barton, setting off down the lawn to the river. "Don't say a word, or it will warn him we're about. We'll take him by surprise—and that boy will feel very sorry for himself in a little while! We can't use the boat as a hiding-place now, unfortunately, because those children know all about it. But it shouldn't be difficult to find somewhere else."

The men went silently down the lawn towards the willow trees that hid the boat. Kit did not hear them. He had felt bored that day, and, having finished his book, he was watching a few rabbits playing on the

146

twilit lawn, peering at them between the weeping willows.

So, although he did not hear the two men coming, he suddenly caught sight of them! He took a look at their faces, and his heart began to beat fast. Both men looked pleased and determined—as if they knew Kit was there! Could they possibly know? Kit took another look at their faces, and made up his mind he wasn't going to hide on the house-boat. No! He didn't feel that would be safe at all. Once these men began to make a thorough search, he would easily be found!

The boy went to the other side of the boat, and slid quietly down the hull to the water. He entered it with hardly a splash. The backwater was not deep, and he could just tread on the bottom of the water. If he kept perfectly still, no one could possibly know he was there.

The men came up to the boat as quietly as possibly. They stood listening for a moment, and then parted the willows for a peep. They could see nobody, of course.

"He must be down in the cabins," whispered Mr Barton. "That's good. We can pounce on him and catch him easily there. You go that side. I'll go this."

The two men went stealthily to the door of the cabins. No one moved. They stood outside the cabin door and spoke loudly.

"Are you there, Kit?"

No answer.

"It's no good not answering," said Mr Barton, beginning to lose his temper. "We know you're there. The boy next door told us!"

Still no answer. "We'll go in and get him," said Paul impatiently. "Come on!"

They both went in. There seemed to be no one in the cabins at all. The men began to strip the bunks and search everywhere for the boy they felt sure was hiding.

And then the Great Idea came to Kit!

It was such a wonderful idea that he could hardly climb up the side of the boat, because he was trembling so much with excitement. He swung himself silently on to the deck and, keeping himself well out of sight, he crept round to the door that led to the cabins. He felt for the padlock and slipped it into place. Then, with a quick movement, he

He slid quietly down into the water

swung the door shut, turned the key in the lock, and locked the padlock, too, so that the door was fast-shut and doubly locked.

The men heard the bang of the door. Mr Barton leapt to open it, but the key turned before he could jerk it open. Then he heard the padlock rattling against the door, too, as Kit let it go, after having locked it.

"Who's there?" shouted Mr Barton, hammering on the door. "Let us out!"

"It's me, Kit!" said Kit. "You wanted to make *me* prisoner, didn't you? Well, how does it feel? I hope you'll find the cabins big enough for you!"

The men looked to see if they could smash the windows and get out—but they were far too small for two grown men to squeeze through. They really were prisoners! Mr Barton completely lost his temper and began to bang on the door as if he were mad.

"Shut up!" said Kit's uncle to him. "You are making too much noise. Let me talk to Kit."

But Kit was not in a mood to listen to anything that his uncle said to him. He sat out on the deck, his heart beating fast, rejoicing because he had so neatly captured his two enemies. Now, if only Robin would come and see him, how surprised he would be!

"I'll wait till Robin comes," thought Kit. "He's sure to come to-night. Then I'll send him back to telephone to the police. I'll keep guard on Mr Barton and my uncle till the police come. Golly, what a row they are making! I hope they don't break down the door!"

It was a good thing the house-boat was so far from the house, or the other man and the caretaker would most certainly have heard the shoutings and hammerings of the two angry prisoners. Kit felt a little anxious as he remembered the strength of the two men. They had broken in the door of the play-room when they had been after him. If they went on like this, they might be able to free themselves. Still, it was getting dark now, so he could easily escape in the darkness and hide somewhere. He wasn't at all afraid—but he did badly want those men to be his prisoners till Robin came. It had been a wonderful idea to lock them in!

Kit sat quietly on the deck, watching the night come on the water. He strained his ears to hear any boat coming. He did so long for Robin to arrive—maybe the Dragon might come too! Wouldn't she laugh to see the surly Mr Barton locked up in the cabin with Kit's wicked uncle!

Kit suddenly pricked up his ears like a dog. He was sure he had heard the distant "plash-plash" of oars. It was getting so dark now that Kit could not see very far. He strained his eyes, trying to make out any boat coming up the backwater.

Then suddenly he saw one, looming up out of the shadows. There seemed a lot of people in it—and there was a man, that was certain. Kit sat tight and made no sound. He was not at all sure whether this boatful of people were his friends! Suppose they were strangers, come for an evening picnic? They might hear the shouting and hammering that the two prisoners set up at intervals, and insist on letting them out! Kit decided to sit quietly and say nothing at all, and hope that the boatload would go by, if it was made up of strangers. They certainly would not see the house-boat, hidden in the willows.

Just then the prisoners *did* set up a shouting. The people in the boat stopped rowing for a moment, and then slid quietly past the house-boat up the back-water.

And then suddenly Kit felt someone pouncing on him fiercely, taking firm hold of his shoulders, and shaking him like a rat!

"I've got one of them!" shouted a voice. "Bring a torch, quick!"

Chapter Twenty-five

GOOD NEWS FOR KIT

AFTER KIT'S father had gone to telephone, the children sat waiting for the Dragon. Mr Armstrong soon came back, a broad smile on his face.

"The police were most interested in what I had to tell them," he said. "They are going off in a car to the house you have described, and I have said we will go round by the river, and prevent the men from escaping that way. You had better come with me, Robin, because I shan't know the right way."

"We're coming, too," said Betty, and Lucy nodded her head.

"No, not you girls," said Robin.

"Why not?" asked Lucy fiercely. "You've had all the fun lately. We haven't had any. We're coming, too."

"I'll come as well, then the girls can go," said the Dragon unexpectedly. "I really feel as if I must see poor Kit as soon as possible. Shall we go up the river now, Peter? It's getting rather dark."

"Yes, we must go straight away," said Mr Armstrong. "Come along. Lead the way, Robin."

So Robin led the way down the drive into his own garden, down to the bottom, and out through the garden gate there. Then across the fields to the river.

He found the boat, and everyone got in. Robin untied the rope and pushed off. The little boat seemed quite crowded with five people and one dog, because, of course, Sandy had come, too. He wasn't going to be left out of anything.

"I hope we find Kit safe and well," said Mr Armstrong anxiously. "I hate to think of him under the very nose of the enemy. They might find him at any moment."

"Kit will be all right!" said Robin. "He's really a very clever boy, Mr Armstrong. I say—I'm awfully sorry I was rude to you that day in the ice-cream shop! But, you see, I was on the lookout for Kit's wicked uncle, and I really thought you were he, snooping round, asking questions."

"That's all right!" said Mr Armstrong, rowing strongly up the river. "You did put me off, of course. I felt sure there was no small boy hiding anywhere in Faldham. I thought I'd got hold of the wrong place, and I went off to another Faldham. But I soon found that my first address was right, and came back to it, as you saw."

"I suppose it is you who is the rich person now, and not Kit?" said Lucy.

"Quite right," said Mr Armstrong. "But Paul won't find it is quite so easy to kidnap me as it is to get hold of a small boy!"

"Now we're passing our little island," said Lucy, peering through the twilight. "We shall soon be opposite the lonely house, where the house-boat used to be."

"Don't speak loudly then," said Kit's father. "Sounds carry a long way over water, you know, and we don't want to warn the men of our coming, if they are anywhere about."

So nobody said a word more for some time. They passed the place where the house-boat had once been moored, and went on to where the little backwater began. It was difficult to see in the twilight. But Robin knew his way well by now and guided the boat deftly into it.

"Whereabouts is the house-boat?" whispered Mr Armstrong.

"Hidden in that enormous pair of willow trees," whispered back Robin. "You can only just see them, sir. I say—what's that?"

It was a noise of shouting! It seemed to come from the house-boat. Then there came a sound of hammering. Mr Armstrong stopped rowing at once and they all listened.

"Mr Armstrong! I believe they've got Kit locked up in the cabins!" whispered Robin in dismay. "That's somebody shouting for help, I think, though it's all rather muffled—and that really does sound like somebody hammering on a door trying to get out. Oh, I do hope Kit is all right!"

"Look here—I think I'll take the boat quietly past the house-boat and moor it a little way up," said Kit's father. "It's quite likely they've left somebody on guard on deck, and, if so, we don't want to warn them we're here. Now—not a word from anyone!"

Very quietly indeed, with hardly a splash from the oars, the boat slipped by the house-boat, keeping towards the opposite side of the backwater. Mr Armstrong rowed some way past, and then turned into the bank. The nose of the boat pushed into the long grass, and Kit's father leapt out. He felt about for a tree-trunk, and tied the boat to it.

"Robin, you can come with me," he whispered. "The girls must stay here with Miss Taylor. Now, don't make any noise at all."

The man and the boy crept over the grass towards the big willow trees in which the house-boat was hidden. When they got to the boat, Kit's father peered on to the deck.

"There's someone sitting there!" he whispered. "Somebody on guard, I should think. Well, I'll pounce on him and overpower him—then we'll rescue Kit."

He did not know it was Kit himself sitting there quietly, keeping guard over the two men, who were now quiet again in their cabins! He crept forward on to the deck of the boat, so quietly that Kit did not hear a sound. Then, with a quick leap, he was on him, his strong arms all round the surprised boy, pinning him so tightly that he could not move!

"I've got one of them!" he shouted to Robin. "Bring a torch, quick!"

"Hi! Let me go!" roared Kit, trying to struggle. He thought it must be one of the men from the house. He fought fiercely, but the man's grip was too tight for him to escape from. He shouted fiercely.

"Let me go! Let me go!"

Robin knew Kit's voice at once, and he yelled to Mr Armstrong: "Sir! That's Kit! Let him go!"

But what with Kit shouting, too, Mr Armstrong didn't hear what Robin yelled, and he held the boy in an iron grip. Then, feeling that he was small, he let go one hand and felt round for Robin's torch. He switched it on to see whom he had caught.

The light fell right on Kit's angry face. Mr Armstrong stared down in amazement. Why, it was little Kit, his own son! He gave a shout of joy.

"Kit! It's you, old son! Are you all right? Oh, Kit, I've found you at last!"

Kit's heart beat loudly. It was his father's voice, that he once knew so well! But how could that be? His father was dead. Robin leapt on board and spoke to Kit.

"Kit! It's your father! It really is! He called on the Dragon to-night. He wasn't burnt in that aeroplane crash. He's alive!"

Kit stood up, and father and son faced one another in the remaining twilight. Kit threw his arms round his father's waist, and buried his head in his shoulder.

"Dad!" he said with a choke. "I can't believe it!"

"It's true, old son!" said his father, patting him on the back. "My word, I didn't know it was *you* when I jumped on you just now! I thought you were yelling down in those cabins, a close prisoner!"

The shouting and hammering began again. Robin looked towards Kit. "Who's there?" he said, in surprise.

"Mr Barton and my dear Uncle Paul," said Kit proudly. "They came to see if I was here, I suppose—and I waited till they had gone into the cabins—and then I hopped up and locked them in—used the same padlock *they* had hoped to use for me!"

"Good for you!" said Robin, delighted. "Golly, think of those two captured like that. What fun!"

"I think we'll go and get the police down here," said Mr Armstrong, still with his arm round Kit. "I don't feel quite capable of capturing two madmen on my own! Come on—we'll go and see if the police have arrived yet. I telephoned to them some time ago."

"I'll just slip along and tell the Dragon and the girls what we're going to do," said Robin, who knew that Betty and Lucy would complain bitterly of being left out of the fun again if he didn't go to them. "Shan't be long, sir. I'll join you later. I know the way to the house."

Robin sped back to the girls, and Mr Armstrong and Kit made their way to the house to see if by any chance the police had arrived yet. Robin told the girls in a few words the clever thing Kit had done.

"And there those two men are, captured as neatly as anything!" he finished. "Isn't Kit marvellous?"

But just as he spoke there came a tremendous noise from the house-boat. The two men were making one last bid for freedom, and with all their combined strength were hurling themselves against the door. It broke from its hinges and went flying back, hanging by the locks!

"They're out!" yelled Robin, and ran for the house-boat, thought what he was going to do, he simply didn't know! He couldn't stop the men, that was certain!

The two men ran to hide. They knew it would not be safe to go back to the house. They plunged into the bushes, and were soon well hidden. Not a sound was to be heard. It was really tiresome!

"Oh, I do hope they won't get away!" said Robin. "Oh—who's that? Lucy, go back to the boat at once."

"I've got Sandy," said Lucy. "He'll smell out the two men if I tell him to. Oh, look—is that the police?"

It was. Three men were coming down the lawn with Mr Armstrong and Kit. They hailed the others.

"Hi! What was that noise we heard?"

"The men escaped," groaned Robin. "They're in the bushes somewhere. We'll have an awful hunt for them."

"Sandy! Go and find rabbits, big rabbits!" said Lucy to the eager fox-terrier. "Hurry now!"

Sandy shot off. He felt certain that Lucy meant him to find the men who had just run off. He put his nose to the ground and followed the scent of the men. Sandy would find them if anyone could!

Chapter Twenty-Six

BACK HOME AGAIN—
AND A BIRTHDAY PARTY!

EVERYONE STOOD still, waiting for the dog to bark—and suddenly they heard him: "Wuff, wuff, wuff! Wuff, wuff, wuff!"

"He's found them!" said Lucy, pleased. "Good old Sandy!"

The police made their way to the barking dog. He was standing a little way from a thick bush and barking at it. The police saw that the grass had been trampled round about, and guessed that the men were there.

"Come out of your own accord, or we'll probe for you with sticks," warned the Inspector. There was a moment's silence, and then the two men crawled out, looking very sulky, in the light of the police torches.

"I think we'll go back to the house," said the Inspector. "Take these men, constables."

The two policemen each took charge of a prisoner, and the whole company went up the lawn to the house. The old caretaker was there, and she stared in the utmost astonishment when she saw everyone coming in.

"What next?" she said. "What next? This beats everything. I'll give my notice in to-morrow, so I will!"

But nobody took any notice of her. The two policemen swung the prisoners round to face the Inspector—and then Kit's uncle gave a loud cry. He had suddenly seen Kit's father.

"Peter!" he cried. "No—it can't be Peter! But if it's not—who is it? Peter's dead!"

"No, he's not dead," said Mr Armstrong, in a quiet and very cold voice. "He's very much alive and kicking. And he's going to have a reckoning with you, Paul, for your treatment of his son!"

Paul went pale. He might have been able to lie his way out with the others—but he could not deceive Kit's own father, who had known him and his bad ways for years. He was his stepbrother, and had gone wrong since he was a young man. He lowered his eyes and said nothing.

"As for you," said Kit's father, turning to Mr Barton. "You are a rat and a worm! To take charge of a boy, and accept payment for that charge—and then to bargain with his enemies for his capture! I can tell you, I shall not rest until you have a fit punishment. You will never be allowed to teach young children again, that is certain."

Mr Barton could think of nothing to say. He had never been kind to Kit, so he could not expect the boy to say a good word for him. His wicked ways had found him out at last. He stood there, surly and sulky, giving the Dragon a hard look now and again.

"Well, sir, I'll take charge of these men now," said the Inspector, nodding to the two policemen to take them away. "We've got a car outside. Perhaps you'll see me again in the morning, sir? Thank you."

Mr Barton and Kit's uncle were hustled out of the room. The children heard the front door bang and then a car door. The car engine started up and the big police car roared off into the night, taking the wicked men to prison.

"That's the end of *them*," said Lucy, with a sigh of relief. "Oh, Kit—are you glad to see your father?"

"I should just think I *am*!" said Kit. He had not left his father's side once. The boy simply could not believe that his father really was there. Now he would look after him and be with him. It was simply marvellous.

Betty yawned.

"Time you were in bed," said the Dragon. "Come along. We must all go back."

"I'll just have a word with the poor old caretaker," said Mr Armstrong. "The old thing simply can't make out what's happening."

"There was another man here once," said Robin, suddenly remembering.

"Well, we'll be able to get him, too, I've no doubt," said Mr Armstrong. He went to speak to the old woman, and she grumbled away at him, shaking her old head.

"Nice goings on, these are! I'm right glad Mr Cunningham's come back from abroad. He ought to know about all this, so he ought! I've a good mind to telephone to him—but I don't rightly know how to use the thing!"

"Don't you worry, *I'll* telephone!" said Mr Armstrong. "What's his number? Do you know?"

Soon Kit's father was telephoning to Mr Cunningham, and that gentleman was extremely astonished to hear what had been happening on his house-boat since he had left.

"I'll come over to-morrow," he promised. "We'll meet on the house-boat, shall we? Dear me, I've just remembered—it's my birthday. Tell Lucy I'll bring a cake—not so nice as hers, perhaps, but, still, quite nice. We'll eat it, and drink ginger-beer at eleven o'clock."

"O-o-oh! isn't he nice?" said the children, looking at one another. "I say—maybe we can have the house-boat properly for ourselves again now!"

They went back home in the little boat, sleepy, excited and tired. Mother was home by this time, feeling very astonished and anxious to find none of the children about. She was even more astonished to see Kit and his father—and the Dragon, too!

"What *is* all this?" she cried.

"Oh, Mummy! Do you remember hearing about a boy called Sammy, who was quite dumb?" cried Robin. "Well, here he is."

"How do you do?" said Kit, holding out his hand.

"He's *not* dumb!" said Mummy.

Everyone laughed. Then they settled down to a good old talk, and the children's mother listened in growing astonishment.

"To think all this has been happening under my very nose and I didn't know a thing!" she said, half-indignantly. "Well, well—it's a good thing everything has come right. You might have got yourselves and Kit into serious trouble."

"Oh, no, madam—children like yours get other people *out* of trouble!" said Mr Armstrong, with a laugh. "Now, I'm going to take Kit off to bed. He's tired out. Good night, children. See you to-morrow!"

The Dragon, Mr Armstrong and Kit went to their house next door, and Mummy bundled three excited children up to bed.

"I'll never go to sleep!" said Lucy. "I want to talk till midnight!"

But they were all asleep in a few minutes, and did not wake till the breakfast gong sounded loudly through the house!

"It's Mr Cunningham's birthday party to-day," said Lucy to the others. "I hope he has a nice cake! Won't it be fun to tell him everything."

They were all on the house-boat at eleven o'clock. Mr Cunningham was already there, looking as twinkly as ever. On a table was the biggest birthday cake the children had ever seen! It was really enormous and had pink-and-white icing all over it.

"No candles!" said Lucy, in astonishment.

"I'm too old to have all my candles on," said Mr Cunningham. "I'm forty-two to-day—and no cake would hold so many candles."

"Oh, aren't you old!" said Betty. "Never mind—you're very nice."

"Thank you," said Mr Cunningham. "Now—who will have a slice of my birthday cake with me? What *you*, Sandy! Dear, dear, to think of a dog liking birthday cakes. No, get down and wait your turn, Sandy. Ladies first, please! Oh, Robin, get the ginger-beer, will you?

160

I've put it all in a bucket of ice to keep cool, down in the cabin."

Well, that *was* a feast! Enormous slices of the creamiest birthday cake the children had ever eaten—and iced ginger-beer, so cold that it made their throats hurt when it went down. But, as Lucy said, it was "a very nice sort of hurt!"

Mr Cunningham heard all the story through from start to finish, and inspected the door that had been broken down the night before.

"That's the only damage these children have caused," he said solemnly to Mr Armstrong. "Very nice children, these. In fact, I'm thinking of selling my boat to them."

The children stared at him.

"What do you mean, Mr Cunningham?" asked Robin at last.

"Well," said Mr Cunningham. "I don't want the boat, you know—and you certainly seem to have found a lot of use for it—so I think it would be a good thing if I sold it to you."

"Well, sir, we'd simply love to buy it—but how much do you want for it?" asked Robin eagerly. "I've only got five shillings in my money-box at present. But I've got plenty in the bank."

"I don't want much for it," said Mr Cunningham. "I'm coming back to live in my house here, you know. So, if you would like to buy my house-boat, I would be willing to sell it to you on your promise of paying me at least—at least—fifty-two visits a year! Is that too much, do you think?"

The children had been expecting him to say fifty-two pounds. They stared at him, delighted. "But that's not proper payment," said Lucy, at last. "A visit isn't a payment. We'd visit you for nothing."

"Pardon me, but you *do* pay calls, *and* visits," said Mr Cunningham solemnly. "And that's the payment I'd like. Is it a bargain?"

"Oh, *yes!*" cried Betty joyfully. It would be lovely to go and see Mr Cunningham once a week—he was so nice. And what fun to have the house-boat for their very, *very* own—to play on each holiday—to sleep in whenever they liked.

"Is Kit to share it, too?" asked Betty.

"Of course," said Mr Cunningham. "Though I suppose he will be going back to America with his father, soon, won't he?"

"He'll stay for the rest of the holidays," said Mr Armstrong, and the children gave a whoop of delight. "Then we'll see. I'd like to see a bit of England now I'm here. And, Mr Cunningham, I'd think it very nice of you if you'd pay *me* a visit whenever *you* are in America."

It was a very happy morning. Everyone had two slices of birthday cake each, even Sandy, and as much ginger-beer as they could drink. Then they said good-bye to Mr Cunningham and promised to visit him again as soon as ever they could.

"Don't you get behind with your payments!" he called as they went off in the boat.

"We won't!" cried all the children, and waved wildly at him.

"Well, I'm quite sorry that adventure's over," said Robin.

"*I'm* not," said Kit. "Oh, Dad—it's lovely to have you again. I simply can't believe it's true!"

"It's true all right," said his father, and smiled at the boy beside him. "We're going to have some fun together, Kit—you see if we don't!"

"And we've got the old *Black Swan* for our very own!" cried Lucy, remembering. "Aren't we lucky? Oh, aren't we lucky?"

"We'll have wonderful times on the old house-boat," said Betty. And there's no doubt about it—they certainly will!

THE END

The Treasure Hunters

First published in a single volume in hardback in 1976by
William Collins Sons & Co Ltd.
First published in paperback in 1988 in Armada

Copyright © Enid Blyton 1976

The author asserts the moral right to be identified as
the author of the work

CHAPTER 1

Granny's Old House

Jeffery was sticking some stamps into his album when Susan and John came tearing into the playroom.

"Jeffery! What do you think! We're going to stay with Granny and Granpa in their old, old house!" cried Susan.

"Really?" said Jeffery, surprised and pleased. "How do you know?"

"Because Daddy said so," said Susan, dancing round the room. "Isn't it lovely! John has never been to Granny's, and I hardly remember the house – but

167

you've told us so much about it, Jeffery, that I feel as if I know it inside and out!"

Mother came into the room, and smiled at the three excited faces.

"Yes," she said, "it *is* fun for you, isn't it? Daddy's father and mother are such dear old people, and you will be very happy with them for a few weeks. Daddy is taking me away for a while, because the doctor says I need strong sea air – and Granny and Granpa have offered to have you till we come back."

"Let me see their letter, Mother!" begged Jeffery. He took it and read it.

"We shall so love to have our grandchildren," he read. "Especially as this may be the last year we shall be able to live here. It will almost break our hearts to leave this old house, which has been in our family for three hundred years."

"Oh, Mother!" said Jeffery, looking up in dismay. "Are they really leaving their old home? I thought Daddy said it would be his and ours some day."

"Yes, we thought so too," said Mother. "But you see, since the War, things have been very difficult, and Granny and Granpa have very little money. They will have to sell the old place, and live in a smaller house."

"Well, it's a good thing we're going to stay with them whilst they've still got the old house," said Jeffery. "I remember it quite well, Mother – it's simply lovely!"

"I've never been there," said John, who was the youngest. "Last time you and Susan went I had chicken pox."

"I don't remember it *very* well," said Susan, "but

168

Jeffery has told us all about it heaps of times. I'm longing to go!"

"Well, you haven't long to wait!" said Mother. "You are going tomorrow! So I am going to be very, very busy today, packing for you all!"

"Tomorrow!" cried Susan, jumping for joy. "Oh, how lovely! I must go and pack for my dolls."

Tomorrow came very quickly indeed. In no time at all the three children were packed into Daddy's car, with the luggage behind, and off they went! Mother sat in front with Daddy, and the three children were behind.

"You'll love Granny's old house," said Jeffery, as they sped along. "It's the sort of place where all kinds of things have happened, you know – and where you feel anything might still happen."

"Oh, I *do* love places like that," said Susan, happily. "Are there good walks round, Jeffery?"

"Most exciting ones," said Jeffery. "There is a deep, dark wood nearby, where we can go exploring. And there is a river that flows through the wood and makes part of it very marshy. And there is a lovely farm, where Farmer Timbles lives, and his wife – she's fat and kind, and she makes the most lovely cakes."

"We'll go there to tea then!" said Susan, jumping up and down on the seat. "This will be a lovely holiday."

"I hope you will remember to be quiet in the house, and to be kind and obedient to your grandparents," said Daddy. "They have had a lot of trouble lately, and it is kind of them to have you."

"We really will do our best," promised John. "Jeffery, was there a dog at Granny's? Or a cat?"

"There was a dog called Rags," said Jeffery, who never forgot anything. "He was a darling, but he may not be there now."

"You'll soon see!" said Mother. "We are nearly there!"

"Look! That's the wood I was telling you about," said Jeffery. The children pressed their noses against the car window and peered out. They saw a thick, dark wood with one or two narrow paths running into it. It looked very exciting.

The car turned into a drive between two big gate-posts. On the top of each sat a stone eagle.

"We're here, we're here!" shouted Jeffery, remembering the eagles from his last visit.

The car ran up a winding drive and stopped before a lovely old house. It was long and rather low, with very tall chimneys. The windows shone with leaded panes, and the sides of the house came out to form a sunny courtyard, in which walked some white fantail pigeons.

With a flutter of snowy wings the pigeons flew to the roof, and sat there cooing. "Rookity-coo," they said, peering down at the visitors in surprise. "Rookity-coo!"

"Isn't it lovely!" said Susan, jumping out of the car. The old house glowed red in the sunshine and seemed to welcome the children. It had known many children's feet in the years it had stood, and had heard many children's voices. Now here were more children of the same family, and the house was glad to welcome their pattering feet and to hear their happy calls.

"Granny! There's Granny!" cried Jeffery, and he ran to meet the pretty old lady who stood on the steps to greet them. She was small and round and smiling, and she wore a funny little cap on her white hair.

Granpa came up behind her. He wore a pointed white beard, and had a thick mop of silvery hair. He ran down the steps to kiss Mother.

"Welcome to Greylings Manor!" he said to them all. "It may be the last time we shall welcome you here – but we hope it will be the happiest!"

The children hugged their grandmother and kissed their grandfather. They knew them very well, for the two old people had often been to stay at the children's home. They were fond of them, and were very glad to see them again.

"Isn't it a lovely place, John?" said Jeffery, as he took his brother and sister up to their rooms. "We have been given the two little rooms up in the roof – good! I had one before, and it's so exciting there."

He opened a door. The others went in. They found themselves in a low-roofed room, with latticed windows that looked out on to the sunny garden at the back of the house. The walls of the room were crooked, the ceiling was crooked, and the big beams that ran here and there were crooked too! "It's like a room in a fairy-tale!" said Susan, delighted. "I love the whitewashed walls and the uneven floor. Is this my room or yours?"

"It's our room," said Jeffery. "John and I sleep here, and you have the little room that leads off it.

171

Open that low door there in the corner and you'll see your room, Susan."

Susan opened a low door that came no higher than her shoulder. She stooped and went through it. She came into a small room that seemed like a doll's room! It was almost round, had a ceiling that sloped right down to the floor at one side, and two tiny windows that let in the sun. A white pigeon sat on a small slanting roof outside one window, and cooed softly.

"It's simply lovely!" said Susan. "Oh, I know what you mean when you say this is a house where things might happen, Jeffery! It's like the beginning of a story!"

Susan spoke more truly than she knew. It *was* the beginning of a story – but the children didn't know it yet!

They washed, and then went downstairs. Mother and Daddy were talking out in the garden with Granny and Granpa.

"They don't want to be disturbed," said Jeffery. "I'll show you the rest of the house!"

The other two followed him. It was the most exciting house in the world. For one thing there were three separate staircases! One was the main one, a wide, winding stair that went from the big landing to the hall. Another led from the kitchens to the servants' rooms, and a third, most mysterious, led from a door in the dining-room, behind the wall, and up to the children's room, entering Susan's room unexpectedly from a cupboard!

"How simply thrilling!" said Susan, as she went up the tiny stairway, so narrow and dark, and came out of the little cupboard in her room!

172

There were old family pictures to see – there was great-grandfather, looking rather stern. Great-great-grandmother, looking very pretty indeed in a blue bonnet, stared at them from her frame.

"She's like *you*, Susan," said Jeffery. So she was. She had just the same deep-blue eyes and golden hair.

They were still looking at the pictures when Granny called them.

"Mother and Daddy are leaving now!" she called. "Come and say goodbye."

The children ran downstairs. They hugged their parents, wished them a lovely holiday, and then watched them get back into the car. Daddy started the engine and called to them.

"Be good now! We'll write to you!"

"Goodbye, dears!" cried Mother, and she waved her hand. The car swept down the drive and disappeared out of the eagle-gates. They were gone!

"Our holiday has begun!" cried Susan, and she jumped up and down the steps. The boys turned to Granny.

"Where is Rags? Is he still here with you?" they asked.

"He's out with one of the maids," said Granny. "Look – here he comes! My goodness, he'll be delighted to see so many children to play with!"

He was! He was a rough-haired fox terrier, with bright eyes, a wagging tail, and a black spot on his white back. He tore up to the children, barked loudly, flung himself on each of them in turn, and licked whatever leg or hand he could find.

173

"You're just the same darling old dog!" said Jeffery, pleased. He patted him hard. "We'll go for some good walks together, Rags, old boy!"

"Woof!" said Rags, in delight, and rolled over on his back with all four paws in the air.

"Ridiculous dog!" said Granpa, tickling him with his foot. "I suppose you'll forget all about the old people, now you've got three youngsters to tear about with! Ah – there's the dinner-bell! I'm sure we could all do with something to eat!"

Indoors they all went, and took their places in the long, low dining room. Rags lay down on Jeffery's foot. He was just as happy as the children!

CHAPTER 2

The Greylings Treasure

For the next few days the children and Rags had a fine
time, tearing round the garden, going into all the sheds
and outbuildings, eating peas in the kitchen garden,
and hunting for ripening strawberries.

When Rags was not with them, Whiskers, the big
black cat, sauntered along beside them. The fantail
pigeons disappeared like a cloud of snowflakes when
they saw Whiskers – but at other times they were tame
and would come flying down on the children's shoulders and hands.

"This is such a lovely place," said Susan, looking back at the old house, as she went out of the little white gate that led to the kitchen garden. "How I wish that Granny and Granpa could go on living here, and that it would be Daddy's later on – and ours too, when we are grown up."

"Look – there is a car coming up the drive!" said Jeffery. The three children watched to see who would get out of the car. It might be someone they knew. But it wasn't.

The chauffeur got out and opened the door of the car. A very grandly-dressed lady appeared, followed by a tall man. They went up the steps to the front door.

The children went into the kitchen garden as soon as the visitors disappeared into the house. They thought no more about them at all – until later on in the morning.

Jeffery was playing hide-and-seek with the others. He had gone into a little hedged garden that Granny called her own. In it she had planted all her very favourite flowers, and here her pigeons came to be fed each day from her hands.

Jeffery pushed his way into the middle of the thick yew hedge. He was sure that the others would never find him there! He stayed there, quite still, and waited for the other two to hunt for him.

Whilst he was there Granny came into her garden. She sat down on her white seat, and looked into her little pond, where white water-lilies were showing.

Jeffery thought at first that Granny's footsteps were those of Susan or John, and he kept as still as could be. But when the footsteps stopped, and nobody spoke or called, he carefully parted the green boughs and peeped to see who was there.

"Oh! It's only Granny!" he thought. And then he got a shock!

Granny was crying! Tears ran down her apple-cheeks, and she mopped them up with a tiny lace handkerchief. Jeffery stared in horror. He had never seen a grown-up cry before, and it was dreadful to see tears rolling down Granny's cheeks. Whatever could be making her so unhappy?

He struggled out of the hedge at once. Granny heard him, wiped her eyes quickly, and then looked round in surprise. She tried to smile when she saw the hot, dirty face peeping out of the hedge.

"Oh, Jeffery dear!" she said. "You did make me jump! Are you playing hide-and-seek?"

"Yes," said Jeffery. He ran up to his grandmother. "What's the matter?" he asked. "Why are you crying? Has somebody been unkind to you? Just wait till I see them, that's all!"

He looked so fierce that Granny couldn't help laughing, though she still had tears in her eyes.

"No," she said. "Nobody's been unkind. But – did you see those visitors this morning, Jeffery?"

"Yes," said Jeffery. "Did *they* make you cry?"

"In a way they did," said Granny. "You see – they came to look over Greylings Manor – to buy it – and it made me feel sad to think that Granpa and I will have to go. It has always belonged to the Greyling family – and now it must go to strangers. Poor old house – it will not like that!"

"But Granny, have you lost all your money, or

177

something?" asked Jeffery. "Why must you suddenly go?"

"We haven't *suddenly* lost our money," said Granny. "The family has been unlucky, as the years went by. First, the Greylings Treasure was lost."

"The Greylings Treasure!" cried Jeffery, excited. "What's that? I haven't heard of that!"

"Here he is!" suddenly cried Susan's voice and she came running into Granny's hedged garden. "He isn't even hiding. Catch him!"

"No, Susan, don't," said Jeffery. "I'm not playing now. Granny is telling me something marvellous - about the Greylings Treasure!"

"Whatever's that?" said Susan and John in surprise. They came to sit beside Granny on the white seat. The old lady went on with her story.

"Well," she said, "the Greylings Treasure was brought back from India two hundred and fifty years ago by an adventurous Greyling - Hugh Greyling. He had done a good turn to an Indian Prince, and the Prince gave him some wonderful presents."

"What were they?" asked Susan.

"There were strings of pearls, diamonds set in marvellous metals, a golden cup studded with rubies and sapphires, and other smaller things," said Granny. "There is a book all about this Treasure in the library."

"I shall read it!" said Jeffery, thrilled.

"Well," said Granny, "this treasure was in the Greyling family for some years, and then civil war broke out. You know what civil war is, don't you?"

"It's a war when a country fights against itself,"

said Jeffery. "Families against families. Daddy says it's the worst of all wars."

"It is," said Granny. "Well, in this civil war the Greyling family was afraid that their enemies would steal the Treasure. So Jeffery Greyling – yes, he had your name Jeffery, and he was very like you to look at – well, this old Jeffery of long ago took the Treasure to hide it away safely. He left the house with it – and never came back!"

"What happened to him?" asked John, in surprise.

"Nobody knows," said Granny. "We think he was killed by his enemies. But anyway, the Treasure was never found or heard of again."

"What do you think happened to it?" asked Jeffery.

"Either Jeffery Greyling hid it somewhere in safety, where it was never found again – and then died before he could tell anyone about it, or else his enemies took it and kept it for themselves," said Granny. "But I don't think that is so because somebody would have been sure to have seen the Treasure, and sooner or later it would have been talked about."

"Oh, Granny! Do you mean to say that you think it's still hidden somewhere?" asked Jeffery, in astonishment.

"I sometimes think so," said Granny. "When the Indian Prince gave your great-great-great-great-great-grandfather the Treasure he told him that as long as the golden cup was drunk out of by the Greyling family once a year, good fortune, health, and happiness would remain with the family. But if the cup passed out of the family, and was not used by them, these gifts would pass away too."

179

"It sounds like a fairy-tale," said Susan, who loved magic and mystery. "Granny, did the tale come true?"

"Well, in a way it did," said Granny. "I don't believe in these old sayings of good and bad luck, you know – but ever since the Treasure went, the Greylings have been unlucky. They have lost their money through the years, they have had illness and sorrow – and now, alas, Granpa and I have so little money left that we must give up the old Manor House, and go to live somewhere else."

"Wait a little longer till I'm grown-up, and I'll earn heaps of money and give it to you!" cried John.

"I'm afraid we can't wait as long as that, John!" said Granny, putting her arm round him. "We shall have to go before Christmas. Those people who came today have offered to buy the house at a good price, and to take the two farms, as well, that go with it."

"Dear old Greylings," said Jeffery, looking at the old house, with its tall chimneys. "I'd hate to think it wouldn't be Greylings any more. If only we had that Treasure now, Granny! You could stay here then, and needn't worry."

"I'd like to see that book that tells us about the Treasure," said Susan.

"I'll show it to you when you go indoors," said Granny. So, that evening, the three children pored over an old book, in which were rough pictures of the Indian Treasure. The golden lucky-cup was clearly drawn and the children looked at it in wonder. It had precious stones set around the middle, and all down the handle. Someone had coloured the picture, and the cup shone as if the stones were real!

The children could not understand the reading in the book, for the lettering was very old, and had faded with the years. They looked at the pictures of great brooches and necklaces and pins, and how they wished they all belonged to the family now!

"It's the most exciting tale I've heard," said Susan. "Granny, I feel as if I must go hunting for the lost Treasure straight away!"

"Many people have hunted," said Granny, with a smile. "But nobody has found it. No – I'm afraid it was captured by enemies all those years ago, smuggled away, and then sold. It's gone for ever now."

But Susan wouldn't let herself think that. She loved to imagine all kinds of things. "I shall pretend it can be found!" she said. "I shall pretend to go hunting for it every day! I shall be a Treasure Hunter!"

"We will, too," said the boys, who liked Susan's pretends.

"My three Treasure Hunters!" said Granny, with a laugh. "Well, hunt all you like – but don't get into *too* much mischief!"

CHAPTER 3

Adventure in the Woods

The boys did not really take the treasure hunt seriously, but Susan did. You should have seen her hunting the next day! She tapped the walls of the old house to see if she could find hollow places, behind which treasure might be hidden. She went into the attics and got herself covered with dust and cobwebs, hunting everywhere in the corners.

"You're silly," said John at last. "All these places have been hunted in for years and years. Granny says there only was one secret passage, and that was the staircase to your room, which was found and opened long ago, and isn't secret any more.''

"Children, you really *must* go out of doors,'' called Granny. "It is far too lovely a day for you to spend in the house.''

"But, Granny, we're Treasure-Hunting!'' cried Susan.

"Well, you must hunt outside,'' said Granny. "Go along – out of the house you go, all of you!''

So the three hunters had to go out of the house, and they wandered over to the gate of the kitchen garden. Tipps, the gardener, was there and he waved them away.

"Don't you come in here this morning!'' he shouted. "You ate half a row of my best peas yesterday and you'll just keep out today!''

"Bother!'' said John. "I felt just like a few peas. What shall we do?''

"Let's go treasure-hunting in the wood!'' said Susan eagerly. "We haven't been there yet. We could follow one of those little paths, couldn't we, and see where it leads to.''

"We shall get lost,'' said Jeffery.

"Well, we can take Rags with us,'' said Susan. "Rags always knows the way home. Come on, Rags. We're going hunting! Hunting! Treasure-hunting, Rags!''

"Woof, woof!'' said Rags, thinking that Susan meant rabbit-hunting. So all four of them set off for the woods. They went down the drive and out of the eagle-gates. They turned to the left and soon came to the wood.

They went in under the trees. There was a green light in the wood, very cool and lovely. The trees were so thick overhead that only tiny specks of sunlight got through and these lay like specks of gold on the ground below.

Rabbit-paths ran everywhere. Rags rushed excitedly about, following first one and then another. The children followed quite a wide rabbit-path, thinking it was a real path.

But it wasn't. It stopped at a big rabbit-hole and Rags almost disappeared down it, barking in excitement. The children had to pull him out.

"Well, we can't go down the hole," said John, laughing. "That's where the path leads to. Where shall we go now?"

"Let's go deeper into the wood," said Susan. "It feels mysterious and exciting. You don't know what we might find!"

"Well, you won't find fairies or witches, if that is what you're thinking of," said Jeffery, laughing.

"Listen – what's that noise?" said Susan, stopping suddenly. They all stopped. There was a rushing noise that was not the sound of the wind in the trees.

"It sounds like water," said Jeffery, puzzled. "Oh – of course! I told you there was a river that ran through the wood, didn't I? It wanders in and out and we must be quite near it."

He led the way between the tall trees. The ground became rather wet and marshy, and the children had to tread carefully.

"There it is!" said Jeffery at last. He pointed to where a dark green stream flowed swiftly along between tree-grown banks. The children went to it.

It was deep, and flowed quickly. Susan thought it looked queer.

"Let's follow the banks," she said. "I'd like to see where it goes."

So they followed the stream. It was difficult, because bushes grew so thickly on the bank in some places that they had to leave the stream, go a good way round the bushes and then come back to the water.

It grew wider and shallower as they followed its banks deeper into the wood. It lost its deep green colour and became brown. It bubbled and gurgled, and in its depths quick fishes darted about.

Then suddenly the stream widened out into a large pool, like a small lake. At one end of the pool the stream flowed in, at the other it flowed out.

"Isn't it lovely!" said Susan, in surprise. "I wonder how it made itself into a pond. It looks so round that it seems as if someone made it."

"Whoever would make a lake in the middle of a wood?" said John scornfully. "Ooh look – what a marvellous water-lily that is!"

Water-lilies covered the pond. They were of many colours. The wild yellow one grew there, but deep red and paler pink ones lay on the water also.

"I wish I could pick that deep red lily and take it back for Granny," said Jeffery, looking at the one that John had pointed to.

"It's deep," said Susan, looking into the water. "You couldn't paddle out to it."

Jeffery made his way round the pond, looking to see if there was any shallower place. "There's a big flat

rock here," he said. "And another under the water. I might be able to stand on that, and reach it."

The flat rock was green with slime. Jeffery stood carefully on it, barefooted, and then stepped to the flat stone below – and then he felt about with his foot and said, "I do believe there's another flat stone below this one as well. It's just like steps!"

"They *are* steps!" said Susan, in surprise. She had scraped the green slime off with a stone, and below the slime was white marble! "Look, Jeffery – they are real steps. Steps that somebody put here for the pond."

Jeffery stared down in surprise. Susan was right. Jeffery forgot all about the red water-lily and began to scrape the steps.

"Well, why should anyone build steps here?" he said. "You only put marble steps by a pond if you want to feed swans – or go boating – or if you have a house nearby that you sit in to look over the water."

"Swans wouldn't come here," said Susan. "They like more open water. And there aren't any boats."

"No – but there might have been once," said Jeffery. "I say – I wonder if there ever was a summer-house – or boating-house, or something, near here. After all, if somebody took the trouble to build marble steps here, they might have built a little summerhouse for themselves as well!"

"Let's look!" said Susan. So the three children began to hunt around the pond. The trees and bushes were so thick that it was difficult to make their way here and there.

Suddenly Susan gave a shout. "I say! Look here! What do you think this is?"

The boys scrambled over to where Susan was standing. She was pulling at some thick ivy.

"Look," she said. "There's brick under this ivy. I believe the ivy, the brambles, and the honeysuckle have grown all together here, and hidden a building of some sort!"

The boys excitedly looked about. It certainly seemed as if the great bramble and ivy cluster might be growing over something. They peeped here and there, but they could find no proper building.

"It's like the Castle of the Sleeping Beauty," said Susan, "all overgrown with thorns. Oh, Jeffery, look, look!"

Jeffery and John looked. Rags had gone after a rabbit, and had scraped hard at the bottom of the great ivy tangle. Where he had scraped, stone steps showed – steps that must lead down to the pond!

"So there *must* be some sort of a building beneath this tangle of bushes!" cried Jeffery. "There must! Steps wouldn't lead down from nothing. There must have been a tiny house of some sort here, with steps leading down to the pool. However can we find out?"

"We'll have to borrow an axe from Tipps," said Susan, thrilled. "Then we can chop away the ivy and the other creepers, and see if there's a house underneath."

"Well, there won't be a Sleeping Beauty inside, so don't hope for that, Susan!" said Jeffery, grinning. "I expect it's just a tumbledown hut built by somebody long ago who loved to come and dream in the wood."

"Jeffery, let's go back and get an axe now, this very minute," begged Susan. "Look – when I pull away

188

the ivy here, there is more stone or brick underneath. I *know* there's a secret house here."

"All right," said Jeffery, who was longing to find out more himself. "We'll go back now, this very minute."

So back they went, making their way over the marshy ground. They would never have taken the right path if Rags had not shown them the way! But he trotted ahead, sniffing, and soon led them to the rabbit-path they had first followed.

When they were at last out of the dark, green wood, they scampered along at top speed, up the drive and into Tipp's garden shed. He was there, potting plants.

"Tipps! Would you please lend us your axe?" asked Jeffery. "The one you chop wood with."

"Indeed no," said Tipps. "I'll not lend you something to chop off your fingers!"

"Oh, Tipps! We aren't as silly as that!" said Susan. "Please do lend us the axe. It's for something secret and important - something we found in the wood."

"Oh, well - I suppose you want to chop up a dead tree," said Tipps. "Listen now - I'll lend the axe to Jeffery because he's the oldest and biggest - but none of you are to use it except him. See?"

"All right, Tipps," said Susan and John. Jeffery took the axe, and they made their way out of the shed. But just as they turned their steps towards the front gate, a bell rang.

"Bother!" said John. "That's for dinner."

"Let's miss dinner and go and chop," said Susan, who was always ready to do mad things.

"Don't be silly," said Jeffery, putting the axe

189

carefully into the middle of the yew hedge to hide it. "We don't want to have Granny and Granpa hunting all over the place for us, and Tipps telling them he's lent us the chopper. No – we'll go in and have our dinner – and then we'll spend the afternoon in the wood, chopping!"

So they went in to their dinner. It was stew, and treacle tart, and the three children ate hungrily. It was exciting to think of the axe hidden in the hedge, waiting to chop away creepers that had grown around a secret house.

"How you do gobble today!" said Granpa, in astonishment. "Now, now, eat properly, or you'll be ill!"

"Granny, we found a pond in the middle of the wood this morning," said Susan, who could never keep quiet about anything.

"Did you?" said Granny. "Well, there did use to be one, I believe. There was supposed to be a summer-house there too long years ago, but that seems to have disappeared now. The river has made the wood so marshy that it is no longer a pleasure to walk there, as it used to be years and years ago. Be careful if you go into the wood very far – it is very boggy."

"We'll put wellingtons on" said Jeffery. He frowned at Susan to stop her saying any more. So often she said too much, and then their adventures were stopped by the growns-ups before they had even begun!

They slipped away from the dining room as soon as they could. "I'm going to have a quiet nap," said Granny. "So keep away from the house, won't you?"

190

"Oh, yes, we'll be far away from Greylings this afternoon!" said Susan. She ran to join the boys. Jeffery was taking the axe from the hedge. It shone bright and sharp.

"Come on," he said. "We've got plenty of time this afternoon. We'll see what we can find!"

So off they went again with Rags, who was delighted to go hunting rabbits once more. The children did not find it very easy to make their way to the river, but once they found it, it was easy to follow.

"Look! There's the pool again!" said Susan, jumping for joy, and landing in such a boggy patch that the boys had to pull her out. "Come on! Do some chopping, Jeffery!"

CHAPTER 4

The Little Secret House

Jeffery went to the overgrown clump and began to chop away at the ivy stems. Some of them were very thick. He chopped hard above the steps where Rags had found a rabbit-hole.

He hadn't chopped for long before he gave a shout. "Yes! Look – there is a house of some sort under all this ivy. I'm chopping by the door. Come and pull away the stems for me."

Susan and John went to help Jeffery. He had chopped so hard that he was very hot, and his face was wet.

He took out his handkerchief and mopped his forehead.

Susan and John began to tear away the broken stems of ivy. They were more careful with the blackberry sprays, because they were prickly. The honeysuckle came away more easily, for its stems were thin and brittle.

"Yes!" said Susan, excited. "There *is* a door behind here. Oh, Jeffery! Fancy there being a little secret house hidden under all this ivy and creeper – a house forgotten long ago and never used except by the rabbits."

Jeffery laughed. He took up his axe again. "Well, the rabbits must be getting a shock now," he said. "Stand away, you two. I don't want to chop your heads off!"

"Let *me* have a turn!" begged Susan, who was simply longing to chop too. But Jeffery shook his head firmly.

"Certainly not, Susan," he said. "You know quite well that we promised I would be the only one to chop. I'm the oldest and the biggest, and I know how to use the axe. Goodness knows what *you* might do, Susan, if you began chopping!"

Jeffery chopped hard. Some of the ivy stems were as thick as the trunks of small trees. The roots that these stems had put out held firmly to the door underneath – but once Jeffery had chopped the stems in half, it was easy to pull away the brown roots that clung everywhere.

"Jeffery, we've made quite a hole already!" said Susan, dancing about in excitement. "Oh, Jeffery, hurry! Soon there will be enough room for us to creep through.''

"Well, I'm hurrying as much as I can," said Jeffery. "But it's jolly hard work."

Crash! Crash! The axe cut through one stem after another, and at last there was a hole big enough for anyone to crawl through, about the middle of the doorway. Jeffery twisted a handkerchief round his hand and bent back some of the more prickly sprays that the others couldn't manage.

He poked the axe in through the hole. There was a wooden door behind. "I can see the handle!" said Jeffery, in excitement.

He slipped his hand along the door and tried the handle. It would not even turn!

"It won't move," said Jeffery.

"Let *me* try," said John. "My wrist is very strong – perhaps *I* can turn the handle."

But none of them could. It was stiff with the rust of many many years, and would not move. The three children were terribly disappointed.

"Let's see if we can find a window and chop the ivy away from that," said John. "We can get in through a window."

So they tried to find a window – but the creeping ivy and brambles were so thick that it was quite impossible to guess where a window might be.

Scratched and pricked all over their arms and legs, the children looked at one another and wondered what to do.

"There *must* be some way we can get in!" said John.

"Yes – there *is*!" cried Susan. "I know what to do!"

"What?" asked the boys.

"Chop down the door, of course!" shouted Susan, in excitement. "Can't you chop a big enough hole in the door for us to squeeze through, Jeffery?"

"But do you think we *ought* to do that?" said Jeffery. "I mean – after all, it's a door, and it isn't right to chop holes in doors."

"It can't matter with *this* door." said John, eager to try Susan's idea. "It must be nearly falling to pieces as it is! Go on, Jeffery – chop a hole in it! We'll never get in if you don't. I simply can't wait any longer!"

Jeffery didn't want to wait either. He lifted the axe and chopped at the door with it. The wood was quite rotten and gave way easily. The axe went through it at once. A few strokes, and there was a large hole in the door, through which the children could easily squeeze!

"Good!" said Jeffery, panting. "I say – doesn't it look dark inside there?"

"I guess it's full of spiders and earwigs!" said Susan, staring at the dark hole in the door. "It's a good thing we none of us mind them. Who's going in first?"

Nobody seemed quite so keen on going in after all! It really did look dark and mysterious through the hole in the door. It smelt a bit funny too.

"I believe I've got a candle-end somewhere in my pocket!" said Jeffery suddenly. He always carried a strange collection of things about with him. "You never know when any of them may come in useful," he would say, when the others teased him about them. He felt in first one pocket and then another – and then brought out a candle-end – about two inches of red candle.

"I've got some matches somewhere too," he said.

"Oh, do hurry, Jeffery!" said Susan, always the impatient one. "I want to see inside this strange, secret little house. Fancy finding a house all hidden and covered with creeper, that nobody has been inside for years and years and years!"

Jeffery found his matches, and lighted the candle-end. He held the candle inside the hole in the door. The three children pressed round it to see inside the queer woodland house.

It did indeed look very mysterious. It was full of dark shadows. It looked small, high and round. A bench ran round it, and there was a small fireplace or hearth at the back. A table was against the wall at one side, with something on it. The children could not see what it was.

"Let's go in!" whispered Susan.

"What are you whispering for?" whispered back John.

"I don't know – but it seems funny to talk out loud now!" said Susan, still in a whisper.

Jeffery squeezed in through the hole first. He said "Oh! what's that!" and quickly climbed out again.

"What do you mean? What's the matter?" asked John, half-frightened.

"Something touched my face," said Jeffery. "I didn't like it!"

"It was a spider's web, you silly!" said Susan. She laughed, and the sound seemed to make things bright and ordinary again. "You baby, Jeffery! Fancy being frightened of a spider's web!"

"Well, it didn't feel nice touching my cheek like that," said Jeffery. "You go in first, Susan, if you think a spider's web is so funny! Take the candle!"

So Susan climbed in through the hole in the door, brushing aside the hanging spiders' webs with her hand. She held the candle up and looked round the queer little house.

It had had two windows, but both these were blocked up with ivy and other creepers. The bench round the wall was thick with the dust of many, many years. So was the table. Susan held the candle up and looked to see what was on the table.

"Jeffery, the people who were here last drank out of these glasses!" she said. "There are two here – all dirty and dusty. Oh, isn't it strange to come here and find glasses still on the table!"

By this time the two boys had crept into the little house too, and were staring round in excitement.

"Those glasses are like the very old ones that Granny keeps in the cupboard in the drawing room!" said Jeffery, picking one up. "She won't use them because she says they are old and rare – how pleased she will be to have two more!"

"Look at the fireplace," said Susan, holding the candle to it. "There are the remains of a fire there. What fun it must have been to come to this house on a cold day, light a fire, and sit here in the middle of the wood, with the lovely pool gleaming below!"

"Yes, mustn't it," said Jeffery. "I'd like it myself! I'd love a little secret house like this. The squirrels would come to it – and the robins. The rabbits would peep inside, and perhaps a hedgehog would walk in, and sniff around."

"That does sound lovely," said Susan, delighted. "Poor little house – hidden away and forgotten all these years. Let's make it ours!"

"Oh, yes!" cried the boys, thrilled with the idea.

"We'll clear away the ivy from the windows, and let the light through," said Susan, busy planning as she loved to do. "We'll bring a brush and sweep the dust away. We'll clean up the whole house – and we'll make a fire here one day, and boil a kettle for tea!"

"What fun!" shouted Jeffery, and he jumped for joy. A long spider's thread caught his ear, and he rubbed it away. "I'd like to clear away these clinging cobwebs," he said. "I really don't like them!"

"Let's go home again now," said Susan. "The candle won't last any more. It's running down on my fingers now and the wax is very hot. We'll bring candles here when we come, and keep them on the mantelpiece. Let's take the two old glasses with us."

Off they went back home, carrying the two glasses carefully. They whistled to Rags, who had been chasing rabbits the whole of the time, and then made their way through the dim wood. What an exciting day they had had!

CHAPTER 5

The House Gets a Spring-clean

Granny and Granpa were thrilled to hear about the secret house in the woods, but Granny was not at all pleased to hear of the axe.

"You are not allowed to use such dangerous things," she said to Jeffery. "Tipps is foolish to let you have an axe. You must not use that again, Jeffery."

"All right, Granny," said Jeffery. "But I am really very careful, you know, and after all, I shall soon be twelve!"

"Look, Granny, here are the glasses," said Susan – and she put them on the table. She had carefully washed them, and polished them with a clean cloth. They shone beautifully. Granny gave a cry of delight and picked them up.

"Look, Thomas!" she said to Granpa. "Two of those beautiful, heavy old glasses that we have in my cupboard over there. How lovely! These are rare, now, children, and I am delighted to have them. They are over a hundred years old!"

She put them proudly in her glass-fronted cupboard in the corner of the drawing room. They were fat glasses, short and very heavy – the children wished they could use them each day for their lemonade but Granny wouldn't hear of it!

"Granny, we are going to make that little secret house our very own," said Jeffrey. "We are going to clean it up, and keep a few books and things there. We shall clean up the steps that lead down to the pond – and then, when it is all ready, you must come and have tea with us there!"

"We can boil a kettle on the little hearth," said Susan, jumping round like a grasshopper. "We can make a fire! There's a table there too, and a bench round the wall. Oh, it really is a most exciting little house!"

"Well, I can't see why you shouldn't make it your own house if you want to," said Granny. "Greylings Wood is ours, and the house was ours too – so you can have it for a playhouse, if you like."

For the next few days the children spent all their time in the wood, going to and from their new house, carrying brooms and pans and cloths! Jane the house-maid was quite cross at the disappearance of so many of her cleaning things, and the children had to promise to bring them all back safely when they had finished with them.

Susan took charge of the cleaning, as she was the girl. They all went to the house the next day, and climbed in through the door again. This time they had plenty of candles and two candlesticks. They put two candles into the stands and stood them on the little mantelpiece. They lighted the house up well.

"You two boys had better see what you can do about the windows," said Susan. "It would be a good thing to let some light and air into the house. It still smells old and musty."

"We mustn't have the axe this time," said Jeffery, staring at the windows. "But I could borrow Tipps' little saw, and saw through the ivy stems. It wouldn't take long."

So Jeffery ran back to Greylings and borrowed the saw. He and John took it in turns to saw the thick stems, and soon they were able to pull the ivy and brambles away from the window, and to let in air and light.

There was no glass in the windows – they were simply round holes in the rather thick wall. Whilst the boys were clearing the two windows Susan got busy with the cleaning. The house was dustier than any-where she had ever seen!

Rags was thrilled with the house. He jumped in and out of the hole in the door a dozen times in an hour, and trotted all round the house, sniffing everywhere.

He would have liked to live there always, surrounded by rabbits!

Susan removed all the cobwebs first. They hung down from the roof, they stretched here and there, and were grey with dust. They were soon down! Big spiders scuttled away. A robin hopped in at the hole in the door, and flew to the mantelpiece. He carolled a tiny song as if to say, "I'll help with the spiders!"

But he didn't. He flew out again, and sat on a branch outside, watching the children with his bright black eyes.

Susan swept down the walls with her broom. She swept the mantelpiece, the bench, and table. When she had got all the dust on to the floor, she began to sweep that into her pan.

The dust made the children sneeze. They blew their noses, and then settled down to their work again. It was fun.

"Get some water from the pool, John, will you?" asked Susan, when she had swept up all the dust she could find. "I want to do a little scrubbing now!"

"I'll help you," said John, who liked to scrub.

"Well, I've got two scrubbing brushes here, so you can have one," said Susan happily. It was lovely having a secret house like this, making it their very own.

John fetched a pail of water from the pond. The children had found that there was a complete flight of overgrown steps leading down from the little house to the pool. Jeffery was determined to clean them and uncover them all as soon as he had finished the windows.

There was a lot to do, but the children enjoyed every minute. The sun was very hot in the garden of Greylings, but here in the wood, it was cool and green. The children had brought lemonade with them, and they drank it when they felt too hot.

Susan scrubbed the floor, the bench, and the table. The floor was of brightly-coloured tiles, set in a pattern, and at some time had had a rug over it, for Susan found threads of it still left.

"I say! What a lovely floor!" said Jeffery, looking in from one of the window-holes. "It looks beautiful now! Who would have thought there was a floor like that!"

It took the children three days to get the little house really nice. At the end of that time it was lovely!

Jeffery had managed to get the door to open now, and had cleared away all the creepers over the doorway, so that light came in there as well as in at the windows. Tipp's saw was not so quick at clearing ivy as the axe, but that couldn't be helped.

John had cleared the steps that led down to the pool. He had torn away the creeping roots that hid them, and had cleared them of earth and moss. They were of white marble and shone beautifully. John was proud of them.

Susan had made the house look really lovely. Everything was clean there now. The brightly-coloured tiles shone on the floor. The table and bench were quite clean, and the fireplace was cleared too, and was neatly laid ready for a fire, with paper, twigs, and old wood that the boys had found outside.

They begged an old rug from Granny for the floor.

They brought along a little vase which they filled with flowers for the middle of the table. Susan even brought an old clock that she had found in a cupboard. It had belonged to Granpa, and one of its legs was broken. It had not been worth mending and had been put away in a cupboard.

John mended its leg. Susan wound it up and it went. So to the secret house it was carried, and there it stood on the mantelpiece, ticking away cheerfully!

"I always think a clock makes a house feel cosy and lived-in," said Susan happily. "Doesn't it all look nice? Let's have tea here tomorrow! We won't ask Granny and Granpa yet. We'll wait till we're sure the fire goes all right, and the chimney doesn't smoke. We'll try tomorrow!"

Rags was most interested in the house. He ran in and out, and Susan did wish he could be taught to wipe his feet. He seemed to take a delight in running in the muddiest places he could find, and then walking over the clean floor of the little house!

The next day the children brought along the things for tea at the house. Susan carried a kettle of water to boil for tea. The boys brought a picnic basket full of food. Inside there were unbreakable cups and plates which Granny had given them to keep in their house.

"Isn't this fun!" said Susan, as she put a gay little cloth on the table. "Jeffery, do let *me* light the fire, please, to boil the kettle! After all, I did lay it ready."

Everybody wanted to light the fire, but Susan was allowed to do it. She knelt down and put a lighted match to the paper. It flared up at once. The twigs

204

began to crackle. The wood soon caught fire, and a lovely glow filled the hearth.

But it wasn't so lovely after a little while. Smoke began to pour out from the fireplace, and filled the little house. The children coughed.

"Oh dear! It's smoking!" said Susan. "What a nuisance! Do you suppose we ought to have swept the chimney?"

"Well, I shouldn't have thought the fire was used often enough to make the chimney really sooty," said Jeffery.

Susan poked the lighted wood to the back of the fireplace, hoping that the smoke would soon go up the chimney. But it didn't. It went pouring out into the room. Soon the children's eyes began to smart, and they choked with the stinging smoke.

"Wood smoke is always horrid," said Jeffery, going outside to wipe his streaming eyes. "This won't do, Susan. We'll have to put out the fire. We can't boil water for tea today. We'll have to do that when we've put the chimney right."

"I expect it's stuffed up with ivy stems and leaves," said John. He kicked the fire out, and soon only a few wisps of smoke rose from the hearth.

But it was impossible to have tea in the smoky house. Susan was very disappointed about it. She took the tea outside, and they sat on the steps, looking down to the little pond, and ate their egg sandwiches, ginger cake, and chocolate biscuits there. They drank the water out of the kettle, pouring it into their cups.

"This is really a lovely place!" said Susan. "Look how the sun comes slanting through the trees just there, and lights up the pond. What a lot of water-lilies there are today!''

"There's a red squirrel watching us," said John in a low voice. "Don't move. He's in that hazel tree over there."

The children watched the big-eyed creature. He sat on the branch, his bushy tail curled up behind him. Then with a light bound he leapt to the ground and scampered up the steps to them. Rags saw him and would have pounced on him, but Jeffery had him by the collar.

Susan held out a bit of chocolate biscuit. The squirrel took it in a tiny paw and then bounded into the trees, carrying it in his mouth.

"He likes chocolate!" said Susan. "Oh, isn't he sweet! I'd like to tell him to live in our little house when we are not there. He can be our caretaker!"

As the shadows began to grow longer, one or two rabbits came slipping out of their holes. They sat not far off, washing their ears, bending them down as they cleaned them. The children watched, keeping quite still. Rags whined, and longed to chase them, but they would not let him.

"We *are* lucky to have a little house all to ourselves in the wood," said John. "All the animals and birds will soon be tame for us and we can feed them and make friends with them!"

The robin was already very tame. It took crumbs from Susan's hand, and did not seem at all afraid. A big freckled thrush sat nearby and eyed the children warily, turning its head first to one side and then another.

"It looks at us first out of one eye and then out of the other!" said Jeffery, with a laugh. He threw the thrush a bit of bread – but the robin flew down and got it before the thrush stirred from the branch.

"I could stay here all evening," said Susan. "But I'd really like to see what's the matter with that chimney, Jeffery. I'd like to put it right before Granny and Granpa come to tea!"

"Well, we'll have a look at it now," said Jeffery, getting up. The squirrel bounded up a tree as he moved, and the rabbits shot into their holes, showing white bobtails. Rags raced after them at once, and began to scrape earth into the air in a great shower!

"Have you got the brush here that you had yesterday, Susan?" said Jeffery. "The one with a long handle, I mean. I could put that up the chimney to see if there is anything stopping it up."

"Yes, there it is," said Susan. "In the corner."

Jeffery took it. He went to the fireplace and knelt down beside it. "I expect there is a bird's nest or something stopping it up," he said. "It is a very short chimney, and it should be quite easy to clear."

He put the broom up – and at once a shower of twigs and moss and leaves came down. It all fell into the fireplace. "A bird's nest," said Jeffery. He pushed the brush up as high as he could. Another shower of twigs and moss came down.

"Go outside and see if the brush is sticking out of the chimney," said Jeffery to John. John went out and looked. He came back.

"Yes," he said. "I can just see it. The chimney should be clear now."

"Right," said Jeffery. He pulled the brush down – but the end of it stuck against something in the chimney. Jeffery tugged hard, but the brush-end would not come.

"Blow!" he said. "What's the matter with it?" He put his head up the chimney and felt about with his hand. To his surprise he found something sticking out halfway across the chimney. This was what the brush had caught on.

Jeffery felt round it. It felt like a box or something. He grew excited.

"I say!" he called. "There's a sort of opening in the side of this chimney – a kind of hidey-hole, I should think! And there's something been stuffed into it – something too big for the hole – so that it sticks out half across the chimney!"

"Oh, Jeffery! Get it down, quick, get it down!" shouted John and Susan.

"I'll try," said Jeffery. "It seems to have stuck. No – here it comes!"

CHAPTER 6

A Most Exciting Discovery

He had tugged so hard at the box that it had moved from its place. He slid it out from the hole. It was heavy and Jeffery could not hold it in one hand. The box slid down the chimney and landed in the back of the fireplace with a crash.

"Gracious!" said Susan. "What a funny old box!"

"Isn't it exciting!" said John, almost beside himself with joy. "Is it the Treasure?"

"Of course not!" said Jeffery. "The box is too small to hold the Treasure! But it may hold something exciting, all the same.''

It was an iron box, with a stiff clasp in front. On the top of the box was a raised letter – G.

"G for Greylings," said Susan, tracing the letter with her finger. "This is an old Greylings box. Open it Jeffery, quickly! Whatever can be inside it?"

It was not easy to open. The years had made the clasp very stiff, and Jeffery had to get a knife from the picnic basket to force it open.

"Shake it, John, and see if it rattles," said Susan eagerly. "Perhaps it might have a few old brooches inside."

John shook it – but it did not rattle.

"It sounds empty!" he said. "Oh dear – I do hope it isn't!"

Jeffery took the box from John, and began to work at the stiff fastening. It suddenly gave way, and Jeffery opened the lid. The three children peered inside in excitement.

"There's nothing inside it at all!" said Jeffery in the greatest disappointment. "Look – it is empty!"

So it was. Nothing was to be seen except the sides and bottom of the box itself.

John was puzzled. "But Jeffery," he said, "why should anyone want to hide a box in a secret chimney-hole, if there was nothing in it?"

"How should *I* know?" said Jeffery gloomily. "It must have been hidden there over a hundred years ago. Perhaps more. A silly joke, perhaps."

"It couldn't have been a joke," said Susan, taking the box from Jeffery. "Nobody sticks things up chimneys for a joke! Do you suppose there *was* something in the box – and somebody found it – and put the box back again after taking out the things inside?"

"Well, that's an idea," said Jeffery. "But how disappointing for us!"

Then Susan made a discovery. "Look, Jeffery," she said, holding up the box. "Doesn't it seem to you as if the box ought to be bigger inside than it is?"

"Whatever do you mean?" asked the boys.

"Well," said Susan, "if you look at the outside of the box it seems quite big – but if you look, *inside*, it doesn't look *big enough*!"

"You mean – there might be a secret bottom to it!" cried Jeffery, and he snatched the box from Susan. He examined it very carefully – and then he nodded. "Yes – there *is* a false bottom to it. You're right, Susan. How clever of you!"

"How can we open the secret part?" cried John, going red with excitement.

"I don't know," said Jeffery, busy pressing and tapping to see if he could open it. "My goodness! Suppose there is something really thrilling here after all!"

Susan and John could hardly keep their hands off the box as Jeffery tried to open the bottom part. It was no good – he couldn't do it.

He gave it to John, and John tried. Then Susan had a try. But no matter what they did they couldn't open the bottom of the box.

"It's some clever little trick, I'm sure," said Jeffery, in despair. "Oh, I *do* wish we could find it."

Susan grew impatient. She turned the box upside down and banged it with her fist. It slipped from her knee and fell on to the floor.

"Susan, be careful!" cried Jeffery – and then he stopped, and stared at the box. It had fallen upside down, and as Jeffery stared, he saw that the bottom of the box had slid crooked! Somehow or other in its fall, the secret spring had been touched, and the bottom was now loose!

Jeffery grabbed the box. He pressed on the bottom of it, as he held it upside down. The bottom slid away neatly, and the three children saw a small narrow space inside, hidden between the false bottom and the real one.

And this time there was something inside! Yes, there really was!

It wasn't brooches or anything like that – it was a sheet of thick parchment-like paper, doubled over. Just that and nothing more.

"A bit of paper," said Jeffery, taking it out very carefully. It fell in two as he touched it, breaking at the fold. It was very, very old.

"What does it say?" asked Susan, bending over to see it.

"It's a map," said John. "What a funny old map!"

"So it is," said Jeffery. "But what's it a map *of*?"

"Goodness knows!" said Susan. "And what's this one word on the map – just here? It's such old, old printing that I can't even read it!"

"What's that first letter?" said Jeffery, trying to make it out. "It's a J, I think. J – and that's an R, I believe. J – R – there's no word beginning with Jr."

"J – R – is that an E?" wondered Susan. "It's a funny one! And the next letter is certainly an A. Jrea – worse than ever!"

"And then comes an F," said Jeffery. "Jr – eaf – it must be some foreign language!"

"There are some more letters after that," said John. "I give it up! But I know what we'll do – we'll ask someone who can read old writing, and see if they can tell us what the word is. Perhaps if we know what the word is, we should know what the map means."

"Gracious! Look at the time!" said Susan. "Granny will be wondering whatever has happened to us! We'd better pack up and go home."

So they packed up their things, and, leaving the kettle behind for another day, they went to Greylings, carrying the old box with them. What a find they had had!

When they got to Greylings, they found a car in the drive. "It's the same one that came the other day," said Jeffery, looking at it. "It belongs to those people who want to buy the house."

"Well, Granny and Granpa will be busy with them, then," said Susan. "We'd better go into the study and wait till the visitors have gone."

So into the study they went – and, of course, they got out the strange map, pieced it together once more – and tried to find out what the word said.

"If only we could find out!" sighed Susan. And then a voice behind her said, "And what do you want to find out, little girl?"

The children looked round. They saw that Granny had brought a gentleman into the room – the man who wanted to buy the house. She was showing him the study once more, and the children had not heard the door open.

Jeffery did not want to say anything about the map. He tried to take it off the table – but as it was in half, he only managed to get one piece before the man leaned over the table to look.

"I want to know what that word says," said Susan, in her clear voice. "We've been puzzling and puzzling over it. It's an old map we found today, hidden in this old iron box, up the chimney of our secret house in the woods."

Granny looked surprised. So did the man. He bent over the piece of parchment at once. "Where's the word?" he said. "Ah – well, let me see. That first letter is a T."

"T! We thought it was a J," said Susan.

"T – R – E – A – S——" read the man.

"S!" said Susan scornfully. "That's not S, it's F."

"In the old days the letter S was written like an F," said the man. Then he jumped, because Jeffery gave a shout. He didn't mean to shout, but he couldn't help it. If the first letter was a T – and the fifth was an S – then he knew what the word was!

But he didn't say it. He tried to take the paper out of man's hand – but the man held on to it. "Wait, wait," he said "I haven't finished. T – R – E – A – S – U – R – E. The word is Treasure! How very interesting!"

The three children's faces went red with excitement and joy. "So it's a map showing where the Treasure was hidden!" thought Jeffery to himself. "We can puzzle it out – and perhaps find the Treasure for Granny!"

"May I take this old piece of paper to a friend of mine who is extremely clever at puzzling out old papers?'' said the gentleman, suddenly, turning politely to Granny. ''I could perhaps find out a good deal more for you, Mrs Greyling, and it might be most interesting.''

''Well – its kind of you,'' said Granny, not knowing quite what to do. ''But I'd rather like to keep the paper and show it to my husband.''

''Very well,'' said the man, ''I'll take it with me now, show it to my friend at once, and send it back to you tonight, with a note telling you what he says about it.''

But Jeffery did not want the precious paper to go out of his sight. ''Please, it's mine,'' he said. ''I want it. We found it ourselves.''

''Of course, of course, my dear boy,'' said the man, smiling at Jeffery. ''I quite understand your feelings. I will only keep the paper an hour – my friend is staying at a hotel nearby, and will tell me at once his opinion of it – whether it is genuinely old or not – and if it contains anything of importance to you. Your grandmother has been so kind to me that I would like to do her this little service, if I may.''

Poor Granny could do nothing but smile and thank him. She did indeed think it was kind of him, but she was sorry because she guessed that the children wanted to show her their find and talk about it as soon as the man had gone. But as she hoped he would buy Greylings, she did not like to offend him.

''Take it, by all means,'' said Granny politely. ''It would be kind of you to find out exactly what the paper means – if it *does* mean anything!''

The man patted Jeffery on the shoulder. The boy

was angry, and looked it. What right had this man to go off with their precious paper?

He went almost at once, carrying the parchment carefully in his hand.

The children clustered together as soon as Granny took the man out of the room to his car.

"What did you want to go and tell our secret to a stranger for, you stupid, silly girl?" said Jeffery to Susan. "Now see what you've done! He's guessed it's something to do with the long-lost Greylings Treasure – and he's got the map. At least – he's only got half of it, thank goodness! I was quick enough to get the other half, and hide it behind my back before he saw it. So he won't be able to tell much from *his* half!"

"That was quick of you, Jeffery," said John. "But really, Susan *is* an idiot to go and blurt out our secret like that."

"I'm sorry," said Susan, looking ready to cry. "I didn't think. I really felt so excited."

"Well, Susan, if that's a map showing where the Treasure was hidden, we don't want strangers going after it and finding it," said Jeffery. "I should have thought you would have been sharp enough to keep your tongue quiet."

"Don't grumble at me so, Jeffery," said Susan, who hated her big brother to think she was silly. "I'm very, very sorry, really I am."

"Well, don't say a word another time," said Jeffery. "We must just wait and see what happens now – I hope the man brings back our paper all right."

CHAPTER 7

Mr Pots of Money

Granny was told all about the finding of the box, and she called Granpa to hear about it when he came in. They looked at the old iron box with the big letter G on it. They exclaimed over the secret bottom, where the paper had been hidden. And Granpa longed for the man to bring back the parchment so that he might see the map himself.

"I shan't tell *any*one that we've got the other half of the map," said Jeffery to the others, when they were alone once more. "Not *any*one. This is *our* secret – and if there's going to be any finding of the Treasure, *we're* going to do it. See?"

The other saw quite well and they agreed heartily with Jeffery. They waited impatiently for the man to come back.

"Supposing he doesn't?" said Susan. "Supposing he keeps the paper for himself, and tries to get the Treasure?"

"Oh, don't be so silly, Susan," said Jeffery, who still felt cross with her. "How can he find anything if *we*'ve got one half of the map? Do use your brains."

"I *am* using them," said Susan indignantly. "He might be able to make out enough, just by using his half. It looked to me to be the most important half."

"Here he is again!" cried John, from the window. "And he's got the map. Good!"

The man was shown into the study again, and Granny and Granpa came too, eager to hear what was said.

"I've taken the paper to my friend to puzzle out," said the man, whose name was Mr Potts. "He says there is no doubt at all that it is an old map, which shows the whereabouts of some Treasure."

"Really!" said Granny, thrilled.

"Yes," said Mr Potts, his big moustaches seeming to bristle with excitement too. "But my friend, who is used to dealing with old documents like this, says that there is only half of the real map here. He says there should be another half."

"Dear dear," said Granny, looking round the room as if she expected the other half to come floating down to her. "Now where can that be? In the box, do you think?"

"Quite likely," said the man eagerly. "May I look and see?"

Jeffery gave a secret wink at the others. He handed Mr Potts the box. He felt quite safe in doing that because he knew quite well that there was nothing in the box at all! The other half of the old map was at that moment in the top drawer of the desk in the corner! Jeffery had slipped it there as soon as he had seen Mr Potts coming up the steps again.

Mr Potts shook the box. He opened and shut the false bottom. He peered into the secret hiding-place and scraped round it with a pencil. There was nothing there at all.

"No," he said. "It's quite empty. But I am perfectly certain there must be another half to this old map. Until it is found, no one will be able to hunt for the Treasure. Do *you* know where it is?" he said very suddenly, wheeling round on Susan.

Susan had no idea where Jeffery had put the map. She shook her head. "No," she said, "I don't know where it is at all."

"Do *you*?" asked the man, staring at John. John went very red. Like Susan, he had no idea where the half was but he couldn't help blushing.

"I don't know at all where it is," he said.

Mr Potts turned to ask Jeffery – but that sharp boy had guessed he would be asked, and he had slipped out of the room. He wasn't going to tell an untruth – but he was jolly sure he wasn't going to tell the truth to Mr Potts either!

"I wonder if you children are telling the truth," said Mr Potts, looking at the blushing John.

That made Granny angry. "Mr Potts," she said, "I think you forget that they are my grandchildren. They are all truthful children, I can assure you."

"Sorry, Mrs Greyling," said the man, with a laugh. "This boy went so red I thought he wasn't telling the truth."

"May we have our map back, please," asked Susan, trying to make Mr Potts stop staring at John, who was looking more and more uncomfortable.

"Certainly," said Mr Potts. "Here it is. But it isn't much use to you or to anybody unless the other half can be found."

He gave the map to Susan. "That word is certainly 'Treasure'," he said. "And I should think that if we could find the other half of the map, and piece it together, there's a good chance of coming across the Greylings Treasure. You were good enough to tell me the old story the other day, Mrs Greyling, and I was *most* interested in it!"

"Well, thank you for your help," said Granpa.

"May I ask a favour?" said Mr Potts, smiling very charmingly at Granpa. "If you *should* come across the other half of the map, let me show it to my friend, and he will work it out for you, and help you to find the Treasure. It needs someone very learned in old documents to trace out the meaning of them – and I should be delighted to help you if I could, by getting my friend to do his best for you."

"Thank you," said Granpa again. "We will certainly promise to let you see the other half, if we find it."

"Where did you say you found the box?" asked Mr Potts, turning to Susan.

Susan told him, rather sulkily. She didn't want to tell him any more than she could help, after Jeffery's scolding – but if she didn't tell him, Granny would – so she didn't see that it mattered.

"Very interesting, very, very interesting," said Mr Potts, when he heard about the secret house, and the hole in the chimney. "You are very lucky children! Well – don't forget to let me know if you find the other half of the map, will you?"

He patted Susan on the shoulder, smiled at her most beautifully, and then said goodbye. As soon as he was gone Susan stamped her foot.

"Horrid man! Patting me and smiling at me with a nasty treacly smile! He'd like to get the treasure himself, I know he would!"

Jeffery slipped into the room, grinning.

"Hallo!" he said. "He's just gone! Isn't he dreadful? Fancy Greylings Manor being *his!* I just simply couldn't bear it!"

"He's frightfully rich, Granny says," said John.

"Well, Potts is a good name for him then," said Jeffery, grinning again. "Mr Pots of Money!"

The others laughed. "You were clever to slip out of the room before you could be asked if you knew where the other half was," said Susan. "John went awfully red. I really thought Mr Pots of Money would guess that he knew about the other bit of map."

"Where's the half he brought?" asked Jeffery. John gave it to him "Oh, good – well now we'll be able to fit the pieces together and see what *we* can puzzle out. We may not be clever and learned, like Mr

221

Potts' friend is – but I hope we're smart enough to see what this map means!"

"Let's go up to our roon to look at it," said John. "If dear Mr Potts comes back suddenly, he might see we have two bits. And I say – suppose Granpa sees them! He has promised to let Mr Potts see the other half."

"Well, we musn't let him or Granny see the half then," said Jeffery. "Now remember, Susan – don't you go and give the game away!"

"Of course I shan't!" said Susan crossly. "Don't keep saying things like that, Jeffery."

"Come on. Let's go up to our room and have a good look at the map again," said John. So they set out to go upstairs – but Granny and Granpa were in the hall, near the stairs. Suppose they stopped the children and asked them about the other half of the map, whilst they still thought of it?

"Susan! We'll go up to our rooms by that secret staircase that leads into your room," said Jeffery. "Quick! Come into the dining room before we're seen."

They slipped unseen into the dining room and went up the funny, narrow stairs that wound up to Susan's room. All three children stepped out of Susan's cupboard, laughing.

"It's fun to come up those old stairs!" said Susan. "There's a table in your room, Jeffery. Let's go and put the map there and really study it hard. Now that we know it may be a map of where the Treasure was hidden, it is much, much more exciting!"

Soon the three children were bending over the funny

old document. Jeffery hurriedly stuck the back of the halves together with gummed paper, so that they could see everything better.

"Look!" he said suddenly. "Do you see this half that Mr Potts took away? Compare it with the other half – and you'll see that every line on Mr Potts's piece looks dented – as if someone had run a pencil over every bit of the map! Do you know what has been done?"

"No, what?" asked Susan, puzzled.

"Somebody has traced the map," said Jeffery. "They wanted a copy of it – so they laid tracing paper over it, and pencilled a copy! The lines would show through the tracing paper quite clearly. It's like when we trace maps at school. Mr Potts has got a copy of this! No wonder he was willing to bring it back so quickly!"

"That means he thinks it's a proper map, showing where the Treasure *is*," said John slowly.

"It shows something else too," said Jeffery. "It shows that he means to try and find it! Why would he take a copy of it if he didn't want to find it! No – he believes in Greylings Treasure – and he believes in our map. Thank *goodness* he only saw half!"

"Do you think he may try to get the other half?" asked John solemnly.

"I hope not!" said Jeffery. "But you never know. Do you know what I'm going to do? I'm going to take a tracing of the map myself – and then put the real map into some good safe place so that we don't need to use it. We'll hide the tracing too, except when we use it."

"Do the copy now," said John. "I can see Granny and Granpa in the garden, and Mr Potts has gone. Then we can hide the real map away."

Jeffery got some tracing paper and sharpened a pencil.

In ten minutes he had carefully traced the map on the paper, which he folded and put into his pocket.

"Now we'll hide the *real* map!" he said.

"Where?" asked Susan.

"It had better be somewhere quite simple," said Jeffery. "Difficult places are always searched. *I* know! We'll put the map in your dolls' house, Susan! I'm sure no one would think of looking there!"

Jeffery got some drawing pins, and knelt down on the floor. He carefully pinned the two halves of the map on to two ceilings in Susan's dolls' house – on the bedroom ceiling, and on the kitchen ceiling!

"Nobody, nobody would *ever* think of looking there!" said Susan, in delight. And, indeed, it was a clever place.

The bell rang for supper.

"Now we shan't have any time to work out the map!" said Jeffery. "Bother! We'll do it afterwards, when we're in bed! You can come into our room, Susan, and we'll see if we can work out the map. We'd better wash now, and change into something clean. Hurry!"

CHAPTER 8

Where is the Winding Road?

At supper that night Granny and Granpa asked the children all kinds of questions about the secret house and the iron box. They were really just as excited as the three children.

Jeffery said nothing at all about the other half of the map. Granpa wanted to see the piece that Mr Potts had had, and Jeffery took out his copy of it.

"I've put the map in a safe place," said the boy. "You see, Granpa, if people keep handling it, it will fall to pieces, it's so old!"

"Quite right, my boy," said Granpa, taking the tracing. "Very sensible of you."

The children went early up to bed that evening, for they all so badly wanted to study the complete map and see if they could puzzle it out. As soon as Susan was undressed and had her dressing-gown on, she slipped into the boys' room.

They were already in bed. They had lighted their bedside lamp, and their two heads were close together, looking hard at the map.

Susan climbed into bed beside them and looked too.

"It's an odd sort of map," said Jeffery. "Look at this curving snake thing – it must be a road! And then there are three big trees. Well, those trees are probably dead by now and fallen down. But it's possible they may still be standing in a row somewhere."

"And look at this funny hump-shaped thing," said John, pointing with his finger. "Is it a hill? There aren't any hills like that round here, are there?"

"There might be," said Jeffery. "We haven't explored everywhere yet, you know. And goodness knows what might be in that deep wood of ours! It's almost a forest, it's so thick and so big."

"Then what's this funny little drawing down here?" said Susan, pointing to what looked like a roughly drawn church. "It's got a row of queer little lines beneath it – steps up to it, I suppose."

"It's very odd," said Jeffery, his face red with trying to make out the map. "I read it like this – first we have to go down a winding road or lane. Then we come somewhere where there are three big trees in a line. Then we come to a hump-backed hill. Near there

226

we shall find a little church or building of some sort – and perhaps the Treasure is hidden somewhere about there."

"That sounds splendid, Jeffery!" said Susan, her eyes shining with excitement. "I wonder where the winding road is?"

"We'll get a map of the district," said Jeffery. "It will show us all the winding roads there are. We should come to the three big trees at the fourth bend in the road. If you count, you'll see there are four bends in the drawing."

"Yes. So there are," said Susan. "You are clever, Jeffery! Oh, I'm longing to go exploring now. Where can we get a map to see if there are any winding roads round here?"

"I believe there's one in Granpa's study," said John. "I saw Granpa looking at it the other day. Shall I slip down and fetch it?"

"Yes," said Jeffery. "Go down Susan's little staircase, John. You won't be seen then, perhaps."

John slipped out of bed. He ran into Susan's room, opened her cupboard door, and went down the curious little stair. He stopped at the bottom to listen if there was anyone in the dining room. He could hear nothing. He stepped into the dining room, ran to the door and then crept into the study, which was nearby. He could hear the radio murmuring in the drawing room.

"Good!" thought John. "If I do make a bit of a noise, no one will hear me if the radio is on!"

He opened the glass front of the bookcase. It made a click as it ran back. But nobody heard. John hurriedly looked down the row of books. He was sure the map had been put back there.

It had. There it was. "Map of the Greylings Lands."

He took it out of the bookcase, shut the glass front, which made a most alarming click again, and then ran back to the staircase. He was up it and into Susan's bedroom in a trice.

"Good boy!" said Jeffery, pleased, when John danced in, holding up the map. "You've been jolly quick. But what a row you made! We heard the click of the bookcase up here!"

"Yes, I know – I couldn't help it," said John. "But the radio is on, so Granny won't hear anything. Come on, let's see if we can find this winding road."

They opened the big folding-map. It showed the whole of the land held by the Greyling family. There were the two farms, the Manor House and its grounds, the Greylings Wood, and the roads around and through the property.

"It's jolly big," said Jeffery. "I hate to think of it all going to Mr Pots of Money. He's not the right person to have it. I bet he'd turn the people out of the farms, and cut down all that lovely wood to sell for timber!"

"Look – would you call *that* a winding road?" asked Susan, pointing to a place called Cuckoo Lane.

"It's not *very* winding," said Jeffery. "And it only seems to have three bends, not four. Let's see if there's a road that winds more than that."

They studied the Greylings map from end to end. They looked at every road, every lane. They even studied the field paths that were shown running here and there.

"Well, it's funny, but Cuckoo Lane seems to be absolutely the only road or lane that winds at all," said Jeffery at last. "Maybe we shall find that it has more bends than the map shows. The other roads are either straight, or just sort of wavy – no proper bends."

"Well, you see, it's very flat ground around here," said John. "People can walk straight from place to place. When there are hills, the roads wind a bit."

"What shall we do tomorrow?" said Susan. "Shall we go to Cuckoo Lane, and see if we can find four bends in it – and maybe three enormous trees, and a hill somewhere?"

"Yes – that's what we'll do," said Jeffery. "We'll go tomorrow morning – and in the afternoon we'll ask Granny and Granpa to have tea at the secret house with us. It will be fun!"

There was the sound of someone coming up the stairs to the landing outside. "Quick, Susan – it's Granny!" whispered John. "Get back to bed!"

Susan almost fell out of bed, in her hurry. She shot across the room, slipped into her bedroom and jumped into bed as Granny opened the boys' door.

"I heard you talking, my dears," said Granny. "It's quite time you put out your light and went to sleep. You will wake Susan if you talk like this."

Jeffery giggled. He knew quite well that he wouldn't wake Susan – she was wide enough awake already! He snuggled down under the clothes with John. Granny bent over them and kissed them goodnight.

Then she tiptoed into Susan's room, and softly

kissed her too. Susan didn't make a sound. But you should have heard those three children giggling as soon as Granny went downstairs!

"Susan, I hope we don't keep you awake with our talking!" called John.

"Be quiet, John," said Jeffery. "You'll have Granny back again, if you shout like that. We'd better go to sleep. Well, goodnight, Susan. I expect we'll all dream of the winding lane and the Treasure!"

CHAPTER 9

A Visit to Timbles' Farm

The next day the children asked their Granny and Granpa if they would go to tea at the little house.

"Yes, we'd love to," said Granny. "We're longing to see it! We'll all have tea there at four. What are you going to do this morning?"

"We're going for a walk, Granny," said Jeffery. "Unless you want us to do anything for you?"

"No," said Granny. "It would be nice for you to go for a walk. Where are you going?"

"Along Cuckoo Lane, I think," said Jeffery.

"We'll take old Rags – that is, if he can walk after such a huge breakfast!"

"You shouldn't feed him at meal times," said Granny. "He gets so many scraps now that he's getting quite fat. Aren't you, Rags?"

"Woof!" said Rags, leaping about the room like a kangaroo, excited because he had heard the wonderful word "walk"!

"You will pass near Farmer Timbles' house," said Granpa, looking up from his paper. "Go in and see Mrs Timbles. She will be delighted to welcome you."

The children set off as soon after breakfast as they could. Rags pranced ahead of them, barking at the sparrows in the roadway. Jeffery had with him the copy of the map.

They went down the drive, out through the gates. The stone eagles sat on the gateposts, looking over the road as they had done for three or four hundred years. They were so old that they had begun to crumble away here and there.

Down the road went the children, followed by Rags, till they came to a stile. They climbed over it and went across a large field. There was a stile at the other end, and then a narrow path that ran between two tall hedges.

"We come into Cuckoo Lane at the end of this path," said Jeffery, looking at the big map.

They were soon in Cuckoo Lane. It began at two cottages nearby and then wandered away across a common to Farmer Timbles' house.

"Now, it begins *here*," said Jeffery, standing at the cottage gates. "We'll follow it carefully and count the bends."

They set off down the lane. On one side was a low hedge of hawthorn. On the other there was nothing – the common stretched away, soft and heathery.

"Here's *one* bend," said Susan, as they rounded a corner. "Good! But oh dear – the lane looks awfully straight now, doesn't it, Jeffery? It looks straight almost as far as Farmer Timbles' house."

"Well, maybe it goes past his house, after all," said Jeffery. "There may be a few bends we can't see."

Down the lane they went again, passing a duck-pond and Jeffery thought they might call that another bend. Then, just as it came to Farmer Timbles' house, it wound round to his front gate.

"That's three bends, anyway," said Susan, pleased. "Jeffery, let's just see if the path goes on, before we go and call on Mrs Timbles."

So they went to see if the lane went on anywhere, or whether it stopped at the farm.

To their great disappointment it seemed to stop at the farm gate! Only field paths were to be seen after that.

"Isn't it tiresome?" said Susan. "But perhaps, Jeffery, the old map is wrong – maybe there should have been only *three* bends shown?"

"Perhaps so," said Jeffery. "But what I'd like to see is some big trees! It's rather wild land here – too much common – and I can't see any big tree except that one over there by the farmhouse – and that's not really very big."

"And where's the hill?" asked John, looking all round. "The land is so flat here. I can't see a hill anywhere!"

"It's very disappointing," said Jeffery. "But let's go in and see if Mrs Timbles is anywhere about. She may be able to tell us if the lane ever went any farther than this. After all, this map is very, very old, you know, and lanes can disappear easily enough, if they are not used."

They went into the farmyard. It was a lovely place. Cows lowed in a shed nearby. Pigs grunted in a big sty. Hens clucked all over the place, and from somewhere not far off came the curious sounds of turkeys gobbling.

"There's Mrs Timbles, with the turkeys!" said Jeffery. "Hallo, Mrs Timbles! We've all come to see you!"

Mrs Timbles shut the door of the turkey-house. She beamed at the three children, who liked her at once. She was fat and round, and her face shone like a large, red, polished apple.

"Well, I never!" she said. "The three little Greylings! Welcome, my dears – I'm right glad to see you all! I was wondering when I'd get a sight of your merry faces. How like your father you all are! Ah, I remember him here as a boy – and a monkey he was too! Let all my turkeys out one day, he did, and such a time we had getting them back."

"Did Daddy really do that?" said Jeffery, in the greatest surprise. He couldn't imagine his father doing anything so naughty. "Oh, I must ask him about it!"

"Yes, you ask him if he remembers Mrs Timbles' turkeys!" said the farmer's wife, with a laugh. "It was this very house he let them out of! The rascal!"

"Why don't you let them loose like the hens and the

ducks?'' asked Susan, who felt sorry for the big birds shut up in the house. There was wire-netting round two sides, but they did look very crowded together inside, she thought.

"You mustn't let turkeys touch the ground," said Mrs Timbles. "If they get wet feet, they're done for! But come along, we don't want to stand here talking about my greedy turkeys! You come along in and I'll see if I can find a few cakes for you, and something to drink!"

They followed her into the sunny farmhouse. They sat down in a great kitchen, whose floor was tiled with old red bricks, so clean that it seemed a shame to tread on them. At one end burned a cheerful wood fire. Bright red geraniums flowered on the windowsill, and cups and saucers with a bright red pattern seemed to flower on the dresser!

"It's a lovely kitchen," said Susan, looking round it. "When I'm grown up I shall have a kitchen like this, and I shall live in it like you do. It's nicer than drawing rooms and dining rooms."

Mrs Timbles disappeared into a larder as big as Granny's study. She brought out some ginger buns, some tarts that were so full of home-made jam that they ran over, and a great jug of something that looked a little like lemonade, but wasn't.

"It's nettle beer, my dears," said Mrs Timbles. "Nettle lemonade! Made of the youngest leaves of the hedgerow nettles, according to an old, old recipe that my great-grandmother had from Greylings Manor when she was cook there a hundred years ago!"

The children tasted the nettle drink and thought it

235

was simply lovely. They ate all the buns and the tarts and were very sorry when they were finished. They were too polite to ask for any more. Rags sat beside them, licking up any crumbs that were dropped!

"I'll not give you more to eat," said Mrs Timbles, who knew quite well what the children were thinking. "I've plenty to offer you – but I know you'll not be eating any dinner if you have too much now! And what will your Granny say to me then?"

The children laughed. They loved being in the old kitchen and having such a feast. The farmhouse felt as old as the Manor House.

"*Is* it very old?" asked Susan, looking up at the enormous black beams that ran across the ceiling and in the walls of the kitchen.

"Very, very old," said Mrs Timbles. "As old as Greylings Manor. Ah, children, I'm grieved to hear that the old mistress is going, and the old master. We've belonged to Greylings, we Timbles, as long as anyone knows. We don't want to belong to strangers!"

"Isn't it a pity that the Greylings Treasure can't be found?" said Jeffery. "Then Granpa would be rich."

"The Greylings Treasure has been lost this many years," said Mrs Timbles, gathering up the dirty plates. "Many a man has hunted for that, my dears. But it's my belief it went years and years ago. It will never be found now."

"Is the lane old that goes to your house, Mrs Timbles?" asked Jeffery.

"As old as the house, I guess," said the farmer's wife.

"Did it ever go farther than the house?" asked Jeffery.

"No, never," said Mrs Timbles. "It had no need to. There's no house beyond this one. It only runs between the two cottages down the way, and our farm."

The children were disappointed to hear that. But they did not tell Mrs Timbles why they wanted to know. They got up to see the young chicks and ducklings at the back of the farm, and to look at the lambs frisking in the fields beyond.

"What's that old place just there?" asked Susan, pointing to a tumbledown stone hut, with no roof, not far off. Lambs were playing in and out of it.

"No one knows," said Mrs Timbles. "It's been like that for years. I did hear say that there was something funny about it, but I never found out what. There's not much left of it now."

"Let's go and look at it," said Susan. But there was no time.

"We must hurry back," said Jeffery. "We've been all the morning! Rags, Rags! Stop sniffing about, and come along home!"

They said goodbye to Mrs Timbles, who begged them to come again soon. They hurried down the lane, counting the bends again.

"It's no good, there are only three," said Jeffery. "And one of those isn't much of a bend really. And there aren't any big trees about and I didn't see any hill at all, did you? I looked and looked everywhere, when we went round the farm."

"So did I," said John, looking gloomy. "I'm afraid this lane isn't the right one. Well, we'll have to think again, that's all!"

CHAPTER 10

Somebody Else is Treasure-hunting!

That afternoon the three children and their grand-parents went to picnic in the little house.

Granny didn't at all like the marshy ground she had to cross, and John had to keep putting down handfuls of twigs on the muddiest bits for Granny to walk on.

Rags came with them, of course, quite beside himself with joy at chasing rabbits again. His tail wagged the whole time, and his tongue hung out of his mouth.

"We'll make a fire again this afternoon," said

Susan happily. She loved making fires. "I hope the chimney won't smoke this time."

"It shouldn't smoke now," said Jeffery. "It was the birds' nests and the iron box that made it smoke, because they stopped up the chimney."

Granny and Granpa were amazed when they saw the secret house, and looked at the doorway and windows which the children had cleared by chopping and sawing away the ivy and brambles.

"I *had* heard of this place," said Granpa. "But even when *I* was a boy it had disappeared. I remember looking for it, and thinking it must have fallen to pieces. But it must have been overgrown like this, even then, and I didn't see it."

Susan went to lay the fire – and then she stopped and stared. The fireplace was not as she had left it! It had been full of birds'-nest twigs and leaves and moss. But now it wasn't! The mess had been cleared out of the fireplace, and was all over the floor.

"Look," said Susan to the boys. "Somebody has been here!"

The boys stared at the fireplace. They, too, remembered that it had not been cleared when they had left the day before. How strange!

"Why should all that mess have been moved away from the hearth!" wondered Jeffery. "Well – for one reason only!"

"What?" asked John.

"Because *some*body was hunting all around for something!" said Jeffery. "Somebody has been looking for the other half of the map! Yes – that's what happened. They've looked up the chinmey – and

239

cleared the hearth to hunt for it, too. And look – they've caught their sleeve on this old nail!''

The nail stuck out from the mantelpiece and on this hung a small piece of blue cloth.

"Mr Potts wore a blue suit yesterday," said Jeffery. "And I guess he's been here hunting – and tore his suit! Serve him right!''

"Well, he didn't find much!" said John. "I wish I'd caught him.''

"I don't," said Jeffery. "He might be rather unpleasant! I don't like him!''

The children didn't tell their grandparents what they had discovered. They quickly cleared away the mess, and Susan laid and lighted a fire in the hearth. This time it burnt beautifully and didn't smoke at all. The children were very pleased. Susan put the kettle on the fire to boil.

They had a lovely picnic, except that Rags discovered the chocolate buns, which John had stupidly put on the floor for a moment. Rags quite thought the plate was meant for him, and he ate six of the buns before he was noticed! Then he was driven out of the house in disgrace, and spent his time pawing in the pool at a big fish he could see below the water.

"I know he'll fall in," said Susan. But he didn't. He wasn't fond enough of water for that!

"Well," said Granny, when the picnic was over, "that was a real treat. I think you've cleaned the house beautifully, Susan darling. You will be able to have it as your own hidey-hole whilst you are at Greylings!''

"The pool is very pretty from here," said Granpa, sitting on a step and looking down at the lilies. "I like

240

the bit of the stream you can see too. It winds in and out beautifully between the trees.''

"Yes, doesn't it," said Susan – and then a thought struck her.

It was such a wonderful thought that she went red at once. She beckoned to Jeffery and took him behind the little house. He was puzzled at her excited face.

"Jeffery! Did you hear what Granpa said?" whispered Susan.

"Of course," said Jeffery. "But I didn't see anything in it!"

"But, Jeffery! When he said the stream *winds in and out beautifully*, didn't you think of anything!" cried Susan, forgetting to whisper. "Don't you see? We've been looking for a winding lane – but it's a river in the map, not a lane!"

"Gracious! I believe you're right!" said Jeffery, thrilled. "Yes – why didn't we think of that before? The river, of course. At its fourth bend – goodness, we'll have some more exploring to do tomorrow!"

They told John, who came up to see what the excitement was. He glowed with delight. "Of course, of course!" he said. "We *are* idiots not to have thought of that. Good old Granpa! He gave us the right idea and didn't know it!"

Granny was puzzled to know why the children seemed so excited when they went home that evening. But they didn't say a word! No – this was their own secret, and they meant to do their exploring without anyone knowing.

"And now that we know somebody else is doing a bit of exploring too, we'll keep our secret all the

241

tighter!" said Jeffery, remembering the fireplace in the little house. "Mr Potts has been to our little house – but he doesn't know any more than he did before!"

"Well," said Granny, when they reached home, "that was a very pleasant outing. You were clever to discover that hidden house, children – it is really most exciting. I can imagine how thrilled you were to find the iron box in the chimney too – and the old map. It is a great pity that there is only half of it."

"Well, the other half may turn up," said Granpa. "If so, we'll let that fellow Potts have it and see if his learned friend can make out what it all means. *I'm* afraid it doesn't mean anything."

The children looked at one another, but they said nothing. Susan longed to tell everything, but she knew she mustn't.

They went up to their rooms – and Susan made a queer discovery! She opened one of her drawers to get a clean handkerchief – and to her great surprise she found that the drawer was most untidy!

"Which of you boys has been untidying my drawers?" she shouted to the two in the next room.

Neither of the boys had even been in the room. Susan opened the other drawers – they were none of them as neat as she had left them. She was puzzled.

"I only tidied them this morning," she said. "Granny scolded me yesterday because they were untidy, and I spent ages putting them nice – now they're all higgledy-piggledy again."

Jeffery came to see. Then he went to the big chest of drawers that the boys shared in their room, and opened the top drawer, and the next one.

"Look here!" he said. "Someone has been through my drawers too. This is pretty queer."

Susan went into the boys' room and they looked at one another. They each thought the same thing.

"It's Mr Potts, or somebody belonging to him," said John slowly. "They've been looking for the other half of the map. They guessed we've got it, because I went so red yesterday when they questioned me about it."

"So they came and hunted through our things whilst we were out," said Jeffery. "The burglars!"

"Jeffery! You don't think they've found the halves of the map, do you?" said Susan suddenly.

"Good gracious! I hope not!" said Jeffery. He rushed to the dolls' house and knelt down. He switched on the little electric lamps that lighted the house and looked inside. He gave a sigh of relief.

"No, it's all right," he said. "They're here, safe on the ceilings. It's a good thing we thought of such a good place!"

"Let's go downstairs and find out if Mr Potts called," said John. So they went down. In the hall they found Jane, the housemaid, arranging some flowers.

"Hallo, Jane," said Jeffery. "Did anyone call whilst we were out this afternoon?"

"Yes, Master Jeffery. Mr Potts came, and another gentleman," said Jane. "They said they would like to see you children. They were sorry you were out."

"Did they come into the house?" asked Jeffery. "Or did they go off straightaway in their car?"

"Mr Potts asked if his friend might use the

telephone," said Jane. "So I showed Mr Potts into the dining room and took his friend to the hall telephone. He was there such a time!"

"Was Mr Potts waiting in the dining room all that time?" asked John.

"I expect so," said Jane.

The children ran off. "I bet he *didn't* wait in the dining room all that time!" said Jeffery. "He slipped up the little staircase to Susan's room and had a good hunt round while his friend was pretending to telephone. He's a clever one, is Mr Potts!"

"Jeffery, I don't think you ought to carry the map-tracing about with you," said Susan seriously. "Suppose he caught you and searched you. He'd find it!"

"You're right, Susan," said Jeffery. "Well, I know something to trick dear Mr Potts! I shall make up a false map, and keep it in my pocket! Then, if he does catch me and search me for the map, he'll get on the wrong track – because he'll have a false map to follow!"

"That's clever, Jeffery," said Susan. "You had better do it tonight – and we'll burn the tracing you made, after looking at it very carefully and learning it by heart! We can always turn the dolls' house upside down and study the map on the ceilings, if we forget anything!'

So that night Jeffery made a false map. At least, half of it was quite correct, because Mr Potts had seen the half with the words "Treasure" on it – but the other half was a real muddle!

Jeffery drew four more bends in the river instead of two, on the first half. He drew six more trees, a few small bushes, and then something that looked like a piece of bread-and-butter with a bite out of it!

"Whatever's that?" asked Susan in surprise.

"I don't know!" said Jeffery with a laugh. "Just something to puzzle Mr Potts, that's all!"

He burnt the other tracing, after the three of them had studied it very carefully indeed, and had learnt it so well that any one of them could have drawn it correctly from memory. Then Jeffery slipped the false map into his pocket.

"Now, Mr Potts can find it if he likes!' he said.

"Jeffery, can we go and find the four bends of the river tomorrow?' asked Susan. "I'm longing to do some more exploring."

"Yes, rather!' said Jeffery. "We'll go treasure-hunting again for all we're worth!"

CHAPTER 11

The Children Follow the Map

The next day the three children set off once more with
Rags. They had wanted to stay out to a picnic lunch
but Granny had said no.

"Mr and Mrs Potts have kindly asked you all to
tea this afternoon," said Granny. "So I will take you
in the car. I want you home for lunch, so that you can
tidy yourselves and change into something nice afterwards."

"Oh, what a nuisance!" said Susan. "I don't like
Mr Potts."

"Well, you may like his house and grounds!" said Granny. "He has a wonderful lake, so he tells me, and four boats. He says you can go out in one."

"Oh, good," said John, who loved boating. "That won't be so bad."

"All the same, it's a waste of time when we have so much exploring to do," said Jeffery, as they got ready to go to Greylings Wood.

Rags knew the way very well to the secret house now, and set off on the usual path at once. But Jeffery called him back. "Hie, Rags, old boy! We're not going that way today!"

"Which way are we going then?" asked Susan, surprised.

"We want to find out where the river enters the wood," said Jeffery. "I think we must count the bends from when it enters the trees. I asked Tipps this morning where it went into the wood, and he said we had to go down the road for about a mile – then we'd see it under a bridge."

So Rags and the children went down the road in the sunshine. After about twenty minutes' walk they came to a small stone bridge that spanned the little river.

"Here it is," said Jeffery. "Come on – we'll leave the road here and go into the wood."

There was no hedge, and no railing. The children simply walked among the trees and followed the stream. It ran quite straight for a little way and then curved slightly.

"Is this one of the bends, do you think?" asked Susan excitedly.

Jeffery shook his head.

"No," he said. "We must look for fairly big bends, I think. They were very curved ones in the map."

A pleasant path ran by the bank of the stream for some way. Then the path stopped at an old wooden seat, and the children had to scramble along through an overgrown part of the wood for some time.

Just after the wooden seat the stream took a great turn to the left, almost doubling over on itself.

"The first bend!" said Jeffery, pleased. They followed the curve as best they could, and almost at once the river curved again, this time to the right.

"The second bend!" said Susan. "We're getting on, boys!"

They were in a part of the wood that they did not know – but after they had followed the stream for a little while longer they suddenly came to the piece they knew, that led to the pond by their secret house!

Susan was very surprised. The boys laughed at her. "But, Susan, you must have known that we would come to it some time," said Jeffery. "After all, it's the same river!"

"Yes, I know," said Susan. "But I just didn't think we'd arrive here somehow. Well, there's a fine bend just beyond the pond, Jeffery – that's the third one!"

They scrambled round the pond, and tried to follow the third bend. But it was quite impossible because the ground was so marshy just there that they sank almost up to their knees. Rags hated it. He stood and barked loudly at the children.

"He thinks we're quite mad!" said John. "Come on, Rags, old fellow. Don't get left behind."

Rags ran off round the trees. "We'd better follow

248

him," said Jeffery, pulling his foot out of a muddy hole. "We can't possibly go this way. We shall come to the river another way, and perhaps miss this marshy bit."

So they followed Rags between the trees on drier ground. The dog seemed to know that they did not want to go very far from the water, for, as soon as possible, he led them back to it.

Jeffery stood on the bank and looked up the river, the way they had come. It was almost straight after the third big curve.

"Only one more bend, and then we should come to the three big trees or the humpy hill," said Jeffery. "Come on. It's drier here."

They were now able to follow the stream better. Great beeches grew all around, and the undergrowth was scarce. Some of the beech trees were so old and knotted that they seemed to have queer faces in their wrinkles.

At last the children came to the fourth bend. This was a good one. The river swung round to the right and then the children saw before them a marvellous avenue of trees, planted in two straight rows, with what must once have been a grassy lane between them.

Now the space between them was no longer a lane but was completely overgrown with bushes and under-growths of all kinds. But it was easy to see what a fine avenue it must have been, for the trees still stood there in their places, swaying in their two long rows.

"Somebody planted this avenue a long time ago," said Jeffery. "Perhaps they liked to ride here – or maybe it was a proper roadway at one time, leading to somewhere."

"The only difficulty is – where are our three big trees?" said John. "With so many trees it's difficult to know which are the right three!"

Jeffery stared at the trees. He noticed that they were not so big as some of the others they had passed on their way through the wood.

"I don't think these trees are more than a hundred years old," he said at last. "So they couldn't have been planted at the time that map was drawn. It's three much bigger, much older trees we must look for – more like those enormous old beeches we passed a little time back."

"Do you think it might be three of those that we want?" said Susan.

"Of course not," said Jeffery. "We want three trees *after* the fourth bend in the stream, not before. We must hunt about the place for three enormous old trees. I only hope they haven't died or been cut down."

They made their way through the trees, looking for three together. Susan came across a great old tree, with such a thick trunk that she felt sure the tree must be about three hundred years old! It had a knotty, wrinkled trunk.

"Here's a very, very old tree," called Susan. "Oh, and look – here's another not far off. They are two of the oldest trees we've seen."

"Where's the third?" said Jeffery, looking around. "These two are certainly enormous – and look, Susan, look, John, there's the stump of a third old tree! In between these two we've found – see? There were *three* trees here once – but one must have died and been cut down. Thank goodness its stump was left to show us where it grew!"

The children stared at the two gnarled old giants and the stump of the third. They were in a slanting line, just as the map had shown.

"There are no other trees in a slanting line as far as I can see," said Jeffery, hunting around. "They are either in straight lines, like those in the avenue, or they are just growing anywhere. These must be the three!"

"Well, now we must look for the humpy hill," said John. "How will these trees help us? Do we have to follow the direction in which they are pointing?"

"Either that – or we climb one of the trees and see what we can find!" said Jeffery.

"Climb up the biggest one!" said Susan.

"I'll climb this one and you climb that one," said John to Jeffery. So each boy climbed up one of the old, old trees. They had to be careful because the twigs were brittle, and some of the boughs were quite dead.

But at last they got to the top. And then Jeffery gave a shout.

"I can see something!"

"What?" shouted Susan, at the bottom.

"A humpy hill!" cried Jeffery.

"Ooooh!" said Susan, almost beside herself with excitement. "Where is it?"

"It's in the very thickest part of the wood, I should think!" said Jeffery. "Wait a minute – I've got my compass. I'll set it so that I know exactly in which direction the hill is."

John could see nothing from his tree. His view towards the hill was hidden by Jeffery's enormous

tree. He climbed down quickly. Jeffery climbed down too, slipping on one bough, and grazing his knee rather badly.

But he was too excited to do any more than mop his knee with his handkerchief. "It's funny," he said. "The hill sticks up just above the top of the trees – and it's not got any trees on it at all, as far as I could see. It's just a grassy hill. It's buried so deep in the wood that no one would ever find it unless they knew it was there. Oh I say, aren't we getting on!"

"Have we got time to go and find the hill?" asked Susan, leaping round in joy. She could never keep still when she was excited.

"Stop, Susan," said Jeffery. "You make me feel giddy. Well, I don't think we really *have* got time! But all the same, we'll *make* time! We'll have a *look* at the humpy hill, even if we can do no more than that today!"

He showed the others his compass. "I've got to keep the needle pointing exactly *there*," he said, showing them the little swinging needle in its round glass case. "If I do, and we follow the direction, we are bound to come to the humpy hill. I say – isn't this thrilling!"

They set off in the direction to which the needle pointed – due north. It was difficult going, for the wood grew very thick indeed, and the children had to force their way through. The beech trees had given way to oak, hazel, and birch, and the undergrowth, untrimmed for years, had grown thick and matted.

Soon their legs were scratched, and their clothes were torn. But they would not stop. It was far too exciting!

After forcing their way though the wood for about twenty minutes they came suddenly to the hill. It was very queer, for it had no trees on it at all, and yet there seemed no reason why trees should not grow there. It rose very steeply from the ground of the wood, covered with grass and bracken.

"Well – there's the hill!" said Jeffery in delight. "We *are* reading the map well!"

CHAPTER 12

Rags is a Great Help!

The three children looked at the queer, humpy hill. A rabbit peeped out of a burrow and popped back. Rags was up the hill like a flash of lightning and put his head down the hole.

"Shall we climb the hill?" asked Susan.

"Well, we shall be awfully late for lunch," said Jeffery, looking at his wristwatch. "But we simply must go on a bit farther and see if we can find that church-like place!"

So they climbed up the hill, seeing little rabbit-paths

here and there. When they got to the top they exclaimed in surprise. They were level with the tops of the trees, and they looked over the top of the wood, seeing the swaying branches for miles! It was a lovely sight.

They could see no sign of any little church anywhere. They looked on all sides of the hill, but there was no building of any sort or kind. It was really disappointing.

"I say, I hope we're not going to lose the trail just as we've followed the map so well," said Jeffery. "But I can't see any building, can you, John?"

"No, I can't," said John gloomily. "Let's go down the other side of the hill and hunt around a bit, Jeffery. Perhaps the church was built among the trees, and is hidden from us."

So down the other side of the steep, humpy hill they went, and spied around to see what they could find. They found nothing at all.

It was Rags who found something! He shot after a rabbit that had ventured too near him, and when it rushed under a bush, he rushed after it and began to scrape there for it, thinking it had gone into the ground! Jeffery pulled him out – and then called to the others.

"Come and look here – Rags has scraped out a big old stone, as grey as our gateposts!"

They crowded round to look. They scraped away more of the moss and creeper, and sure enough, it was an old stone.

"I guess that was once part of a wall," said Jeffery. "What *sillies* we are! That old building shown in the map must have fallen down long, long ago! All we shall find will be the great squares of stone, like this one, that it was built of. Let's look.''

They began to hunt, scraping away moss here and there, and pulling away brambles – and at last they found enough stones to show where some building had been. It could not have been a very large building, for the children found a rough outline of the shape, guided by the great stones they had unearthed round about.

"Well, this was the building all right," said Jeffery. "The thing is now – *where* is the flight of steps that led up to it? You remember the lines that looked like steps in the picture, don't you, you two?"

They remembered quite well. "I don't see how there could possibly have been any steps to this building," said Susan, puzzled. "It's built flat on the ground. If it had been built on the hill, there might have been steps leading up to it, as there are to our secret house, from the pond – but you can't have a flight of steps if you build on the ground itself!"

Jeffery was puzzled and disappointed. It was too bad that they had found everything except the steps! He looked at his watch and gave a shout. "Goodness! It's one o'clock already – and lunch is at one. We *shall* get into a row! Come on – we must go at once. We'll come back tomorrow."

"Isn't there a shorter way home?" asked John, thinking with dismay of the very thick wood they would once more have to force their way through.

"Well, if there is, we don't know it!" said Jeffery. "Hie, Rags! Where are you going? Come back!"

Rags was trotting off in another direction. He took no notice of Jeffery at all.

"RAGS!" yelled Jeffery angrily. "Don't pretend to be deaf. Come here! You'll be lost if you go wandering off by yourself when we're so far from home!"

Rags stopped and looked back at the other. He cocked his ears up, and put on a most cheeky expression. But he didn't come back.

"I'll go after him and get him," said Jeffery, angry. "He'll make us later than ever."

So he ran after Rags – who at once began trotting off again in the opposite direction. It was most annoying. Jeffery called and shouted, and ran after the little dog, but he still would not come.

Then Jeffery noticed that Rags really did seem to know the way he was going, and he stopped and thought. "I say!" he called. "I think old Rags knows another way home! After all, he's lived here all his life and gone rabbiting in the woods hundreds of times. I expect he knows all the shortest ways home. Shall we follow him?"

"Yes," said Susan. So all three children followed Rags, who wagged his tail, very pleased. He led them through the wood, leaving behind the very thick part, and then, most unexpectedly, came out at the field behind Farmer Timbles' house! It was most astonishing.

"Good gracious!" said Jeffery, amazed. "Who would have thought we were so near the farm? Well, that's jolly good, I must say – we can run home all the way from here, instead of scrambling through the wood. It will be a shorter way to come tomorrow too."

They set off home at a trot, and arrived at a quarter to two, dirty, tired, hungry and with their clothes torn and scratched. Granny was very cross indeed.

"You naughty children!" she said, coming out of the dining room and catching them just as they were creeping upstairs to wash and change. "Three-quarters of an hour late! You don't deserve any dinner at all! And just look at your clothes – and what *have* you done to your knee, Jeffery?"

"Oh, nothing much, Granny," said Jeffery, looking down at his badly-grazed knee, which he had forgotten all about. "I climbed a tree and slipped as I was climbing down again. Really it's nothing."

"I give you five minutes to wash and put on something clean," said Granny. "If you are not down by then I shall send out the dinner and you can have bread and butter instead."

They all shot upstairs, and soon taps were running and clothes were being hurriedly changed. They rushed into the dining room just in time!

"Now I don't want you to speak a word," said Granny, still very cross with them. "Eat your dinners, and try to make up for your bad behaviour."

So they ate hungrily, and didn't say a word. Granpa had had his dinner and was in the garden, smoking.

"You will be ready at three o'clock to go with me in the car to Mr Potts' house," said Granny, when they had finished. "It is nearly half-past two now. Wash again, a little more carefully, bind up that awful knee, Jeffery, do your hairs properly, put on your best things, and be down in time. You had better begin to get ready now – it is nearly half-past two."

"Bother Mr Potts," grumbled Susan, as they went upstairs. She was very tired with her exciting morning, and would have liked to take a book and go and read in the hammock.

At three o'clock they were all ready, looking very clean, neat and well-dressed. Jeffery had bandaged his knee with a clean handkerchief.

"Now, are we all ready?" said Granny, appearing down the stairs. "Yes – you look nice, all of you. Now please behave yourselves, and don't climb trees or anything this afternoon!"

The children were glad to see that Granny was smiling again. She was never cross for very long for she was very sweet-tempered. They all got into the car and set off.

Mr Potts' house was more like a mansion. It was simply enormous, and the grounds were marvellously laid out. There was the lake that Granny had told them about, and a few small boats moored at the bank.

Mr and Mrs Potts greeted them all very heartily. Mrs Potts was rather fat, and had more rings on her fingers than Susan had ever seen anyone wear before. She had six ropes of pearls round her neck, and bright earrings dangled in her ears.

"They must be very rich people," said John to Susan, in a low voice. "I wonder what they want to buy Greylings for, when they've got an enormous place like this?"

The children were told that they might go out in the boat, with Mr Potts to help them to row. They would much rather have gone by themselves, but it would not have been polite to say so.

They all got into the little boat. It was painted red, and was very pretty. There were two pairs of oars. Jeffery took one pair and Mr Potts took the other.

"It's quite a way, to row round the lake," said Mr Potts. "I'll show you some ducks' nests, and a little waterfall we've made."

It certainly was quite a long way round the lake! John took the oars after a bit, and then Susan had a turn. They saw three ducks' nests, all with eggs in, and came to the little waterfall, which was very pretty.

Mr Potts talked a lot. He tried to be very nice to them indeed. He noticed Jeffery's bandage, and spoke to him about it.

"Hurt yourself, Jeffery?" he asked.

"Nothing much," said Jeffery.

"He did it this morning," said Susan, who always liked to talk when she could. "He was climbing a most enormous tree – right to the very top he went – and when he came down, he slipped and grazed his knee badly."

"A most enormous tree?" said Mr Potts. "And where was that? In the wood?"

"Yes," said Susan. "Ever so far in the wood. We followed . . ."

She stopped and gave a cry of pain. John had punched her in the back to stop her saying any more. He knew what Susan was like once she begun talking. She never knew when to stop!

"Dear me, why did you stop your sister telling me about your adventures this morning?" asked Mr Potts "I am most interested. Do go on, my dear."

But Susan would say no more. She bit her lip and

hoped that Jeffery wouldn't scold her afterwards. Why was she so silly as to tell things she had much better say nothing about?

"Well, we'd better be getting back," said Mr Potts, seeing that none of the children was going to say any more about their morning adventures. "I'm afraid this is rather a dull afternoon for you, after all your tree-climbing this morning!"

But it wasn't so dull after all – because something most unexpected suddenly happened!

CHAPTER 13

Mr Potts is Clever

Mr Potts and Jeffery rowed back to the bank. Susan got out first, and then John. Then Jeffery stood up – but suddenly the boat wobbled violently – and Jeffery fell straight over the side into the water!

It wasn't at all deep – Jeffery could stand quite easily. But he got a shock and came up gasping and spluttering. Mr Potts looked *most* alarmed and grabbed him at once. He pulled him into the boat and then helped him to the bank.

"Oh, Jeffery, are you all right?" cried Susan,

who had been really frightened.

"Of *course* I'm all right!" said Jeffery, half cross at the fuss. "I can't imagine how I fell in. The boat rocked like anything and I lost my balance, that's all."

Granny and Mrs Potts came hurrying up when they saw what had happened. Mrs Potts was dreadfully upset.

"Oh, my dear boy, you are so wet!" she cried. "Come along in at once and take your wet things off. Mr Potts has some shorts you can have, and a vest and pullover. Dear, dear, I *am* sorry this has happened."

"Now don't get upset, my dear," said Mr Potts to his wife. "*I'll* see to the boy. He won't be any the worse for his wetting, and I can easily get him dry clothing. Come along, Jeffery – we'll see what we can do for you."

Susan and John went with Jeffery. Mrs Potts sank down on a garden seat, looking quite pale. Granny found that she had to comfort her, because she really looked as if she would burst into tears!

"Such a thing to happen!" she kept saying. "Such a thing to happen!"

Mr Potts took the children into an enormous kitchen, where three maids were at work. They were astonished to see the children with Mr Potts, but at once saw what had happened.

"I'll take his wet clothes off, sir," said a kindly-faced cook, bustling forward.

"No thank you," said Jeffery firmly. "I can take them off myself. I hope I shan't make your kitchen floor too wet, though."

He stripped off his wet clothes, and took the big warm towel that Mr Potts offered him. It wasn't long before he was quite dry. Mr Potts picked up the wet clothes and went through the door with them. "I'll get you some dry ones," he said.

"Oh, sir! Let *me* take the clothes!" cried the house-parlourmaid, running after him. "I'll dry them and press them."

But Mr Potts took no notice of her and disappeared quickly. The cook went to the scullery, and the third maid went into the garden. The house-parlourmaid followed Mr Potts after a minute, and the children found themselves alone.

"Jeffery! You *were* a silly!" whispered Susan. "It's the first time you've ever fallen out of a boat!"

"And so would *you* fall out if the boat was rocked violently just as you were standing on one foot, ready to step out," answered Jeffery crossly. "That boat was rocked on purpose – by Mr Potts. He *wanted* me to fall in the water!"

"Oh, Jeffery! But why?" asked Susan, horrified.

"So that I would have to change my wet clothes under his eyes – and he could take them away – and run through my pockets to see if he could find any signs of the *map*!" said Jeffery.

The other two stared at him in silence. They hadn't for one moment thought of such a thing – but now they saw that it was very likely to be true. After all, the clothes had been whisked off by Mr Potts, although it was the maid's job to take them and dry them.

"But, Jeffery ——" said John, beginning to

giggle, "you had the false map in your pocket – the one we made up!"

"I know that," said Jeffery with a laugh. He pulled the big towel round him more closely. "Old Pots of Money will have to use his brains to work out *that* map, won't he!"

"What a good thing you didn't have the proper tracing in your pocket," began Susan. But Jeffery nudged her, for he had heard footsteps. The house-parlourmaid came back with some dry clothes – some rather big shorts belonging to Mr Potts, a vest, and a yellow pullover.

"Has Mr Potts got my wet clothes?" asked Jeffery.

"Yes, he has," said the maid rather indignantly. "He won't let me hang them out, he's doing them himself!"

Jeffery winked at the others. "Well, I've no doubt he has some good reason for seeing to them himself," he said. The others giggled. They knew what Jeffery meant. But the maid didn't, and she looked annoyed. She tossed her head, sniffed, and went to join the cook in the scullery.

Jeffery felt rather odd in his big clothes. Granny laughed when she saw him. Mrs Potts patted him kindly and said, "Well, I expect you'd all like some tea now. I can see Edith bringing it out on the terrace. Come along."

They went to the magnificent terrace that over-looked the lake – and there, set out on low tables, was the most scrumptious tea that the children had ever seen.

There were great ripe strawberries, and rich cream.

There were the most exciting sandwiches imaginable, honey in the comb, looking like golden syrup, a chocolate cake as big as a Christmas cake, little iced cakes of all kinds, a jam sandwich stuffed with cream as well, and a dish of the most exciting biscuits. And, to end up with, the maid brought out a tray full of strawberry and vanilla ice creams.

"Well, this was worth falling into the pond for," said Jeffery, as he ate his second ice cream, and wished that he could manage a third.

"I'm so glad you enjoyed your tea," said Mrs Potts, who had eaten just as much as the children. Susan thought it wasn't surprising that she was so fat, if she ate gorgeous teas like this every day. She wished she could have tea like that every day herself – but Granny would say it wasn't good for her, she knew!

The car came round for them after tea and they said goodbye and thank you, and got into it. Mr Potts promised to send Jeffery's clothes back the next day.

"That will just give him nice time to dry our false map and copy it out!" said Jeffery, with a grin, as they sat in the car waiting for Granny to finish saying goodbye.

They drove home, feeling rather full up. Granny gave a sigh as they turned in at their stone gateposts. "Dear old Greylings Manor!" she said, as the beautiful old house came into sight. "I am sorry to think you will soon no longer be ours. Mr Potts will be your master instead!"

"What does old Pots of Money want to buy your house for, Granny?" asked Jeffery. "His own is far bigger and grander."

"Jeffery! Don't call him that!" said Granny,

looking half-shocked and half-amused. "You must call people by their right names."

"Well, it *is* his right name," said Jeffery. "He *has* got pots of money, hasn't he?"

"Yes – I suppose he has," said Granny. "He doesn't want Greylings Manor for himself though – he wants it for his daughter, who is soon getting married."

They swept up to the steps and jumped out. "Now you'd better go and do something quiet," said Granny. "After that enormous tea you won't want to climb trees or run races, I hope. And if you don't come to supper, I shall quite understand. I am sure you can't possibly manage any more to eat today!"

But, dear me, by the time that supper was on the table, the children were quite ready for it! Granny seemed very surprised indeed, but she gave them just as big helpings as usual.

The next day a parcel arrived for Jeffery from Mr Potts. It was his clothes, all dry now, and neatly pressed. He ran his hands through his pockets. Everything was there – string, handkerchief, two bits of toffee, an unusual stone he had picked up, a pencil stump, a broken rubber, a notebook – and the map! Yes, that was there as well.

"Carefully copied, I'm quite sure!" said Jeffery, putting it back again with a grin. "Well, Mr Potts may be smart – but we're smarter! I didn't guess he'd get me into the lake – but we were ready for him, anyway. We did that map just in time for him!"

"I wish tomorrow would come quickly," said Susan. "I do want to hunt round that ruined building again – what's left of it! I simply can't *think* why there are those steps shown on the map, if there are none to be seen by the building."

"Perhaps they are not steps," said Jeffery.

"Well, what else can they be?" asked John.

"I can't think!" said Jeffery, frowning. "No – they *must* be steps. But yet there never, never could have been steps there, if the building was set on the level ground, as it seems to have been."

John was thinking hard. He looked up. "I suppose, Jeffery, there couldn't have been steps leading underground from the building, could there?" he asked. "You know – steps going down to a cellar, or something, from *inside* the building?"

Susan and Jeffery stared at John in surprise. Then Jeffery smacked his hand down on a nearby table. "Of course!" he said. "Of course! *That's* what we've got to look for! Steps going *down* from the building – not steps going *up* to it! Good for you, John!"

"Tomorrow we'll take forks and spades," said John excitedly. "We'll probe all over the ground and see if we can uncover a floor of some sort. And then we'll see if there are any signs of steps going underground!"

"Now I shan't be able to go to sleep tonight!" said Susan, her eyes shining. "I shall keep on and on thinking of tomorrow!"

But she did go to sleep, and she dreamt of finding a wonderful place where beautiful treasures were stored – but just as she was going to take what she wanted, Mr Potts popped up and drove her away! Susan woke up with a jump, feeling very angry with Mr Potts.

269

CHAPTER 14

A Thrilling Morning

The next morning Jeffery went to ask Tipps to lend him a garden fork and two spades.

"I got into trouble over lending you the axe," said Tipps. "I don't think I'd better lend you anything else."

"Oh, go on, Tipps, please do," begged John. He saw Granny in the distance and called to her. "Granny! May we borrow some gardening tools, please? Tipps says he had better not lend them to us."

"Well, so long as it's not an axe or a scythe," said

Granny. "I'm glad to hear you want to do some gardening!"

"Dear old Granny's got remarkable hearing," said Jeffery. "Nobody said a word about doing any gardening! Anyway, Tipps, let us have the things we want, now that Granny says we can."

They marched off with the tools, hoping that Granny wouldn't call them and ask where they were going to garden. Jeffery slipped indoors for his torch. He thought that if they *did* find steps going underground, they would want a little light to see them!

"We'll go the short way," said Jeffery. "We won't scramble all through the wood again. Where's Rags? Hie, Rags, come on – you can take us the way you took us yesterday!"

As they marched down the drive to the gates, Mr Potts' car came in. Mr Potts saw the children and stopped the car.

"I just came to ask if Jeffery was all right after his wetting yesterday," he called, showing all his white teeth in a wide smile. "But I see you are, Jeffery. Dear me, wherever are you going with those spades and forks?"

The children couldn't think what to say. Then Jeffery spoke up.

"We're going to the farm," he said. This was quite true. They had to pass the farm – and they meant to call in for a moment to see Mrs Timbles.

"Oh! You're going to help the farmer, are you?" said Mr Potts. This wasn't exactly a question, so nobody answered it. But John, of course, went as red as a tomato. He always did if he felt awkward or guilty about anything. Mr Potts noticed his red face at once.

"Have you found the other piece of that map?" he said suddenly.

Now this was a very difficult question to answer. If Jeffery said yes, Mr Potts would ask him for it and would see that it was different from the copy he had found in Jeffery's pocket. If he said no, it was an untruth, and Jeffery, like the others, hated untruths.

The three stared at Mr Potts, quite tongue-tied – and then Rags saved them! He suddenly saw a stray hen and barked loudly at it. He rushed at it, and the frightened creature fluttered into the hedge.

"Excuse us, sir – we must rescue the hen!" cried Jeffery gladly, and he darted off. The others went too and left Mr Potts in his car, looking annoyed.

"Quick, Rags, scare the old hen through the hedge," whispered John, "then we can squeeze through after it and disappear!"

Rags was delighted to find that for a change the children were encouraging him to bark at a hen, instead of scolding him for it. He went completely mad, barked his head almost off, leapt round like a kangaroo, and made the hen almost faint with fear. The children made as much noise as they could, too, shouting to the hen and to one another, as they pretended to shoo away Rags and catch the poor hen.

They squeezed through the hedge, and although they could hear Mr Potts calling to them, they took no notice and shouted all the more loudly. At last they began to giggle. Jeffery hurriedly picked up the hen, and tore off with it, afraid that Mr Potts would leave the car and come after them.

272

But he didn't. They heard the car going up the drive. Jeffery set the hen down when he came to the hen-run, and it ran to join the others, squawking out its adventures at the top of its voice. Rags barked joyfully. He had had a wonderful time.

"Poor old hen!" said Susan, sorry for the clucking bird. "But it did save us from a very awkward moment, Jeffery."

"It did," said Jeffery. "Come on. We'd better slip off quickly before old Pots of Money catches us again."

So once more they set off, this time without anyone stopping them. They came to Farmer Timbles' house, and stopped for a few minutes to talk to Mrs Timbles. She was most astonished to see their spades and forks.

"What in the world are you going to do?" she asked.

"It's a secret, Mrs Timbles!" said John. "We'll tell you all about it one day."

"All right, I'll wait till then!" said the farmer's wife. "Would you like some of my new cakes?"

"Well, if you'd let us take a few with us, we'd be *very* pleased," said Jeffery. "But we can't stop long today, because we have a busy morning in front of us!"

"I'll pop some into a bag for you," said Mrs Timbles kindly, and she did. The children were thrilled when they saw her put at least twelve cakes into the bag for them.

They set off again with Rags, who was very much interested in the bag of cakes. Jeffery sent him on in front, hoping that he would be sensible enough to take them the way they had come yesterday.

He did take them the right way. He was a very clever dog, and loved trying to read the children's thoughts. He trotted ahead, and it was not long before the children came to the humpy hill, and found the place where they had uncovered so many old grey stones the day before.

"Now the thing to do is to jab about with the fork and see what we can feel underneath all this moss and stuff growing on what must have been the floor of the building," said Jeffery. So, taking the long-pronged fork, he began to jab strongly here and there.

Each time he jabbed, the fork struck something hard. He stopped, and looked at the others. "There must be a proper floor all underneath here," he said. "A tiled floor perhaps, like our secret house has. We'll clear it if we can."

Jeffery was right. Under the moss, the grass and the bracken was a tiled floor. The tiles were small, and even after so many years were still bright in colour. Rags helped as much as he could, scraping away with his feet in excitement.

After a great deal of hard work the children had most of the floor uncovered. Many of the tiles were broken. Some were missing altogether.

Then John uncovered a flat slab of stone, quite different from the coloured tiles.

"Look!" he said. "Here's something different. A big slab of stone – and it's got some old pattern on it."

Susan and Jeffery came beside John to see what the pattern was. Jeffery gave a shout.

"Don't you know what the pattern is, sillies? It's the

Greylings eagle – just like the ones on the gateposts, only flat instead of rounded. That shows this was a Greylings building.''

"Why do you suppose they laid a flat stone here suddenly, in the middle of the coloured tiles?'' asked John. "It seems odd to me.''

"It *is* odd,'' said Jeffery, "But I bet I can explain the oddness! I guess there's the flight of steps underneath that slab!''

"Oooh, really?'' said Susan and John in delight. "Goody!''

"The thing is – how are we going to get it up to see?'' wondered Jeffery. "It looks jolly heavy. I wonder if there's an iron ring or anything that we can pull it up by? Let's clear the whole slab properly and see.''

They cleared it from end to end – but not a sign of any iron ring was to be seen. Jeffery stood on the slab and jumped on it to see if he could make it move.

The slab moved at once. There was a creaking, cracking noise as if something underneath was breaking, and Jeffery leapt off the slab in alarm. The children stared at it. Something below the slab of stone had given way, and it was lying all crooked, a little below the surface of the ground.

"Now what did it do that for?'' said Jeffery. "It did give me a shock when it moved like that – and did you hear that funny breaking noise?''

"Perhaps, Jeffery, the stone is placed on wooden supports or something,'' said John. "And maybe they have rotted with the years, and when you jumped on the stone, the wood cracked and gave way.''

"I think you're right,'' said Jeffery, kicking at the

275

stone with his foot. "I don't like to tread on it again. I wonder how we could move it?"

"There's a big stone over there, that was once part of the wall," said John. "I think we could all three carry it between us – then we could drop it down on the slab and see if that would move it!"

"Good idea," said Jeffery. They went to the big square stone and with great difficulty lifted it up. They staggered with it to the slab, and then, at a word from Jeffery, dropped it right on to the flat stone.

The result was most startling. The heavy stone struck the slab, which at once gave way, and, with a crash, it disappeared entirely, taking the heavy stone with it! The children found themselves staring into a big black hole!

"Golly!" said Jeffery, in the greatest astonishment. "Look at that!"

"The flight of steps must be down there," said John excitedly. He bent over to see. Jeffery took out his little torch and flashed it downwards into the hole.

It was a deep hole, with an old stairway leading downwards. "So we were right!" said Jeffery, in delight. "John! Susan! Down there is where the Greylings Treasure is hidden! I'm sure of it!"

Susan was so excited that she almost fell down the hole. Jeffery pulled her back. "Don't be silly," he said. "The whole place is rotten with age – if you miss your step you'll crash down there and hurt yourself. Look – can you see the slab of stone right down there, on the floor and the other stone beside it?"

Yes, they could see them both. They examined the entrance too, where the slab had been, and saw that the flat stone had rested on wood, which, as John had said, had become rotten, and had given way when Jeffery jumped on the stone.

"I want to go down the steps," said Susan. "Jeffery, do let me be the first one."

"Certainly not," said Jeffery. "Those steps may look all right, but they may be quite rotten too. *I* shall try them first."

"Well, be carefull, then, Jeff," said John anxiously. Jeffery stuck his torch in his pocket and sat down at the entrance to the hole. He tried the top step with his foot. With a crack it broke away at once, and the splinters went down below. Jeffery tried the next step. That broke too. The steps were as rotten as deadwood in a tree struck by lightning.

"Blow! The steps are no use at all," said Jeffery. "They wouldn't bear the weight of a mouse!"

"Well, how shall we get down then?" asked Susan, so anxious to explore underground that she simply could not keep still.

"We'll have to get a rope," said Jeffery. Both the others looked most disappointed at once. They couldn't bear the thought of going home and leaving the exciting hole even for an hour!

"Couldn't we jump down and chance it?" said John.

"Don't be so stupid," said Jeffery. "You'd break your leg to start with, and you'd never climb out again! Rags, go away. You'll fall in."

"Well, let's go home quickly and get the rope," said

John impatiently. "Anyway, it's almost dinner time. We'd better not be late again – though I'm sure we shall. We can come back after dinner."

"Come on, then," said Jeffery, and he turned to go. "Gracious! We *are* late again! Run!"

CHAPTER 15

An Unexpected Punishment

They hadn't gone very far before a thought came into
John's head. "I say," he said, stopping, "do you
think we ought to leave that hole open like that?
Suppose anyone came along and saw it – and got
down before we did?"

"Yes – you're right, John," said Jeffery. "We
ought to have thrown bracken and branches over it to
hide it. Let's go back and do it quickly – it won't take
a minute!"

But a great surprise awaited them as they made their

way back through the trees. The sound of voices came to them!

Jeffery put his hand on Rags' collar at once, in case he should bark.

"Sh!" he said to the others. "Don't make a sound. Take Rags, John, and I'll creep up and see who it is."

Jeffery crept silently from bush to bush, keeping himself completely hidden – and at last he came in sight of the ruined building. He had a dreadful shock! Mr Potts was there, with another man! They were looking in the hole and talking in excitement.

"Those children are smart!" said Mr Potts. "They've found the very place. That map in the boy's pocket was wrong. We've been on a regular wild goose chase this morning, following goodness knows how many bends in the river! It's a good thing we heard their voices, and came to see what they were doing!"

"We'd never have found this by ourselves," said the second man. "This little hill is well-hidden, and the old building is fallen to pieces. Those are the steps shown in the map, Potts – no doubt of it. But they're quite rotten. We'd better come back again with a rope."

"Well, those kids will be back after lunch," said Mr Potts, rubbing his chin and thinking. "Let me see – how can we stop them? I know! I'll get my wife to phone up the old lady and invite the children to go for a picnic somewhere! Then they will be out of the way. I can't come back here after lunch, as I've business to see to – but we'll be here early in the morning before those kids are about."

"Well, come on then," said the other man. "I wish

we knew a short way back – I hate wading in that marshy bit! I'm soaked to the knees!''

Jeffery couldn't help grinning. He wasn't going to show them the other way back! He waited until the men had disappeared round the humpy hill and then he shot back to the others. He told them all he had heard. They listened in rage.

"*Well!*" said Susan. "So he thinks he'll get the Treasure before we do, does he? He thinks he'll get us nicely out of the way for the rest of the day! Well, he won't. We'll refuse to go to the picnic!''

"Quite right," said John. "We've simply *got* to get here this afternoon. Then, when he arrives early to-morrow morning, he'll find nothing at all!''

"I say, we *must* go!" said Jeffery. "It's five to one! You know what a row we got into yesterday!''

They simply raced home, carrying the spades and fork, hoping Granny wouldn't be too cross.

But she was. She was very angry indeed, and worse, still, Granpa was in a rage too.

"Half-past one!" said Granpa, as they trooped into the hall. "Is that what you call being punctual? Two days running! Disgraceful! Really disgraceful!''

"We're awfully sorry, Granpa," said Jeffery.

"Being sorry isn't enough," said Granpa, looking really fierce. "Your Granny orders nice meals for you and then you keep the whole household waiting like this.''

"It is really very naughty of you all," said Granny. "I've a good mind to send the dinner out and make you have bread and butter – but I'm sure you are all very hungry, and I don't like to do that.''

281

"But you'll be punished all the same!" said Granpa, looking very fierce still. "Oh yes! You'll go up to your rooms after lunch and there you'll stay for the rest of the day. You'll have your tea up there and no supper! Bad children! I'm angry with you!"

Granpa stalked out of the hall and the children stared after him in dismay. What! Spend the rest of the day in their bedrooms, when they had such important work to do after lunch? They couldn't!

"Granpa!" called Jeffery. "Please forgive us. Just this once. You see. . . "

"I never listen to excuses," said Granpa. "You'll just do as you are told and say no more."

Susan began to cry with tiredness and disappointment. She stamped her foot. "It's too bad, it's too bad!" she shouted. "Granpa, you're unkind! You ought to listen to Jeffery."

"*Susan*!" said Granpa, in a shocked voice. "Don't be rude. I shall send you all up to your rooms immediately if I have any more nonsense."

Susan didn't want to make the boys lose their lunch, so she wiped her eyes and said no more. They went meekly into the dining room and sat down.

"You musn't make Granpa angry by arguing with him, Susan," said Granny, serving out big helpings of cold meat, potatoes, and salad. "You have really been very thoughtless, coming in late again like this, and you deserve to be punished. Now I don't want to hear a word from any of you. Eat up your dinner quietly."

Granny took up the paper and sat down. The children were very hungry indeed, and they ate quickly. Just as Granny had finished ladling out the raspberries and cream for pudding, the telephone bell rang.

The maid came into the room after a minute. "Mr Potts on the telephone, Madam," she said. Granny got up and went into the hall. The telephone was in the hall cloakroom. Granny left the door open, and the children could hear every word she said.

"Good afternoon, Mr Potts," she said. Then she listened. "Oh, it's very kind of Mrs Potts to offer to take the children for such a lovely picnic, but I'm sorry to say they can't come. No, they really can't, Mr Potts. . . . No, they are not ill . . . as a matter of fact, they have been rather naughty, and they have been told to keep to their rooms for the rest of the day. What? Yes – I'm afraid they will be indoors – they will not be allowed out at all . . . so you see they can't possibly go to the picnic – but please thank Mrs Potts for me. Another day perhaps."

Then Granny listened again as Mr Potts spoke for some time.

"Well, I'm glad you have really decided to buy Greylings," said Granny. "Yes – the papers will be ready for us to sign tomorrow. Our lawyer will be here, and if you like to come tomorrow morning at ten o'clock, the whole matter can be finally settled. Yes . . . yes . . . goodbye."

Granny put back the receiver. The children longed to speak to one another and say what they thought, but they had been told not to talk. Oh dear! So everything was to be settled at ten o'clock tomorrow morning. It was dreadful. Tears trickled down poor Susan's face and fell into her raspberry juice.

Granny came back. "Mrs Potts wanted to know if

you could go for a picnic with her this afternoon," she said. "Now you see what you have missed by being so silly!"

"I don't want to go picnicking with Mrs Potts," said Susan. "I'm glad we're not going! I don't like Mr and Mrs Pots of Money!"

"Susan! Don't talk like that!" said Granny sharply. "Mr Potts is buying Greylings Manor, and you will have to be polite to him if you ever want to come and see the old place again."

"Granny! Please don't let him buy it!" said Jeffery. "Granny, we're going to find the Treasure for you, really we are!"

"Don't talk nonsense, dear," said Granny. "I suppose you are thinking of that old map? Well, I'm sure it doesn't mean anything at all."

"Oh, but, Granny, really we . . ." began Jeffery, but Granny wouldn't let him say any more.

"That's quite enough, Jeffery," she said. "Have you all finished? Well, go up to your rooms then. And remember that you are to stay there for the rest of the day. Tea will be sent up to you, but you'll have to go without supper – and I do hope you will remember that when you are guests in somebody's house the least you can do is to be punctual for meals!"

"We're very sorry, Granny," said John humbly, hoping that Granny would change her mind. "Couldn't we just stay in our rooms till tea time and then take Rags for a walk?"

"Certainly not," said Granpa, who had come in at that moment. "I never heard of such a thing! Go along now – and can I trust you not to leave your rooms – or must you be locked in?"

"You can trust us," said Jeffery, his cheeks going red. "We promise to stay in our rooms for the rest of the day."

"Very well," said Granpa. "I trust you. The Greylings never break their word."

The children went upstairs slowly and sadly. They sat in the boys' room and looked at one another dolefully.

"This is the worst bit of luck that could happen!" said Jeffery. "Who would have thought that Granpa would be so fierce?"

"Well, what about Granny?" said John. "She was fierce too. And all the time we're trying so hard to find the Treasure for them."

"Yes, but grown-ups don't think of things like that," said Jeffery. "Oh, do stop crying, Susan. I can't think where you get all your tears from. I really can't!"

There was a scraping at the door, and Rags whined outside.

"The dear old dog!" said John, jumping up. "He wants to share our punishment too! Good old Rags."

Rags came in and jumped up on to Jeffery's knee. He licked the boy's chin.

"Jeffery, I suppose we can't possibly go to the woods?" said John, in a timid voice. "I feel as if we *must* – don't you think Granpa would understand, once we had got the Treasure?"

"I know enough of Granpa to know that he would rather lose the Treasure than have any of us breaking our word," said Jeffery. "We've given our word of honour, John, and we can't possibly break it. Don't even think of it! It would be an awful thing to do, and I'd hate myself for it."

"Yes – you're right," said John, in a miserable voice. "Oh, how I wish Mr Potts was at the bottom of his own silly lake!"

That made Jeffery laugh. "That's where he tried to put *me* yesterday!" he said. "Well, old Pots of Money knows we are safely out of the way now, picnic or no picnic – so he's safe to attend to his business this afternoon. If only we could have borrowed a rope and gone down that hole – we'd have been down it by now if it hadn't been for this silly punishment!"

"I'm tired," said Susan. "I'm going to lie on my bed and have a nap."

But no sooner had she laid herself down than an idea came to her. She jumped off her bed and ran to the boys.

"I've got an idea!" she said.

CHAPTER 16

An Underground Adventure

The boys looked at Susan. "What is it?" asked Jeffery doubtfully. He didn't think there *could* be any good ideas just at the moment.

"Well, listen, Jeff," said Susan. "We've promised to stay in our rooms for the rest of the day, haven't we?"

"Yes," said the boys.

"But we haven't promised to stay in them all night long!" cried Susan. "Mr Potts is going to explore that underground place early in the morning – well, why can't we go *tonight*? We can take torches. We shall be quite all right. It would be just as dark down in that hole in the daytime as in the night, so it won't make a bit of difference, really."

"Well! That *is* an idea!" said Jeffery, really thrilled. "Why didn't we think of it before? Of course – we shan't be breaking any promise if we go there tonight. We'll go!"

"We'll go!" shouted John, and he banged his eiderdown so hard that the feathers flew out of it.

"We'll creep down Susan's secret stairs so that no one will hear us!" said Jeffery.

"We'll take our touches! We'll find a strong rope! We'll get the Treasure before old Pots of Money!" shouted John.

"Sh!" said Susan, delighted that her idea was thought so much of. "You'll tell everyone in the house what we're going to do if you shout like that!"

"I feel much happier, now," said John. "What shall we do till tea time, Jeffery?"

"I think we'd better try and have a nap," said Jeffery. "It looks as if we shall be up half the night!"

So they all three lay on their beds and shut their eyes. The smell of the early roses outside the window came in. Bees hummed loudly. Everything was peaceful, and soon the children, happy again now, were fast asleep. They had worked so hard that morning, digging and scraping, that they were really tired out.

They did not awake until Jane, the housemaid, came knocking at the boys' door with their tea. She came in and set the tray down on the table.

"And what have *you* been doing to get sent to your

rooms like this?" she said. "Late for lunch, I suppose. There's nothing that makes your granpa crosser than that!"

"Oooh, what a nice tea you have brought us, Jane!" said Susan, looking at the tray of things. "Egg sandwiches – my very favourite ones! And what are these – potted meat. Thank you, Jane!"

"And ginger biscuits and seed cake!" said John. "Well, I shan't mind going without my supper now."

"You'll never be able to eat all this," said Jane. "Ring when you've finished and I'll fetch your tray."

"Thanks, Jane," said Jeffery. Jane left the room, and the three children drew up their chairs and began their tea.

They enjoyed it. They talked about what they were going to do that night. It was very exciting.

"I think we'd better keep slices of that seed cake for tonight," said John. "We shall be awfully hungry if we go exploring at midnight!"

So they cut three enormous slices and put them in the top drawer of the chest. Then they rang for Jane.

"Good gracious!" she said, when she came in and saw what a lot they had eaten. "Nearly everything gone! *You* won't miss your suppers!"

She went, carrying the tray. The children found some cards and played Happy Families until seven o'clock. Then Granny came in.

"Well," she said, "I'm sorry to have had to punish you like this – but you will please remember in future not to be late for meals, won't you?"

"Yes, Granny," they all said.

"You had better go to bed now," said Granny.

"You are not coming down to supper. I will say goodnight – and I hope tomorrow you will turn over a new leaf, and we shall all be happy together again. It upsets me to have to treat you like this – but I promised your mother I wouldn't spoil you. You are usually such *very* good children!"

They kissed their Granny goodnight and listened to her going down the stairs to the hall.

"It's not worth while getting undressed," said Susan.

"Yes, we'd better," said Jeffery. "Granny may come up again for something – or even Granpa – and we don't want to get into any more trouble. We can easily dress again about midnight."

So they undressed and got into bed. But none of them could go to sleep! They talked to one another and listened to the hall clock chiming the hours and the half-hours.

"Granny's gone to bed now," said Susan. "I heard her door click. It must be eleven o'clock."

It was. The clock struck eleven almost at once. The children talked again until midnight – and then, when the hall clock chimed, they slipped out of bed.

"Don't make a sound," said Jeffery. "If we drop anything on the floor it may waken Granny or Granpa."

So they were very quiet indeed. They were soon dressed. Jeffery took the slices of cake out of the drawer and they all ate them. The cake tasted delicious at that time of night!

"We had some supper after all," said John, with a grin.

They took their torches, and opened Susan's cupboard. The top of her secret stair was there, and one by one they crept down the tiny winding stairway to the dining room. They crept out of the dining room and went to the garden door at the side of the house. It was locked. They unlocked it and stepped outside.

"Good! There's a bright moon," said Jeffery. That was lucky. The moonlight lay on the ground like pools of silvery water, and everywhere was bright.

"Where is Rags?" asked Jeffery. Jane had taken him down with her at tea time, and he had not come back.

"In his kennel, I expect," said John. So they went to the kennel and there was Rags, staring at them in delighted astonishment. What! A walk at this time of night! Well, he was quite ready for it! He slipped out and joined the children.

"Now for a rope," said Jeffery. They went to Tipps' shed and shone their torches round. They soon found that there was quite a big coil in one corner. It was thick and strong, just what they wanted.

Jeffery picked it up. It was heavy. He flung it over his shoulder, and thought he could carry it quite easily like that. Then, with Rags at their heels, they set off for Timbles' Farm, for that was the shortest way to the ruined building.

They had to use their torches in the wood for it was dark there. They arrived at the hole, and pulled away the branches and bracken that covered it. Mr Potts had put them back, for he did not want anyone else to find the hole.

"I'll go down first," said Jeffery. He tied the rope

291

to a tree-trunk nearby, and then let the other end fall down the hole. Then he let himself carefully down the rope, swung on it, and slid down slowly to the ground below.

"Come on!" he shouted to the others, flashing his torch around. "There's a passage here. It smells a bit musty, but it's all right – not blocked up, or anything."

The other slid down the rope. Jeffery helped Susan, who was so excited that she might have fallen. They all three switched on their torches and looked around.

In front of them was a narrow passage, with the roof just above their heads.

"I believe it leads into that hill!' said Jeffery. "You know – the little humpy hill."

He was right – it did! The children followed the passage, which was very narrow in parts, and at last came out into a curious oblong room, hewn out of the very heart of the hill!

It was strange to stand there in the light of their torches, and look round at a room where no one had been for many, many years.

"This must have been a hiding-place for the Greylings at some time or other," said Jeffery. "In the old days people were often ill-treated because of their religion, and maybe this room was a hidey-hole for long-ago Greylings. It's a marvellous place – right in the heart of a wood – and in the heart of a hill!"

"Where is the Treasure, do you suppose?" asked John, looking round. They flashed their torches everywhere. The room was furnished very plainly with strong wooden benches and an old narrow table. On a shelf old plates and mugs still stood, dusty and cobwebby. The floor was tiled like the floor above. There was no fireplace at all.

"I can't see anywhere for Treasure to be hidden," said Jeffery. "I say! Wouldn't it be too disappointing to have come all this way, to the very end of the map, and find that the Treasure wasn't here after all!"

"Jeff, look – there's an old wooden door in that corner," said Susan suddenly. She shone her torch there and the boys saw what she meant. They had not noticed the door before, because the walls were of earth and the door was as brown as the earth.

"I say! I wonder if that's a cupboard or anything!" said Jeffery, in excitement. He went over to the door. It was fast shut, and seemed to be bolted on the other side.

"Funny!" said Jeffery. "How could it be bolted the *other* side. People wouldn't bolt themselves in a cupboard surely!"

"The door is as rotten as those steps were," said John. He aimed a kick at the lower part of the old door. It gave way and the wood broke at once. John kicked again, and soon there was an enormous hole in the door!

Jeffery put his hand in at the hole and felt about for bolts. He found them but they were too stiff to undo. So he and John kicked at the door until it had almost been kicked away, and the three children could easily squeeze through the hole.

It wasn't a cupboard. It was the entrance to another passage, a little wider than the first one, and leading in the opposite direction.

"Come in – let's see if we can find anything here," said Jeffery. He walked a few steps and then came to a stop. In his way, stopping up the passage, lay a great wooden box, with bands of iron round it. The lock had rusted, and the lid was loose.

The children shone their torches on it and looked at one another, very thrilled. Was it – could it be – the Treasure, at last?

CHAPTER 17

The Treasure at Last!

"I hardly dare to lift up the lid in case the box is empty!" said Jeffery, in a whisper. Nobody knew why he whispered, but it seemed the right thing to do. He lifted up the lid – and then, oh what a marvellous sight!

The Greylings Treasure lay in an old box! Somehow or other the dust and the damp had kept away from the box, and the Treasure shone undimmed. Great brooches, wonderful necklaces, jewelled pins – and loveliest of all, the wonderful Greylings cup made of pure gold, with its handle and the middle studded with precious stones! Jeffery lifted it out.

"Look!" he said. "Oh, look! The very cup that we saw pictured in that old book. The lucky-cup! It's been here for years and years. Oh, what will Granny say? She'll be rich! She won't need to sell Greylings after all!"

Susan began to jump up and down in excitement. She forgot that the roof was so near her head and she jumped right into it. But she was so happy that she didn't even feel the bump. She knelt down by the box and put her fingers among the jewels.

"Pearls for Granny! Brooches for Mummy! Lots of lovely things for everyone," she said. "Oooh! This is wonderful! How clever we are, aren't we, Jeffery?"

"I think we are rather," said Jeffery. "After all, people have been hunting for this lost Treasure for years and years - and now three children have found it!"

"Won't Mr Potts be angry when he hears that we got here first and found everything!" said John. "And he'll be angrier still when he finds that Granny won't need to sell her dear old house to him after all! Oh! I'm longing to get home and wake up Granny and Granpa and tell them everything!"

"Listen," said Jeffery suddenly. "What's that noise?"

They all listened. "It's Rags barking," said John, in surprise. "What's he barking at?"

"Suppose somebody is coming through the woods," said Susan, clutching Jeffery. "Suppose it's Mr Potts and the other man, coming at night? What will he say when he finds us here?"

296

Jeffery ran back into the oblong room, and then made his way down the first passage. He shone his torch up to the top of the entrance hole. Rags looked down, wagging his tail. He gave a short yelp.

"Is there somebody coming, Rags, old boy?" said Jeffery. "Come on down with me. Jump!"

Rags jumped into Jeffery's arms. He was very glad to be with his little master. Jeffery listened and at last heard something. It was the sound of people scrambling through the wood! In the silent night the sound could be heard very clearly.

Jeffery thought quickly. There was no time to get out. Was there any good hiding-place up the second passage for them? Could they take the Treasure with them and hide it? But how could they carry that heavy box?

He took out his pocket-knife and cut a good piece of loose rope from the rope that hung through the hole. It might be useful. Then, hearing voices coming nearer, he shot back to the others.

"Sounds like Potts and one or two more," he said. "Come on. Let's see if this passage has got any sort of hiding-place for us."

"How are we going to take the Treasure with us?" asked John.

Jeffery quickly tied the rope round the big box. He knotted it at the top, leaving two long ends, which he looped firmly. He gave one loop to John and took the other himself.

"We can carry the box between us," he said. "It's too heavy for one person – but we can easily carry it like this, swung on the rope."

"Good idea," said John. "Get out of the way, Rags, old boy. You don't want this box on your head!"

Susan had crept to the old room and had listened to see what was happening. She heard somebody at the entrance to the hole.

"Hallo! Look here!" came Mr Potts' voice. "Somebody's dropped a rope down. I didn't see it this morning, did you?"

"No," said another voice. "I suppose those kids aren't down there now, are they?"

"They'll be sorry for themselves if they are!" said Mr Potts, in an angry voice. "Making false maps and trying to throw us off the trail – stupid little idiots!"

Susan waited to hear no more. She fled up the second passage to tell the boys.

"Oh, here you are," said Jeffery impatiently. "We wondered where you were. Don't go disappearing like that just when we've got to escape."

Susan told the boys what she had heard. The three of them set off up the second passage, the boys carrying the box between them.

"I only hope this passage *leads* somewhere!" said Jeffery. The underground way ran straight for some time then turned to the left. It was dark, musty, and low. The three torches threw a bright light in the dark tunnel.

The passage suddenly split into two ways – one to the right and one going straight on.

"Blow!" said Jeffery. "Which way ought we to go, I wonder?"

John anxiously shone his torch up first one way and

then the other. "The right-hand way seems a bit wider," he said. "Let's go that way."

"Right," said Jeffery. "Susan, have you a handkerchief? Well, throw it down on the ground just a little way up the *other* passage, will you?"

"Whatever for?" asked Susan, in surprise.

"So that old Pots of Money will think we've gone up that way, and follow the wrong path," said Jeffery.

Susan laughed. "You *are* clever, Jeffery!" she said. She threw her little white handkerchief down on the ground a little way up the passage. Then the three of them, with Rags nuzzling against their legs, took the right-hand tunnel.

It went on for ages. Once they came to where part of the roof had fallen in, and had to climb over a heap of stones and earth.

"I feel like a rabbit running through a burrow," said Susan.

"With foxes behind us," said John.

"Oh, don't!" said Susan. "I hope Mr Potts has gone up the wrong passage."

Mr Potts had! He and his friends – there were two of them this time – had jumped down the hole, found the strange underground room, and squeezed through the broken door that led up the second passage. But when they came to the splitting of the ways, they caught sight of Susan's handkerchief, just as Jeffery had hoped they would.

"They've gone up there," said Mr Potts. And up the wrong passage they had gone! But before they had gone very far the passage came to an end in a small cupboard-like room, whose walls were of stone. It was quite empty, though, hundreds of years before, it had been used for storing and hiding many things.

By the time that Mr Potts and his friends had turned back and gone to follow the children's passage, the three treasure-finders had got a long way ahead.

"I simply can't *imagine* where this is leading us to," said Jeffery, putting down the box for a moment. It was really very heavy, and though the two boys were strong their arms were aching badly.

They went on again after a bit. Rags ran ahead, thinking that all this was a fine adventure! Every time he turned round his eyes gleamed like the head-lamps of a small car in the light of their torches.

Suddenly the passage came to an end – and facing the children were a few rough steps of stone.

"Hallo – look at this!" said Jeffery. "We've come somewhere at last."

John shone his torch overhead. The stone steps led to a square stone slab that lay flat in the earthy roof above their heads.

"Why, it looks as if there's a slab of stone at the entrance here, just like the one we moved," said Jeffery.

"But not nearly so big," said John. "Get up the steps, Jeff, and try to heave up the stone with me."

Both boys went up the steps. They bent double and heaved with their backs against the slab. It seemed to move a little.

"Jeffery! John! They're coming! I can hear them!" suddenly cried Susan. "We shall be caught. Oh, do hurry!"

There was the sound of voices and footsteps to be

heard a good way along the passage. Jeffery and John pushed at the stone slab with all their strength. Rags ran back along the passage, barking loudly and fiercely.

"That's right, Rags! Keep them there! Don't let them pass!" shouted Susan. Rags felt grand. He tore down the passage till he saw Mr Potts and his friend and then the plucky little dog stood in front of them, barking, growling, and showing his teeth. He would *not* let them pass!

The children heard Mr Potts' voice shouting to them.

"You naughty children! What are you doing here at this time of night? Call your dog off. He's making himself a nuisance!"

The children didn't say a word. Jeffery heaved up with all his might – and the roots of the grasses that had been clinging to the stone slab and keeping it tightly in place, all gave way. The stone lifted up – and Jeffery put his head out into the cool night air!

"Golly! It's open!" said John, thrilled. "Just in time too! Come on, Jeff – hand out the box. Susan, come along. Leave Rags there to bark and give us a start!"

The children all climbed out of the hole. They stood there in the bright moonlight for a moment, wondering where they were. And then Jeffery suddenly knew!

"We're near Timbles' Farm!" he cried. "Look – there it is, down there, beyond the field gate. Do you know where we are – we've come up inside that funny little ruined stone hut we saw the other day in the field. We wondered what it was! Fancy! There's

301

an underground way between the old building in the wood and this one – and we've found it!"

"Oh, do come on," said John, who was very much afraid of being caught. "Let's go down to the farm and wake Mrs Timbles up. She'll look after us!"

"Come on then," said Jeffery, thinking it would be very nice to see plump Mrs Timbles. They half-stumbled, half-ran down the slope of the field, the boys still carrying the box between them.

When they came to the pig-sty, Jeffery put the box down. "Let's hide the Treasure here," he said. "Nobody would guess it was in a pig-sty!"

The others giggled. It seemed funny to hide treasure with the pigs – but as Jeffery said, no one would ever think of looking there!

So under the straw of the pig-sty went the old box. The pigs grunted sleepily in surprise. Jeffery stood up and stretched his tired back.

"Look! There are Mr Potts and friends," he said. "Let's go and wake the farmer! I feel as if I'd like a grown-up on our side now!"

CHAPTER 18

Safe at Timbles' Farm

In the bright moonlight the children could see the three men running over the sloping field. What the men were going to do the children couldn't imagine – perhaps they would take away the Treasure – perhaps they would be very angry indeed – they might march them all the way home, and tell some dreadful story to Granny and Granpa.

"Come on, let's bang on the farm door," said Jeffery. "No one will find the Treasure in the pigsty."

They ran round the farmhouse, and Jeffery banged on the big knocker there. The sound thundered through the night. Crash! Crash! Crash!

A window was flung up and the farmer looked out in astonishment.

"Who's there?" he shouted.

"It's us!" shouted back Jeffery. "We're in trouble – somebody is chasing us. Let us in!"

"Good gracious – it's the Greylings children!" said Mrs Timbles' voice, and her head appeared by the side of the farmer's. "I'll go down and let them in, Fred."

In half a minute the big bolts were being drawn back, and the great wooden door was opened. The children pressed inside and Jeffery banged the door. He could see the three men coming up the path.

"Now, my dears, what is all this?" said Mrs Timbles, in the greatest astonishment. She looked very queer because she had on an enormous white nightgown, with a pink shawl thrown over it, and her hair was hanging loose round her plump red face.

Before the children could answer there came another knocking at the door. Mrs Timbles jumped.

"Bless us all!" she said. "Who's that now?"

The farmer came into the hall; he had pulled on his breeches, and put on some bedroom slippers. He looked just as amazed as his wife.

"Fred! There's someone at the door again!" said Mrs Timbles.

"Ay! I can hear them," said the farmer. "I'll open before they knock my door down."

The children went into the big kitchen with Mrs Timbles. She lighted the oil lamp, and poked the fire which still showed red.

"Why, you're shivering!" she said, looking at them. "You can't be cold this warm night."

"We're shivering with excitement," said Jeffery. "Oh, Mrs Timbles, take care of us, won't you?"

"Of course, of course," said Mrs Timbles, in still greater surprise. "You're safe here."

The farmer brought Mr Potts and his two friends into the kitchen. Mr Potts looked very angry. He glared at the three children, who stood close to fat Mrs Timbles.

"Now what's all this about?" asked Farmer Timbles, looking sternly at the three men. "Have you been frightening these children?"

"Let me explain," said Mr Potts. "I have bought Greylings Manor, and . . ."

"You haven't bought it yet!" said Jeffery.

"Don't interrupt, my boy!" said Mr Potts. "The final papers are being signed tomorrow – but I regard myself as the owner of Greylings lands now. Everything is settled."

"Well, what's all that got to do with you being out at this time of night?" asked Farmer Timbles.

"My friends and I are interested in the old ruins belonging to Greylings," said Mr Potts. "Naturally those belong to us, as well as the house and grounds. Well, we have been doing a little exploring, and these children have very strangely and rudely been trying to interfere with our affairs. My friend here is an authority on old books, china, jewellery, and so on, and I have promised to let him have any old Greylings property to examine."

"You're not telling the story truthfully," said Jeffery, boiling with rage.

"My dear boy, don't be rude," said Mr Potts. "As you can see, Farmer, these children are quite out of hand. Well, we have been looking for some old things that belong to the property – and we have reason to believe that these children have stolen them tonight. This is a very serious matter, Farmer, as you will see – but if the children are willing to hand us back our property now, we will not make any more trouble about it."

"They didn't bring anything in here with them at all," said Mrs Timbles. "And let me tell you, sir, that these children are not the sort to steal! I never heard of such a thing!"

"Mrs Timbles! It was the Greylings Treasure we found!" said Jeffery. "It's Granny's and Granpa's! It doesn't belong to Mr Potts. We found it tonight! They were after it too – these three men!"

"The Greylings Treasure!" said Mrs Timbles, in the greatest surprise. "Well, I never did! The Greylings Treasure! Are you sure, Master Jeffery?"

"*Quite* sure," said Jeffery. "We looked it up in an old book, and saw the pictures of some of the things – and they were there, in the old box!"

"Well, my boy, you must let us have the box," said Mr Potts. "I tell you, I have bought Greylings, and anything found on the property is mine. You will get into serious trouble over this, if you don't give me what belongs to me."

"That's so," said one of the men.

"I don't care!" Jeffery almost shouted. "You shan't have it!"

"Well, Jeffery, give us the box to put somewhere safe just for tonight," said Mr Potts. "Then tomorrow we will all go into the matter with your Granny and Grandfather. You will see that I am right. Now, be a sensible boy and tell us where you put the Treasure."

"Well, lad, I think maybe you'd better do that," said Farmer Timbles. "If this gentleman *has* bought the property, you'd better be careful."

"I will *not* give up the Treasure!" said Jeffery.

"No, we won't!" cried Susan and John. They were all quite certain about that.

"Then we shall find it ourselves," said Mr Potts, looking furious. "And you will get into trouble, all three of you. I'll see that you do – you interfering little wretches!"

The men went into the hall and out of the front door. They began to hunt about in the moonlight for the box of Treasure. The children flew to the window of the front room and watched them. Would they look in the pig-sty?

They did go to it – but the sty smelt and the men didn't even open the gate. They did not think for one moment that the children would have chosen such a peculiar place!

Mr Potts suddenly grew tired of the search. "Come on," he said to the others. "We'll have something to say about this tomorrow!"

To the children's great delight they saw the three

men going away. Then, and not till then, did they pour out their extraordinary story to Mrs Timbles and the astonished farmer.

Jeffery and John went out to the pig-sty to get the box. It was covered with straw, and did not smell very nice – but who cared for that! How the children enjoyed Farmer Timbles' surprise when they opened the box and displayed the marvellous things inside! Mrs Timbles too, could not believe her eyes. She would not even touch the things – she just stared and stared at them, saying, "I never saw such a thing! Never in my life!" over and over again.

"So, you see, we've got the lost Treasure at last!" said Susan, jumping round the kitchen like a frog. "Isn't it awfully exciting, Mrs Timbles?"

"I never heard of such a thing!" said Mrs Timbles, and her plump face looked even redder than usual with the surprise and excitement.

"Well, I'm going to take you children back home," said Farmer Timbles, getting up.

"Oh, couldn't the little things stay here for the night?" said Mrs Timbles. "They'll be tired out."

Jeffery did not at all like being called a little thing, but he was so delighted at the thought of staying the night at the farm, that he felt he didn't mind anything. The children looked at the farmer anxiously.

"Well, let them stay if you want to," said Farmer Timbles. "I'm not wanting to dress and go out at this time of night! We will telephone to the Manor early tomorrow morning, before the children are missed."

So that night the children cuddled down in soft

goose-feather beds at Timbles' Farm. They were terribly excited and terribly tired – but very, very happy. They didn't care what Mr Potts said – the Treasure was theirs!

CHAPTER 19

Good Luck to the Greylings!

The children's grandparents were immensely astonished when the telephone rang early the next morning,
and the news was told to them. At first they simply
couldn't understand it – but when they heard Jeffery's
voice on the phone, telling them that he had found the
Treasure, the two old people sat down and stared at
one another in astonishment.

Farmer Timbles told his wife to give the children
some breakfast, but for once the three were really too
excited to eat anything. They swallowed down the

310

creamy coffee that kind Mrs Timbles made, and then begged the farmer to take them home in his pony-cart.

They were afraid of meeting Mr Potts on the way home! They wanted to get the Treasure safely to Greylings Manor. So Farmer Timbles put the fat brown pony in the little cart, and brought it round to the front door.

He and Jeffery put the box in the cart. Then they said goodbye to Mrs Timbles and climbed into the little cart themselves. It was a bit of a squash but nobody minded.

"Gee up there!" said Farmer Timbles, and the pony trotted down the farm lane. "Clickitty-clack, clickitty-clack," went her hooves.

Granny and Granpa were waiting excitedly for the children. They really couldn't believe it was true! They had telephoned to a friend of Granpa's, an old man who was very wise about long-ago things, and knew whether they were real or not.

He had arrived just before the children came. His name was Mr Frost, and his hair was as white as his name. He, too, was very excited, for if the children really had the old Greylings Treasure, it was very wonderful.

The pony-cart clattered up the drive. The children sprang out, and the farmer lifted the old box on to his shoulder. Granny opened the front door and the children rushed to meet her.

"Granny! We've got the Treasure!"

"Granny! We've had such an adventure!"

"We've found the Treasure, Granny!"

"What a noise!" said Granny, and she led the way

to the study, where Mr Frost sat talking to Granpa. Granpa had got out the old book that showed the Treasure, and he and Mr Frost were examining the pictures carefully.

Farmer Timbles put the old wooden box gently down on the table. "It's been in the pig-sty," he said, with his large smile. "I'm afraid it doesn't smell very good."

Nobody minded that! Granpa flung back the lid and everyone looked inside. For a moment there wasn't a sound to be heard. Then, to everyone's surprise, Granny began to cry! She cried quite quietly, and the tears rolled down her soft pink cheeks one after another.

"What's the matter, Granny?" asked Susan, in alarm, putting her arms round the old lady.

"Nothing, dear – just tears of happiness," said Granny. "It's so wonderful – just as we were thinking of selling Greylings, you find the Treasure!"

Mr Frost looked quite amazed. With his long thin fingers he took first one thing and then another out of the box. Soon the table was covered with precious jewels, and the wonderful golden cup shone in the midst of them.

"Yes," said Mr Frost, in a low voice, "yes! This is all old – very old. Wonderful stuff. Marvellous! And to think it has remained unspoilt and undiscovered all these years!"

"It is worth a lot of money?" asked Susan.

"It is worth a fortune!" said Mr Frost. "It is almost priceless! This cup alone is worth thousands of pounds."

"Ooooh!" said the children, and looked with wide eyes at the dull gold of the carved cup, with its precious rubies and sapphires shining and glowing around it.

"But I shan't sell this cup," said Granpa. "The famous Greylings cup, found after so many years! It is unbelievable! The lucky-cup is back where it belongs!"

"Granny, you won't have to sell Greylings now, will you?" asked John.

"No, we shan't," said Granny. "We shan't have to leave our dear old home – it will be your father's – and yours – and your children's!"

"Mr Potts said that it was his, last night," said Jeffery. "I knew he wasn't telling the truth."

"Well, he almost was," said Granpa. "Except for my signing one document, and Mr Potts signing another, the sale was completed. I'm not sure even now that we shall not have some difficulty in drawing back from the sale. We shall see what our lawyers say. I have no doubt that we shall find a way out all right."

"It seems to me that this man's strange behaviour will not sound too good when it is told to your lawyers," said Mr Frost suddenly. He had listened very carefully to all that the children had said. "I think, my dear sir, that you will find Mr Potts will not want anything said about his behaviour, and will not make any more trouble."

"He did make Jeffery fall into the lake," said Susan. "We are sure of that."

"Yes. He is not a charming friend to have at all!" said Mr Frost. "I shall be interested to hear what he has to say about all this."

313

Susan, who had been listening impatiently to all the talk, suddenly went quite mad! "But we've got the Treasure, the Treasure, the Treasure!" she yelled, dancing round like a top. "Nobody can take that away from us! It's ours, it belongs to the Greylings! Hurrah! Hurrah!"

She took up two pearl necklaces and hung them round her neck. She pinned two enormous brooches to the front of her frock. She put an enormous bracelet round her wrist, and took the golden cup into her hand.

Everyone watched her and laughed.

"*I've* got the Treasure! *I've* got the Treasure!" she sang, and danced round the room again. Just at that moment the door opened, and Jane showed in Mr Potts and his lawyer! Susan almost bumped into them.

Mr Potts stared at Susan in amazement when he saw all the jewellery she wore. "The Greylings Treasure!" he said. "So you *did* find it after all! I began to think last night, when we hunted round the farm for it, that you had made up the tale of finding it, just to annoy us!"

"It was in the pig-sty, the pig-sty, the pig-sty!" chanted Susan.

Mr Potts suddenly remembered Granny and Granpa and bowed stiffly to them.

"I have brought my lawyer to hand you my cheque for Greylings," he said. "And, Mr Greyling, as your property is now mine, I also claim the Greylings Treasure."

The children held their breath. What would Granpa say to that?

Granpa offered the box of cigarettes most politely to

314

Mr Potts. "I'm afraid," he said, "that there will be no sale. I can't accept your cheque, as now that the Treasure has been found, there is no need for me to part with Greylings Manor. I very much regret that you have been put to so much unnecessary trouble. I shall be pleased to pay you whatever sum our lawyers agree upon to make up for the trouble you have been put to."

"But this won't do, this won't do!" said Mr Potts, in a rage. "You can't get away with things like that! I'll soon show you that you can't behave like this to me."

"Mr Potts," said Granpa, in a voice like icy cold water, "if I have any nonsense from you, my lawyers will hear my grandchildren's tale of your very peculiar behaviour this last week – and I do not think you would want that made public. I quite understand your disappointment over the sale – and over the Treasure – but I do feel very glad that Greylings Manor is not going to belong to your family! I think, if I may say so, that it deserves a better fate!"

Mr Potts listened to all this with a furious face. He went red – and then white – and then red again. He tried to speak. He swallowed hard. He looked as if he were going to burst – and then, with a noise that sounded like the squawk of an angry hen, he stamped from the room. His lawyer followed him, looking worried.

The front door banged. There was the noise of a car being started up. It sounded as angry as Mr Potts had looked.

Then the car drove off down the drive. Everyone heaved a sigh of relief.

"Horrid man!" said John.

"I feel rather guilty about him," said Granpa. "The sale *was* almost completed – and I would have considered myself bound to go on with it, if it had been any other man. But I have heard such strange tales about Mr Potts lately that I feel he is not the right owner for Greylings – and now that I have heard how he has scared you children, and tried to get the Treasure for himself, before the sale was really completed, I am glad we have defeated him!"

"Oh, Granny! Oh, Granpa! Isn't everything lovely!" cried Susan, who was still wearing a great deal of jewellery. "Oh, I'm so happy! Greylings belongs to Greylings – and we can go on coming here as often as we like!"

"You certainly can!" said Granny, hugging the excited little girl. "You all deserve a reward for being so clever!"

"We've got our reward," said Jeffery. "We've got the Treasure. Oh, Granny, it *was* such fun hunting for it! You nearly stopped us finding it yesterday, though, when you sent us to our rooms!"

"Poor children!" said Granny. "No wonder you were late for lunch! You should have told us all that you were doing, and then we would have understood!"

"Well – it was rather fun having a secret," said John.

"Woof!" said Rags, who had been quite bewildered by all the excitement. He had hidden under the table, and now he came out and licked Jeffery's legs.

"Rags was a *great* help, Granny!" said John, patting the little dog. "We simply couldn't have done without him."

"I think," said Granpa, beaming round at everyone, "I think that such an exciting day needs a celebration – what about going out to the ice cream shop and ordering the largest and most delicious ices they have?"

"Oooh, good!" shouted the children – and off they all went in the car to eat chocolate, strawberry, and vanilla ices – and what do you think Granpa did? He had taken with him the golden Greylings cup – and he had it filled with iced ginger-beer at the shop!

"Now we must all drink from the lucky-cup!" he said. "Just as the Greylings did long years ago. And each year we must all meet and drink from it again, and we'll hope that good fortune and happiness will come to everyone of the Greylings family!"

Then all of them drank from it and said the same words – "Good luck to Greylings – and may it always belong to – a Greyling!"

Victoria .

Victoria

victoria